SWEET THIEVES

So much to steal, so little time...

Brian Wallace

www.brianwallacebooks.com

Sweet Thieves

© 2016 by Brian Wallace

ISBN-13:   978-0991355631
ISBN-10:   0991355636

For all you Sweet Thieves out there...

3

It's a matter of life and death.

2212 Bismuth Vale

1

Thief at the Scene

The crash was horrific.

Even before he caught sight of the mangled vehicles and shattered glass sprayed across the pavement, Kent knew it was going to be bad. A head-on collision on the freeway? No one was going to be walking away from this one.

Kent slowed down and pulled his rig to a stop. About fifteen cars back and completely penned in, he set the parking brake and turned off the radio. To either side his mirrors danced red and blue with the lights of emergency vehicles racing past, and the urgent wailing of sirens let him know that more were on the way.

Kent unclasped his seatbelt and leaned back to dig the phone from his pocket, the screen lighting up at his touch as he called in to let the dispatch manager know what was going on.

"Were you involved?" asked Mrs. Sullivan.

"No," said Kent, looking out at the mess up ahead. "But I'm going to be here a while. All three lanes are blocked and traffic is already backed up behind me as far as I can see."

"What happened?"

"Not sure," Kent replied, "but it looks like someone came all the way across the median. The grass is all torn up."

"Probably some idiot texting," grumbled Mrs. Sullivan.

"I don't know," Kent shrugged unconsciously.

There was a brief pause as Mrs. Sullivan consulted the driver schedule on her desk. "OK," she said, "I'll call McCormick's, the Décor Depot, and Grady's to let them know what's happening. Those are your stops today, right?"

"Yeah. But I already hit McCormick's and the Depot."

"Already?" Mrs. Sullivan sounded surprised. "Well then I'll just call Grady's. Any guess as to how long you'll be stuck?"

Kent didn't answer. The phone in his hand was completely forgotten as he caught sight of the accident victims.

"Kent!" Mrs. Sullivan snapped. "Do you have any idea when you'll be moving again?"

"Oh…" Kent murmured to himself. "This is bad."

Mrs. Sullivan softened, hearing the horror in his voice. "What's wrong?" she asked.

"I can see them," said Kent.

"See what?"

"The bodies in the vehicles," Kent whispered, his voice sounding far away. "I can see them…"

Mrs. Sullivan scrunched her face in disgust and turned away from the phone.

Sitting high up in his rig, Kent had an unobstructed view of the entire scene. He saw the short black streaks on the asphalt from their failed attempts to stop. He saw the trail of debris that linked both vehicles to the point of impact. He saw the victims hanging in their seatbelts, all of them sickeningly still – three in the smashed remains of a blue minivan and a fourth slumped over the wheel of a small pickup truck.

Kent was staring right at him when the pickup driver raised his head.

"He moved!" Kent shouted into the phone.

"Who?" Mrs. Sullivan asked in alarm.

"I just saw him move!" Kent cried out, half-standing in his seat.

"Who moved? Who did you– " Mrs. Sullivan pressed.

"No!" Kent screamed, cutting her off. "It's on fire!"

"What's on fire?" Mrs. Sullivan demanded, but the only response was the sound of an abandoned phone rattling on the floor of the cab.

Kent leapt from his truck and sprinted toward the accident. He didn't stop to think. He didn't pause to consider what he was doing. He just raced in, pointing and screaming for help, vaguely aware of the smell of hot asphalt and gasoline.

Kent never reached the truck.

A moment later it all went up in a huge fireball.

When Kent came to and pried his cheek from the pavement he was sprawled out on the ground fifty feet from the blast, pinned beneath the body of the cop who tackled him.

Beside him lay the man from the pickup, along with the paramedic who had hauled him out. The man looked dead.

The paramedic sliced the man's shirt away and immediately went to work trying to revive him. At the same time, a firetruck let loose with a blast of water that slammed into the burning pickup like a sledgehammer. Steam mixed with the smoke in a great billowing hiss and a thick gray canopy swept up and hung over the road.

"You got him out?" Kent shouted to the police officer, barely able to hear himself over the crackling thunder of water on fire.

"Yeah, we got him," the officer nodded, his face clearly conflicted. "But you almost got yourself killed. And us!"

Kent didn't know what to say. He hadn't really thought it through when he took off running toward the wreck. No, scratch that. He hadn't thought at all. He could barely even remember what had happened. It felt like he should apologize, but he wasn't sure what for.

Kent's thoughts were suddenly shredded by an awful scream as the man from the pickup regained consciousness. The sound was pure agony, and the paramedic struggled to restrain the man as he thrashed in pain.

That is when Kent saw it.

Inexplicably stitched on the paramedic's sleeve, so understated that it could easily be overlooked… the mark!

Kent blinked in disbelief.

The rest of the world fell away, the shattered glass and smoke and flashing lights fading into the background as he was suddenly unable to see anything else.

It was the last thing he expected. Kent squinted hard, his mind struggling to accept such a wild coincidence, but the familiar symbol continued to jump out at him each time the medic moved his arm.

There was no doubt that it was the mark. He'd seen it enough to know. But why was it here? How had it ended up on the medic's sleeve? There was only one rational explanation…

He must be one of them.

Of course! That made perfect sense. If the rumors were true – if the sweet thieves really were able to steal pain – then there didn't seem to be a more logical place for one of them to be. After all, the paramedic had literally just snatched someone from the flames. He'd saved a person's life. If that wasn't stealing pain, then Kent didn't know what was. And there on his sleeve was their insignia.

This was definitely one of them.

Kent wanted desperately to get the paramedic's attention, but with the firetruck blasting away and the man from the pickup writhing on the ground and the officer holding him down there was nothing Kent could do but watch and wonder. Who was this person? Was he really a sweet thief? Was there any truth to the rumors he had heard?

Kent's questions remained questions, for suddenly several more medics rushed in with a stretcher. The interaction that followed was rapid and efficient, and an instant later the paramedic was gone, speeding away in the back of an ambulance with the man from the pickup.

Lying there on the asphalt, with the ambulance siren fading in the distance, Kent was no longer thinking about McCormick's or Grady's or shipments of tile adhesive. None of that mattered. Not compared to this.

He'd seen an actual sweet thief at work…

Kent was struck by the fact that there was no applause. It was such a clear act of courage! Where was the roar of the crowds? With stadiums and theaters packed each week, it seemed absurd that no one would be there to cheer when a genuine hero actually showed up. Yet there were no fans or camera crews to be found as the paramedic came and went. The thief didn't even notice. He just stepped into the throat of tragedy and, without a spotlight or a trophy or a pat on the back, he stole life out of death. It was powerful. It mattered.

Kent was in awe. As far back as he could remember, he couldn't recall ever having done anything that significant, and that was something that definitely needed to change. The sooner the better.

Long after the ambulance and the firetruck left; long after the tow trucks hauled away the twisted steel and the police cleared the street of orange cones and bright red flares; even after Kent climbed back up in his rig and drove away... he could still see it all. The wreckage. The medic. The clandestine mark stitched upon the medic's sleeve. The images flashed through his mind on a loop, and he was more determined than ever to find out what the mark was all about.

When Kent got home late that night, he parked outside the apartment complex and walked straight to the mailbox. He was tired, but there was no way he wasn't going to check. Not after what he'd seen earlier on the freeway. Sure enough, there was a package waiting for him.

It was a plain golden brown padded envelope – exactly like the eight others he had received over the last three months. And just as it was with the others, there was no return address. "The Den" was the only thing written in the top left-hand corner.

In the center of the envelope was a cream-colored label bearing his name and mailing address, the words appearing as if they had been pecked out on some ancient typewriter.

The only other identifying feature on the envelope was the postmark. It was local.

Kent snatched the envelope from the mailbox. There were a few other letters inside, but he left them where they were and closed the door. He would deal with them later. Turning the small key in the lock, Kent spun away and hurried toward his apartment.

What kind of odd trinket would he find inside the package this time? He looked down at the envelope excitedly. The others had seemed so random. A patient ID band from a hospital... A tiny glass vial of water... A spent bullet casing... One package was even empty. There was never any explanation. The only thing that tied them together, other than the identical envelopes, was the mark.

The mark was the constant. It was etched or stitched or stamped somewhere on every mysterious item he'd received. Even the empty envelope had it, the telltale symbol drawn inside in what appeared to be red lipstick. The whole thing had Kent thoroughly puzzled, and now today he had seen it out in the world. It was no longer a mysterious game showing up in the mail. Something bigger was going on. On the sleeve of a paramedic at the scene of a random accident… there was no way anyone could have staged that. Yet at the same time somehow it felt like his seeing the mark was anything but an accident.

Now here was another package, and as he tore open the seal he knew he was about to see it again. The mark of the sweet thieves.

So what did they want? Was there anything to the stories he'd heard? They were clearly trying to contact him, but why? And why did it feel like they had what he had been searching for his whole life? Again Kent longed for a moment alone with the paramedic. If he could only ask him a few questions, he could surely shed some light on the whole thing.

Of course, maybe it would make more sense now for Kent to just go find out himself. For as he dumped the contents of the latest package out onto his hand, his heart skipped a beat. Inside the package was a faded old note.

And this time there was an address.

2

Mail Call

"This is it?" Kent couldn't even begin to disguise the disappointment in his voice.

"I take it you were expecting more," observed the tall figure leading him down the hall.

"Much more," Kent replied honestly.

"I see," the escort remarked without looking back. "Well that is something you'll have to get used to, should you decide to stay. The budget is tight around here."

"I get that," Kent shrugged. "I just assumed that you would have connections."

"We do..." she replied firmly. "But things are lean. It always looks like we might run out – like it might not come together this time."

"That doesn't seem right. It seems like you ought to have plenty. To be backed up. Supported, you know?"

"Oh, we are. You'll see." The escort stared straight ahead as she walked. "It's just hard. It's supposed to be."

"Why?"

"Later," she said, striding briskly down the hall.

That didn't sit well. If they expected him to leave everything behind and join them, he wanted more reassurance than 'you'll understand later.'

He was given none.

Kent looked back over his shoulder toward the thin slivers of light slipping in between the blinds near the door where he had entered. It was a quick little motion, almost nothing at all, but it did not go unnoticed.

"That's a bad habit to start out with."

"What do you mean?" Kent asked the unnecessary question, his tone that of those who know they are guilty.

"It's awfully dangerous to enter a battle looking backward."

"I wasn't..." His objections died on his lips. There was no point in lying to this person.

The escort walked on without another word.

Kent glanced around at the drab surroundings and scowled. He had been so excited to finally see this place, but now that he was here he reeled at the pathetic shabby reality of it all. The hall smelled musty, like old paint and plaster. The floorboards squeaked beneath his feet every time he took a step. And there was more than one exposed pipe that appeared to be held together by nothing but flaking rust and duct tape.

There was no way this was going to work.

So what was he still doing here?

Kent pressed further down the hall. He did not stop, for unlike his eyes and his mind, his feet were not put off in the least by the look of the place. They were tracking something real, and they trailed the escort like a pair of bloodhounds, carrying Kent along as they went. He could not see what they were after, but the hounds lunged forward and would not heel. They could smell it: Meaning. Substance. Purpose! The scent hung heavy in the air, hiding behind every dingy stain, lodged thick in every crack, swelling all around until it pried the peeling paint from the walls.

Kent went along for the ride. He was only looking, after all. He would give this crazy thing a try and see how it went.

Deep down, however, he knew it was much more than that. That's why he'd kept up the chase as long as he had. There was a line here. He wouldn't be able to jump back and forth forever. Neither camp was going to be alright with that. At some point, he was going to have to choose.

Grimacing at the sight of the rundown headquarters, Kent doubted that this would be his choice. It felt like he was walking into the losing team's locker room to sign up.

As if hearing his thoughts, the escort turned around. "Doesn't look like much, does it?"

"No." The reply was flat. He didn't even have the heart to lie politely.

For a moment the escort said nothing, just considered him in silence. It was as if she was giving him time to decide. Finally she spoke, "Would you like to turn back?"

"I don't know." He was one gentle shove from bolting for the front door and leaping back out into the sunlight. One little pebble on a scale. A single gust of wind is all it would take...

If the escort was troubled by his indecision, she did not show it. She simply waited, unmoved. There was something about her – a profound sense of calm; a serenity so powerful that she seemed untouchable. Far from the conquering hero who rides in, dispensing justice and making everything right by the strength of their arm, she was more like an old stump; beaten down and weathered to the point of indestructibility. The full host of earthly ruin and tragedy could be poured out upon her and she would remain unshaken. It was an entirely different kind of strength, and the newcomer shuddered with fearful envy when he imagined the price that must have been paid to own it.

In the end it was her tranquility that Kent latched onto, for it was precisely the kind of strength that he had always craved but had never found out in the world.

He took a deep breath and nodded forward.

The escort's eyes shone for a moment before she turned and began walking once more.

The doubts continued, but Kent no longer listened. He would see this thing through, at least long enough to find out what was at the end of this hallway. Maybe then he would turn around and run.

Maybe.

The door at the end of the hall, like everything else here, was much thinner and more fragile than he expected. It looked like one good shove would break it down. The hinges on which it hung would surely be torn loose if pulled too hard. He wondered why they had bothered to hang the door at all. A curtain or a bed sheet would have been more formidable.

With reverent hands the escort gently opened the door, then stopped and stood to one side. "This is as far as I go."

Kent paused, gave the escort a quick glance, and stepped through.

The room he entered was not large – maybe ten feet across and twice that side to side. There were no furnishings to speak of. There was no hook for a coat, no table for coffee, no place to sit down and be comfortable. That is not what this room was for.

A single bank of fluorescent bulbs buzzed monotonously overhead. One of the bulbs was out, one was missing, and the two that remained were dimmed by piles of fly corpses that were trapped in the plastic covering. It matched the rest of the decor seamlessly.

The only other distinguishing feature in the room was a large mirror mounted on the wall to Kent's left. It looked like a scene right out of a bad cop movie, and he imagined that there was someone on the other side of the mirror watching him. Maybe that's why he was so startled when a voice actually addressed him from behind the glass.

"You are here," the voice said matter-of-factly.

"I'm here," Kent confirmed. He had no idea who he was talking to, but it seemed the appropriate thing to say.

"Why?"

Kent balked. Were they joking? It's not like he was standing out on a street corner or wandering through a shopping mall. People didn't just end up in places like this by accident. "What do you mean, why?" he asked pointedly.

There was no answer.

Kent bristled. Mind games were definitely not what he was looking for.

"I'm here to help," he stated at last.

"What do you mean?"

Kent clenched his teeth, annoyed at his interrogator's seeming inability to grasp the obvious. "The world is broken. I want to help."

"Why?"

That was it. Kent was at his limit. One more inane question and he was leaving. "Because I want to matter."

"And you think that will happen here?" asked the unseen voice.

"I don't know... maybe. I've heard rumors."

"I see." There was a long pause. Kent thought he heard papers rustling. "And are you willing to do what is required?"

"I guess that depends on what is required," Kent replied.

"Fair enough. What won't you do?"

Kent thought for a moment. "To matter for real?"

"Yes."

"Nothing."

"Then it doesn't matter what is required."

They had a point.

"Then I guess I'm willing." Kent said the words casually, but he meant them. If it truly mattered – if it would actually make a difference in the world – he was ready to do anything.

"Do you know what we do here?" the interrogator asked from behind the glass.

Kent thought about what he had seen and heard, glancing again at the scribbled address in his hand. "You steal pain."

"That's right. Is that what you want to do?"

"I think so," Kent muttered.

"I'm afraid that's not good enough," said the one behind the mirror. "Divided hearts are dangerous. There's too much at stake." The voice paused, then offered up the final terms, "Yes or no; the choice is yours."

"What if I'm not sure?" Kent challenged.

"The door is behind you."

It was an ultimatum, but for some reason Kent found that strangely refreshing. In a world full of half-truths and double-talk, the sound of accountability was unexpectedly delicious.

"No halfway?"

"No."

"Can I think about it?"

"Haven't you been thinking about it?"

"Hardly anything else."

"Then what is the point?"

"Of thinking?"

"No. Of thinking more."

"You don't want me to think about it?" Kent pushed again, thinking he had them cornered.

"Not if that is all you ever do. Few things are more tragic than a life spent thinking through every little thing while doing nothing at all. There comes a point when you have to choose a direction and go. Or not. But if you don't, then this conversation is over."

"So I can't come back later?"

"For what? To say these same words all over again?" Behind the mirror there was the sound of a pen being laid down on a table. "Look, we're going to level with you. There is a lot for you to learn and a long way for you to go, and you won't see any of it if you don't start walking. Every day that you wait leaves you further behind."

"So I have to choose now?"

"You don't have to do anything," said the mirror. "Choose now."

Kent's heart burned. He wanted to plunge in, to dive off the cliff into the unknown. But the step was daunting. It would be so much easier to slip back into the comfortable life he was used to. A steady paycheck and a decent apartment; his big screen TV and high-speed internet; Thursday men's league at the gym and happy hour every Wednesday after work... It was all set up for him to slip easily through the years, and he couldn't do it anymore. Not without a piece of him dying.

"I'm in."

The instant the words left his mouth, Kent was flooded by a sudden awareness that something inside of him was finally right. Sadly, the sensation faded almost immediately.

"You are Number One."

The voice behind the mirror sounded somehow richer.

"Excuse me?"

"Number One," the voice repeated. "Your first assignment will be waiting for you on your way out."

"I'm Number One?"

"Yes."

"That doesn't make sense."

There was no reply. The sound of a chair scraping on the floor and a door softly closing was all he heard from whoever was behind the mirror. Then the room went silent.

Kent frowned, puzzled. He couldn't be Number One. Others had taken this path before him. He was sure of that. He had seen one of them just yesterday with his own eyes, and that was only the one he knew about. There were probably dozens, if not hundreds more. He must be far down the list somewhere. Still, that is what the voice had said…

Number One.

3

Head-on Collision

Number One stepped outside, hurried down the stairs, and quickly crossed the street. He didn't pause to open the folder tucked underneath his arm. He just continued up the sidewalk, cautiously looking around to make sure he wasn't being followed.

A few people drove by, but no one even gave him a second glance.

It was all so strange.

Driving to the den that morning, Kent had fully expected to find bolted doors and armed men waiting to pat him down to make sure he wasn't wearing a wire. He even sat out in his car for a half hour after he arrived, trying to mentally vaccinate himself against the apprehension that comes from being around dangerous men who know dangerous things.

There was none of that.

He may as well have been at the grocery store. The post office was more intimidating.

With his assignment hidden away in the sealed folder under his arm, Number One slipped down an alley nearby. He had been so concerned with the covert nature of the morning's interview that he had pulled off the street and tried to park out of sight. Now he laughed at himself as he saw the edge of his bumper peeking out from behind a dumpster in the alley. He really had gotten a little carried away.

Shaking his head and chuckling, he walked over and reached for the welcome anonymity of his car.

The door handle bent and creaked the same way it always did. The worn and curling floor mats caught the heels of his shoes just like every other morning. Almost blissfully reassuring, the comfort of normalcy wrapped him in a cocoon of things familiar. The pile of gum wrappers in the cup holder. The vents pointing every which way. The ridiculous plastic blue feet hanging from the rearview mirror, still smelling faintly of manufactured vanilla. It was all the same. Life could continue. Nothing had changed.

Nodding and smiling, Kent turned the key.

Silence.

He tried again. There was a click and then nothing.

Number One slammed his hand on the steering wheel as a whole host of problems came rushing on. It was amazing how quickly his mind flipped through the images. Mrs. Sullivan's fury when he showed up late to work. Tow trucks and mechanics. His bank account draining out before his eyes. A heavy net flopped around him, all from one little turn of a key.

"OK, calm down," he said out loud, letting out a breath that it felt like he had been holding all morning. He sat for a minute with one hand resting on the bottom of the steering wheel and the other slowly rubbing his forehead. Then he glanced up at the dash and laughed in disgusted relief.

To the left of the instrument panel was the tell-tale switch, and the headlights, though lifeless now, were still turned on. "You moron," he scolded himself. Still, he gladly let the larger net of worries drift off and accepted the smaller one. A dead battery would be little more than a hiccup in the day. He reached for his phone, ready to get things back in order.

It was not there.

His pockets were empty.

Kent closed his eyes in disbelief. He knew exactly where the phone was – charging on the counter at home where he left it!

With a deep sigh he climbed out of the car and tossed the assignment, still unopened, onto the seat beside him. Then Number One made his way back out of the alley onto the main street that ran through town.

It took much longer than he thought it would to find someone willing to give him a jump start. Parked in the shadows as he was, the first three people he flagged down were unwilling to accept his invitation to "just follow me down this alley." After half an hour of fruitless searching, he finally embraced his humiliation and went back to the building he had come out here to visit in the first place, only to find the door sealed and the windows dark. Though he knocked loud and long, there was no response. Frustrated, he shambled back down the concrete steps and returned to wandering the streets.

As time ticked by, his desperation must have been starting to show, because people were no longer even slowing down or cracking their windows to hear him. They either scowled at him and shook their heads or pretended to be fascinated by something on the other side of the street as they drove by. A few even sped up.

In the end, it was an unlikely hero that saved the day. She was so small and old that he almost didn't even bother lifting a hand. There was no way she was going to stop.

But she did.

"What's the matter? Are you lost?" she asked sharply. Her tone sounded almost rude, but he recognized it as something else. It was direct and unapologetic – the way his grandma spoke.

"Dead battery," he explained.

Her eyes peered around, obviously searching for his vehicle, though he wondered if she could see past her steering wheel at all.

"Where's your car?" she snapped.

"Back in the alley." Kent stared at the ground, feeling like an idiot.

He looked so sheepish that the woman was not the least bit afraid. She was dealing with a child. "Why in the world would you park back there?"

Number One had no answer.

The old woman reached up with long, skinny fingers and pulled down on the gearshift beside the steering wheel. Then, without another word, she slowly nosed her big boat of a car into the alley. It was difficult for her to maneuver close enough for the cables to reach from battery to battery, but the fifth time she backed up and pulled forward finally did the trick. A moment later both cars were idling.

"Thank you so much."

"Be more careful next time," she wagged a finger at him.

"What do I owe you?" he asked.

The old woman's eyes widened in surprise. She was about to tell him that he didn't owe her anything, but suddenly thought better of it.

"Lunch," she answered.

"What's that?" Number One wondered if he had heard her right.

Now she was confused. Surely this poor boy couldn't be that stupid. "What is lunch?" she asked.

"Oh, lunch!" he cried. Quickly, he thought it over. He needed to get going. He'd already lost the better part of the morning and was dreading the tongue-lashing he was going to get for being late to work without calling in. Still, he owed her. "Sure," he said at last. "Where would you like to eat?"

There! That was that. Damage control with Mrs. Sullivan would have to wait. Number One was going to lunch.

He just hoped it wouldn't take too long.

4

Diner of Destiny

"Well, I just have to say this is a nice thing to see!" The waitress beamed at them.

Number One sat in a little booth at a tiny diner in a town too small to have its name on the state map. The old lady said that they served the best soup she'd ever had, so he followed her for forty minutes on winding country roads to a place with a hanging sign that was nothing but spray paint on plywood.

"What can I get you two to drink?"

"I'd like a nice cup of hot tea, dear," said the old woman. She sounded more and more like his grandma with every word.

The waitress nodded and turned to Kent.

"Coffee. Thanks."

The skirt of her cornflower blue uniform twirled as the waitress spun away in stockings and white sneakers, and Number One quickly got lost in the menu. Chicken fried steak. Hash browns. Onion rings. It was a grease lover's paradise. The only problem he was going to have here would be narrowing it down to one choice. Apparently, the old woman would have no such problem. Her menu was closed, lying flat on the table.

She peered at him expectantly.

The waitress returned with their drinks and placed two steaming mugs down in front of them. "Cream and sugar for you two?"

He asked for cream, she asked for honey, and a moment later they were alone again.

"Do you know what you want?" asked the old lady.

"No. I'm not very good at this part," Kent admitted, grinning. "But I get much better once the food arrives."

The old woman chuckled and Kent relaxed back in his seat.

"How about you?" he asked.

"The soup."

"Ah yes, of course. I forgot."

One lowered his menu and the waitress hurried over, taking their order as they poured out honey and cream.

Outside the wind picked up, drawing an eerie, groaning whistle past the diner and setting the faded plywood sign to rocking. The loose ends of the chains thunked gently against the wood like something knocking to come in.

Number One heard none of it. He had no idea what was coming for him, no clue that the world was shifting, reality bending to invite him in. It was still just another day, just another set of small choices that shape the ins and outs and curves of life. The world was still the world he'd always known.

The waitress brought the soup.

Number One leaned in over his bowl and blew across the surface, making ripples in the broth and sending the thick noodles swirling. Clouds of steam billowed up, the aroma so rich and enticing that his hands fell to his lap and a contented sigh escaped his lips. If this soup tasted even half as good as it smelled, the old lady's claim would soon be his as well.

For ten long seconds he just sat there with his eyes closed, enjoying the feel of the savory steam as it warmed his face. The whole dead battery fiasco suddenly seemed worth it. Then he looked up eagerly, reached for his spoon, and froze.

His hand hovered over the table, fingers empty; thoughts of soup vanishing faster than the clouds of steam above his bowl.

What he saw made no sense.

As if he was looking at the world through strange goggles or an odd magnifying glass, everything seemed just a touch out of focus. Not blurry at all — just focused elsewhere. And while the diner and everything within were still as real as ever, there was now something else as well, something that should not have been there at all... birds.

Vaporous and vague around the edges, dozens of miniature raptors circled and swooped, diving savagely into and out of the old woman as she sat and ate her soup. Kent rubbed his eyes in astonishment, but the birds remained, diving and plucking and flying back out, gulping down bits and pieces of their victim as they went.

One looked down, eyeing his soup suspiciously, but quickly realized that he had yet to take a bite. He redirected his gaze toward the cup of coffee in front of him. Finally, nervously, he looked back at the old woman. They were still there, those horrible birds. Violently they dove in and tore away, then whirled around to dive again. What were they? Who was this woman?

She caught him staring at her, so he blurted out the first thing he could think of that wouldn't make him sound completely crazy. "Thanks again for stopping to help me."

The old woman flashed a quick smile, shining for an instant before fading back behind wrinkles and clouded eyes. She appeared not to notice the birds as they continued their assault.

"Can I ask you a question?" Number One asked, trying to conceal his fear and confusion by dragging his spoon in thoughtless circles through the soup.

"May I," she corrected.

One nodded automatically. "May I ask you a question?"

"Of course," she replied.

"What made you stop?" he asked.

Again the old lady glanced up, but this time she did not fade. She peered at him intently for a while, as if she were making up her mind about something. She turned her head slightly, looking hard at him from the top corner of her left eye. Then she did the same from the other side.

One felt like he was being measured, and he had the strange desire to pick up one of the cheap paper napkins from the table and try to cover himself.

Finally, after glancing carefully around the diner once more, the old woman put down her spoon, dropped her hands into her lap, and leaned forward into her own cloud of steam. The swirling birds scattered and flew off, circling distantly as her mouth formed the words.

"The Sweet Thief," she whispered.

Three little words.

One's head spun. The bench beneath him felt as if it had come loose from the floor. It was the last thing he expected her to say. How did she know about that? Had she been following him? She obviously knew why he was there that morning! Someone must have set him up. They were likely surrounding the place even now! He shot a panicked glance out the window.

No one was there.

The old woman recognized the look on his face. "You know who I mean, then?"

Unsure of what to do, One nodded.

Instantly he questioned his decision. Perhaps he should have played dumb. After all, he didn't know this woman. Too late. The nod was out and he could not get it back. There was nothing left to do but wait for the consequences. He looked toward the doors, expecting to see them burst open at any moment and for guards to swarm the place. But nothing happened. The other guests continued to eat. The waitress kept on chatting with one of the cooks behind the counter. The steam rose from their bowls. Everything seemed fine – except for the birds, of course.

The old lady smiled and sat back, apparently satisfied.

Number One, however, was far from satisfied. "You know the Sweet Thief?" he whispered frantically.

She looked around again, obviously conscious of their surroundings. Then she smiled and leaned in, reaching across the table to take his hand. "Oh, yes!" The words flowed from her lips so peacefully that they almost resonated, and Kent watched as one of the birds that was again swooping down on the woman suddenly went limp and fell to the floor, landing with a small splat and becoming nothing more than a smudge on the tile.

"How?" he asked, mystified.

The lady seemed surprised by the question. Then her face took on the same expression she had worn earlier. She was dealing with a child.

"What number are you?" she asked.

His jaw dropped, astonished at how much she seemed to know. Was it safe to reveal his number? Should he even be telling her anything? Kent didn't know what to do. Perhaps he should just change the topic. They could talk about the weather. Or he could ask about her grandchildren.

In the end, though, he could not deny it… he trusted her. "I am Number One," he murmured quietly. He felt funny saying it. The title felt too big.

"That is wonderful!" cried the old lady. She squeezed his hand, genuine excitement and joy lighting her face. "I am so thrilled for you!"

Another three birds fell helplessly. The flock was thinning.

She gave his hand one last little pat before retreating and tending to the rest of her soup.

Neither of them said another word about the Sweet Thief. They did, however, end up talking about the weather, and grandchildren, and the challenges she had faced moving out west as a young woman, and how hard it was trying to keep up with the changes in the world now that she was old. The more that she shared, the more the birds fell. So Kent kept talking and asking questions until finally she stood up.

"Young man, thank you for lunch. It's time I went home." Then, smiling at him knowingly, she whispered, "You keep up with your assignments!"

With those words and another small squeeze of his hand, the old lady left the diner. The swarming birds were far fewer and flew further away.

Number One heard the high ringing chime of the bell above the door as she left, and turned his head to face the window beside the booth. As he watched her shuffle to her car, Kent realized two things. She had been right about the soup, and he had been wrong about the world.

Nothing was the same.

Nor would it ever be again.

5

The Assignment

The waitress brought the check.

Kent held out his credit card.

The old lady pulled away.

Like cogwheels all the pieces turned, each of them moving in perfect time with the knocking of the chains against the plywood sign outside as the wind blew past the diner.

Kent gazed out through the window, waiting for the waitress to come back with his card. He wasn't used to the sensation of momentum that was sweeping him along, but he liked it. He felt alive, the rhythm of the universe spinning around and through him. It was as if, for this one rare moment, he was moving with the current of creation.

The waitress returned and Kent sprang up from his seat.

"Wow," the waitress exclaimed. "It looks like you have somewhere to be."

Kent smiled back at her. "You know, I think I finally do." He leaned down and wrote in a nice tip on the credit card receipt, signed his name with a flourish, and headed for the door.

Number One was across the parking lot in a flash. Pulling up on the creaking handle, he slipped eagerly into his car. It was time to find out what this was all about.

The folder was there, silently waiting for him in the passenger seat.

One leaned over and snatched it up, then ripped the seal open with the enthusiasm of a little kid on Christmas. Dropping the detached tab into the cup holder full of gum wrappers, he turned the folder upside down and a thin spiral notebook fell out into his hand.

Kent tossed the empty folder back onto the seat beside him and turned the notebook over in his hands.

It wasn't much to look at. The plain green cover was creased in several places as if it had been repeatedly stuffed into a backpack or something similar, and there was a faded coffee stain on the back. The advertisement on the front boasted seventy pages, but as Kent flipped quickly through he saw that about half of those had already been torn out. Of the thirty or so that remained, only a handful had been written on.

Turning the green cover around to the back, he quickly propped the notebook up against the steering wheel. His eyes leapt to the first page.

What is it about this place?

What is it that makes my underskin tremble with anticipation and fear each time I approach?

I shouldn't be here; that much is clear. I should be back on the mail route. I should be out there defending the code — that sacred litany of the carriers — the long-hallowed and cherished words that whisper a challenge to the rain and sleet and gloom of night.

That is, after all, who I am: a carrier. Third generation, as a matter of fact. First my grandfather, then my father, and now me. We wear the sidewalks and bear the conversations of our people. I am proud to do it.

Of course, it is different than it used to be. The paper that for so long ushered words from here to there has been largely replaced by faster, lighter forms, and our job has become less than what it was — more an arm of business now than of humanity. Oh, we still carry the occasional sentiment. Our role is not without heart. But like I said, it is not what it was. Like all good things, we had our moment.

Then the earth spins and hurls it all away.

Adapt or die is what they tell us. So now we carry more for less. We get there faster and earlier, racing against an unavoidable fate, plodding on like the last dinosaurs down trails of fading glory.

I am still proud to do it.

I love my uniform. The sharp crease in my collar. The bag upon my shoulder. The sewn on badge that tells the world who I am. It reminds me every morning that I matter. Maybe less now than before, but maybe not. What does the world know?

I pull my hat down until it feels just right. I lace up my shoes. I set my eyes to the route. And when you get your mail every day all year long, so efficient and accurate that you almost never stop to doubt it, that is me.

Never late. Ever faithful. I am a postman.

I am so reliable that you normally don't even notice me, rarely think about me, never really know me at all...

I walk to music. Always have. In the early days I whistled as I walked. I whistled the songs I heard on vinyl as a boy. I couldn't take grandpa's turntable with me on the route, but eventually I saved up enough money to buy a small radio that fit in neatly with the letters in my bag. It made the load a bit heavier, but it was worth it. The music carried me as I carried it, and I hummed along happily with the sounds that they had somehow taught to come dancing on the air to meet me.

How did it work? How did brass and strings and the human voice all live together in that one black box? I couldn't tell you. It was a mystery to me then and it's a mystery to me still. That doesn't make me love it less.

What a delight it was when they figured out how to let me record my favorite songs myself. To be able to capture music with the push of a button and then wear it around on my belt? It felt like more power than a person should have. Of course, that never stopped me from using it.

My first walkman was one of the best birthday presents I remember unwrapping, and I enjoyed it every day until the tape gasped and died, sliced to ribbons by the rainbow shine of CD's – which died themselves soon after when it all went digital.

Today I walk with an iPod, carrying 1517 near-perfect songs in the pocket on my shirt. Crazy world. Even now, I know it's not the end. Soon they will figure out how to get rid of the wires altogether. Skip the ears. Send the music straight to my brain. Give me songs I can taste and touch and smell.

For now the music is in my pocket, and I'm content with that. It gives my feet a rhythm as I journey up and down the sidewalks, stepping over the concrete cracks like the skips and pops on an old record. They aren't in the music anymore, but I can still feel them. There in the sidewalk. There in my steps. There in the many little chips that the years have taken out of me. You can make it sound as good as you want, but the cracks are still there. Always there. So once in a while, not often, but once in a while, I switch the music off and just whistle. The cracks seem smaller then.

Why I ever crossed the line? I'm still working on that one.

We know not to do it. It's a federal offense — one that to the carriers is akin to heresy, adultery, and murder. If there are seven deadly sins to the Catholics, there are three or four to the carriers, and at the top of that list, the very top, is the one commandment we all know...

You simply do not open mail.

Not a frayed edge. Not a worn flap. Not letters or tubes or boxes. No matter how curious, no matter how much one might stand to gain, the seal formed by glue on paper is the line without which the entire system is undone. The security of the mail is paramount to its worth. We all get it. So we don't do it.

Then I did.

What was I thinking? I don't know. I don't remember what it was that sparked the fire in my belly, that strange and irresistible draw that makes us do the things we know we will regret. I don't remember why it was this one that did me in, when so many times I had turned away in innocence.

It doesn't matter now.

The tattered envelope was directed to an abandoned house on the outermost loop of my route. I carried it up the walk, pressed the cracked doorbell, and listened for the dull chime behind the door. I checked the slot that I had checked a hundred times before. Still sealed. There had been no one home since the last renters skipped town four months earlier.

To be honest I knew there was no point in trying to deliver it, but I am a creature of habit. I would rather just do my route, sing my songs, and step over all the same old cracks. Change is painful. So I kept on doing an extra ten purposeless steps every day. It wasn't hurting anyone. Besides, I knew the day would come when someone would be back in that house and I'd have to add it in again. It was a nice enough place. It wouldn't stay empty forever. So I kept my routine like a dog returning to an empty bowl, knowing that one day it would be full again.

It was empty that morning, though, and that poor paper finch in my hand was left without a branch on which to light. It fluttered back into my bag and chirped the whole way as I drove back to the office. Its song was irresistible. I couldn't whistle loud enough to keep from hearing it.

I parked my truck.

I grabbed my bag.

I pulled out the letter.

Whenever I find an envelope with no return address, it always makes me wonder. Is it secrecy? Is that why the sender doesn't put anything in the top left corner? Surely they know how to do it. Maybe they just forgot. Or maybe it's just sheer laziness. Perhaps it is a show of independence, a passive aggressive rebellion against the powers that be, even as they use the system to send their words around the world. I don't know. It's better for me not to think too much about those things.

All I know is that there was no return address on that little envelope, which means I should have taken it inside and put it in the dead-letter bin. That is what is expected, taught, demanded. That is my job. That is what I had always done before, and since.

This once, however, that is not what I did.

To be fair, I never broke the seal. The envelope was torn, a hole in the side so big that the corner of the folded note was hanging out. So I never really opened the mail. But I did coax the note out through the hole.

31

A moment later it lay open in my hand, faded and yellowed with age.

"It's a matter of life and death.
2212 Bismuth Vale"

I read the words. I saw the mark.

Perhaps there is nothing else I could have done.

I suppose if I hadn't I would not be here, but here I am, so surely I did. Whether or not I could have done differently involves a knotted mess of concepts like predestination, free-will, chaos theory, and a bunch of other considerations I would put more time into if I thought they mattered more. The fact is they don't. I stand here staring eye to eye with nothing but what is. Reality. The here and now. All day every day.

It doesn't matter what else I might have done.

Here I am.

2212 Bismuth Vale

If I were to draw out from among the sketchings in my imagination a blueprint for the perfect hideout, this place would be it. It was completely regular and altogether not, at once both inconspicuous and intoxicatingly mysterious. Walls full of secrets. Narrow doors that closed the way to sites of meetings that might change nothing at all, but that might just alter the course of human history. Hidden thoughts and files marked "secret" were the mortar in the walls, and from the concrete steps out front to the dark alley that ran around back, the whole place smelled like destiny. But it was not a clear scent. It was hazy — so that while you could feel the beast coming through the trees, you could not quite make out what manner of beast it was.

Did this place have answers? Yes it did. But behind each door lurked both the promise and the price. For that reason no one came here by accident.

No one but me.

Maybe not even me.

Now it's not unusual to get vibes from certain houses. In my line of work, it's hard not to. I approach hundreds of doors every day, stepping up to the portals where people enter and exit their private sanctuaries. I get a whiff of each one regularly enough to recognize different scents and flavors. Like clothing or sheets, a house will eventually take on the essence of those within; the aroma of the occupants' souls seeping from the foundation and popping up like grass in the yard. That is why two houses built side by side in identical styles can come to feel totally different from one another over the years. It's the touch and quality of the people who live there that coat the walls like unseen paint, and the colors are as varied as a box of crayons.

Some have nothing to hide. Welcoming and unguarded, those homes make it easy to come and go, and I whistle my way up to the door and back without a second thought. Other homes have thick scars and deep wounds. They bristle at my approach like a chained dog in the yard. I waste little time when delivering to those places. Then there are a few that are just plain evil. I can feel the invisible claws lurking inside, and while some people evidently enjoy such suffocation, I do not. I drop their mail and go before a door can be cracked or a curtain pulled back.

I thought I had seen it all.

So why was I now so stuck in place; my feet a thousand pounds each and tar on my toes?

A short handrail pointed the way up three worn concrete steps to the door, but even though I wrapped my fingers around it, the best it could do was prevent my retreat. It drew me no closer to the summit.

What was I to tell them? 'Um... hello. I opened your mail and here I am...' Ridiculous! That is what this was. It was time to walk away and forget the existence of the little yellow note. Just refold the paper, stuff it back in through the hole in the envelope, and bury it in the dead-letter bin where it belonged.

'It needs to be delivered.'

It is none of my business.

'Delivering mail is your business.'

But I wasn't supposed to open it.

'How do you know that?'

It is not mine!

'That is exactly why you read it; to find out who it belongs to.'

This is preposterous.

'They need help.'

Not my help!

'Obviously your help. The message came to you!'

Only by mistake.

'How do you know that?'

We've been through this. The letter is not mine! Besides, I have no idea what any of this is about.

'Only one way to find out.'

Curiosity killed the cat.

'You are not a cat.'

Look, how would I explain myself, handing them a letter with no address on the envelope? What if they asked how it got open?

'You tell them the truth: you found the letter already torn open. Then, if they object, you simply explain that you are a mailman and that you are trying to deliver the mail.'

I guess that makes sense...

'Right then, up you go.'

Wait! No! This is absurd.

I turned to leave. It was simple. All I had to do was release it. Let the questions remain questions. Remove the hand from the rail, about-face, and walk away whistling. Back to normal.

Wishful thinking. The current was too strong. I stepped away four times, and four times I turned back; back to that cursed door. I shake like one betrayed every time I think of the hands that planed and hung that door. Would that they had been sick that day, or that the sun had scorched the forests from which the wood was drawn. Anything to keep that door from standing in the world.

It would have been more productive to wish against everything and nothing all at once. The door remained, and I was drawn to it as if by gravity itself. Unyielding, insistent, victorious, the door hauled me in. Three slow steps and I knocked. I should have knocked soft, but much practice had made me swift and efficient.

They heard, and came.

6

Thieves' Wages

Number One dropped the notebook onto the seat beside him.

What kind of assignment was that?!

His body was still in the parking lot outside the old lady's diner, but his mind was beating down the door of a silent building forty minutes away, screaming for answers. He had no idea what to do with the folder they had given him. He expected a name and a photo and a description of what he was supposed to steal. What he found was more like someone's private journal.

But whose journal was it? Kent had no idea. He didn't know any mailmen. He didn't even write letters. How was he supposed to know what to do?

The letdown was crushing. Having just seen the otherworldly birds, and with the old lady's potent words still fresh in his mind, he had been entirely convinced that this was it. Purpose was waiting! He had rushed out to his car, at one with the pulsing of the universe, breathless with anticipation, thrilled to feel the world finally bending to reveal the overarching and all-important destiny that would be consummated with the opening of this folder! Then… nothing.

It made no sense.

A rambling journal entry in a tattered notebook? Surely that wasn't what this had all been about. Kent wondered if he'd been given the wrong folder by accident.

He shook his head and glanced down again. There was no doubt that whoever owned the journal was somehow tied to the thieves, for the address they had written there was the same one Kent had visited that morning. But the assignment itself…? Kent couldn't find one sentence that even remotely hinted at what he was supposed to do.

Who was the mailman?

What was Kent supposed to steal from him?

His mind raced, trying to find something to latch onto, but again and again he came up empty. With a weary sigh, he wiped his face with his hands and let his head fall back against the headrest. He'd had enough for one day. Casting one more dubious glance at the notebook in the seat beside him, he leaned forward and turned the key.

The engine roared to life.

It should have been a long drive. An hour and a half of asphalt slipping beneath him should have been plenty of time to figure a few things out.

Kent blinked and was home.

Climbing numbly from the car, Number One scuffed up the short sidewalk and fumbled with a fistful of keys. His mind was too busy chasing other things to make sense of the shapes and colors of the keys, so he shoved them blindly, one by one, toward the lock. After two failed attempts he found one that worked and he stumbled inside. A second later his jacket found its way to the high-backed chair just inside the door. He tossed his keys onto the narrow island that separated the kitchen from the living room and sent the cryptic notebook spinning across the tiny apartment to land on a small couch along the far wall. Then he grabbed a peach from the kitchen and began to head for his room.

Not even halfway there, Number One pulled up short.

Kent stood in the living room just in front of the kitchen counter, his hand in his pocket and a befuddled expression on his face. He couldn't for the life of him figure out why he had a pocketful of coins.

He almost never used cash anymore. Plastic was easier. The few bills in his wallet had been there for weeks. He didn't actually buy anything with them. And coins? Coins were nearly unheard of.

It was so rare for Kent to have coins in his pocket that the coin jar on his dresser - a mottled red and blue clay heart that his niece had made in her junior high pottery class - hadn't needed to be emptied in over a year.

So why were there coins in his pocket?

One frowned in confusion, trying to recall even one time throughout the day when he would have dealt with actual currency. There was lunch at the diner, of course, but he distinctly remembered using his credit card to pay for that. Apart from the diner… there was nothing. He had bought nothing else all day. In fact, he thought back four and five days and could not recall a single transaction involving cash; not one instance that would explain the coins being there.

He rattled his pocket, perplexed.

There were coins.

But how? From where?

Intent on putting this new mystery to rest, One scooped up the contents of his pocket and drew them out.

He opened his hand, expecting to see the familiar shine of nickels and quarters. As he looked down at his palm, however, a powerful chill raced up his spine. Only his desire for answers kept him from throwing the coins to the floor and fleeing the apartment.

Lying flat in Kent's hand were five dense, heavy coins, each about the size of a quarter. But they were not quarters.

They were dark. Much darker than the color black, the coins seemed to gobble up the light around them. And they were cold on his skin; a terrible, empty cold.

One leaned in close to get a better look, moving them around with his finger, and noticed that there were markings etched into both sides of all five coins. He squinted and raised his hand closer, trying to make out the details. It was difficult to see, as the void of light around them obscured the engravings, but by tilting them just so he was able to make out the image.

Birds…

Each coin displayed the likeness of one of the vicious birds he had seen swooping down on the old woman in the diner. So wild and mad in flight, so merciless and destructive in their tearing and gulping, the birds were now held frozen in his hand.

Over each bird was stamped a single word. 'Ligatio.'

Still unsure what he was seeing, Kent flipped one of the coins over and looked at the back. The symbol in the center of the coin jumped out at him. He had certainly seen that before.

Above the familiar mark was another word. 'Redimere.'

Dazed by what he saw, One shuffled over and slumped down on the couch. The path was pulling him forward faster than he could run.

He sat for a while, staring at the blank wall across the room.

In one hand he clutched a half of ten coins, the markings clearly indicating some kind of connection to the old lady who had helped him that morning. With the other hand he reached out and retrieved the notebook beside him on the couch.

Not sure what else to do, he read it again.

The mailman. The music. The note. The den.

What did it all mean?

He trailed the mailman through his journal once more, struck again by the precipitous walk up the steps. That part was all too familiar. The rest of the journal, though, seemed pointless.

Was it a code? Some kind of metaphor?

If not, if the mailman was a real person, how was he supposed to find him? Should he just start following postal workers around until he found one who… who what? Who listened to music and whistled?

This was insane.

And what of the coins?

That question would have to wait.

Kent's train of thought was suddenly broken by the loud buzz of his phone rattling on the floor. Evidently it had vibrated itself right off the counter under the constant barrage of calls from his boss throughout the day. How many times had she called?

Kent pushed himself up off the couch and walked over to pick up the phone. He looked at the screen. Sure enough.

"Hello?"

"Where are you?!!" the phone exploded.

"I'm very sorry, Mrs. Sullivan." Kent tried to sound remorseful, but after what he had seen in the past twenty-four hours, it was hard to get too worked up. Some things just seemed less relevant than they had a few days ago.

"Do you have any idea what you did to us today?"

Kent swallowed an unexpected smile and fought off a powerful urge to point out how the world would keep spinning quite nicely without a day's worth of tile adhesive being shipped to northern Omaha. He tried to focus instead on making things right. It was his job, after all. "Yes ma'am. I'm very sorry."

"I've been calling all day!" Mrs. Sullivan continued, still raging. "Why haven't you picked up your phone?"

"I had car trouble," One explained. "And when I went for my phone to call in, I realized that I had left it at home. I am really sorry. It was a crazy day."

"That's right it was a crazy day!" Mrs. Sullivan shouted. "Mainly because I was answering calls and e-mails all afternoon about how unprofessional I am and how our customers are threatening to never order from us again because they can't do their jobs. And why can't they do their jobs, Mr. Hentrick? Because you didn't do yours!"

"Yes ma'am."

"So where were you?" she demanded.

It was a question he had known was coming. Compelled to think the situation through a hundred different ways throughout the day, One was prepared with the simplest answer of all: He didn't have to tell anyone where he had been.

"I had a personal appointment this morning before work, but when I got back to my car it wouldn't start. I couldn't call for help because I didn't have my phone, and it took over an hour to find someone who was willing to give me a jump start. I tried to find a way to call in and let you know what was going on once I realized that I'd left my phone at home, but it's as if pay phones don't even exist anymore." Kent kept talking, hoping that she would not think to ask where he had gone after that. He was in no way going to tell her about invisible birds and mysterious coins and journals from mailmen he did not know. "Anyway, I'm very sorry. My immediate thought was about how my mistake would inconvenience our customers, and that is not something I ever want to do." Kent slowed down as his explanation came to an end. "I'm also extremely sorry for making your day such a mess. There just seemed to be nothing I could do to get myself back on track."

One paused and waited. Listening closely, he heard Mrs. Sullivan take several slow breaths.

When she spoke again she had softened considerably. "Your record up to now has been spotless. At the same time, this cannot happen again. So here's what we'll do... This is obviously going to be a write-up, but I am willing to flag it as personal emergency leave with extenuating circumstances, provided you come in early on Monday and double up your run."

"Yes ma'am."

"And the next time you fail to show up and I don't receive a phone call or a carrier pigeon or a smoke signal telling me why, you will be finding someplace else to work. Do we understand each other?"

"Yes ma'am."

There was a click and the line went dead.

After she hung up, One took a few minutes to go through the absurd number of messages that were piled up on his phone. He couldn't help but smile at the increasing level of panic in each one. The drama rose like a pointless tidal wave, and by the time he got to the eighth message he was dying. How did people let themselves get so upset about things that didn't matter? He didn't know where the thought came from, but an image sprang up in his mind of Egyptian contractors stressing out about pyramid construction deadlines. It was very cartoonish, and one of them definitely had Mrs. Sullivan's voice.

Chuckling to himself, Kent chose 'delete' twelve times. He thought about saving the last message, just in case he ever needed to reference his boss's near-hysterical tone at a roast or in court. In the end, however, his love for a clean slate won out, and his in-box went empty.

Kent slipped his phone back on the counter and began his nightly ritual. Tossing a burrito in the microwave, he threw on a T-shirt and a pair of shorts and wandered out to eat while staring down at the coffee table in the living room. The trail of clues he had received in the mail was there, all carefully arranged and patched together with his own scribbled notes about what he thought each one might mean.

Nine packages. Nine odd clues. Nine places on the table.

The last of them was in the middle – the folded note, faded and yellowed, opening to reveal a simple address. Pressed into the paper was the mark, the one that kept showing up like breadcrumbs on the trail.

One ran his thumb along the back of one of the coins in his hand. The mark was there as well. He knew it well enough now to see it with his eyes closed. And when he closed his eyes he saw something else; the paramedic's sleeve… and the man who had been pulled from the flames. There was no doubt. From now until the day he died, he would never forget that.

Life pulled out of death.

It was the single most important thing that he had ever seen.

7

Bringing in the Loot

The sound of the rain outside went silent as Kent stepped in and closed the door. He took a moment to ruffle his fingers through his hair and carefully wiped his shoes on the mat. Then he looked up and found the escort waiting for him. She smiled in greeting and Kent took a step forward to follow her down the hall. One step was all he managed.

Freezing in place, Number One raised a hand to his face, slowly drawing his fingers down his cheeks toward his chin. "What in the...?"

The hallway couldn't possibly be larger than it used to be. It had only been one day! Besides, there wasn't a hint of drywall dust anywhere. No splintered studs, no forgotten hammer left behind... No work had been done here. Yet somehow it was different.

Kent was sure he had come to the same address. He'd walked up the same steps and entered through the same door. Yet there was no denying the strange and simple truth – the hallway was larger. There was now ample room for him to walk beside the escort, whereas before he had felt almost entombed as they walked in single file. He didn't understand.

The size of the hallway was not all that had changed. It was brighter as well. New lights overhead? Fresh paint? No. Neither. It just was. Some of the dinginess had been rinsed away, but there was no reasonable explanation as to how or why.

If those had been the only changes, that would have been enough to mystify him. But there was one more difference that really sent him reeling.

One hadn't seen them on his first visit. He was absolutely certain of that. The walls had been bare. He distinctly and clearly remembered that. Bare, drab, dingy walls.

Now there were portraits.

Portraits lined both sides of the hallway, each portrait successively larger than the one before. The first few were so small that they appeared as little more than specks, mere dots upon the walls. A few steps later the portraits were the size of small tiles. As One stumbled after the escort toward the other end of the hall, the portraits grew in size until he was able to make out tiny faces staring back at him – one face per frame.

There seemed to be no rhyme or reason as to what sort of people were pictured in the portraits. There were women and men; old and young and middle-aged; people from every time period he could think of and from more races than he knew existed. Culture colored each portrait, as clothing and settings provided clues as to when and where each person lived. But there were no dates, no names.

How many were there? He looked back over his shoulder and could still see the door through which he had entered, but despite the short distance he knew that he had already passed more portraits than he could fully examine in a lifetime. One was baffled.

Where had all these portraits come from? How had they been hung so quickly? He considered asking the escort how there had been time to put up so many portraits, but the question seemed hollow and out of place. In the end he said nothing, stepping over to the wall instead.

The escort paused and waited in silence. It was as if his interest in the portraits was expected.

The faces at the point where One stopped were the size of his own, and he stood nose to nose with a young man whose liquid eyes seemed as if they might blink at any moment. There was maturity and depth in those eyes; a bearing that was striking to see. And though the tribe to which the young man belonged had not existed in over a thousand years, his portrait was brimming with life.

Kent stepped closer. He was determined to solve at least one of the mysteries that had recently swept into his life, and he peered around the sides of the portrait in the hopes of discovering how they had been hung so quickly. As he inspected the frame, however, the answers he hoped to find danced mirthfully away.

One's legs wobbled so hard that he nearly went down.

On top of the frame, piled up against the wall, was an impossibly thick layer of undisturbed dust. This portrait had not been hung last night. It was put up ages ago. Though the walls on which it had been mounted could not be more than a few decades old, this portrait had been here for centuries.

There was no getting his head around this one. One turned toward the escort demandingly, but was met with that same tranquil smile.

The escort said nothing.

It was clear that no explanation was forthcoming, so Number One turned urgently back to the wall. No longer aware of himself or of how outrageous his behavior had become, and desperate to know what in the world was going on, he reached out, took hold of the frame, and lifted the portrait from the wall.

The escort raised her eyebrows slightly, but she did not stop him. The newcomer's boldness would be allowed, so long as no damage was done.

Kent watched as the dust floated softly to the ground, then looked up to find that the space behind the portrait was much darker than the rest of the wall. He scowled thoughtfully, as yet one more piece of evidence suggested that this portrait had been here for a very long time.

Number One turned his attention to the work of art in his hands. The canvas was thicker than he expected. He wasn't sure, but he didn't think it looked like fabric. Curious, he ran his fingers gently over the back.

Kent recognized the texture at once, and the touch of it brought forth an image as striking and real as the portrait itself. In his mind he saw the young tribesman at work tanning and stretching the hide, then pulling it over and pinning it down on the face of the shield.

One blinked, shocked at the vividness of the image. It was as if he was standing beside the young man in the middle of his village, watching as the hide was folded around and pinned to the frame and then painted with an assortment of berry-blood dyes. How such primitive methods could render such a lifelike image was baffling.

It had hung here ever since, on display for over a thousand years, suspended from the wall by a crude bone peg and a length of catgut.

Impossible? Obviously.

Unreasonable? Of course.

But — like the dark coins in his pocket — it was.

With a reverence he felt all the way to his bones, One hung the portrait back in its place and stepped away. The sacred was all over his fingers. He looked over sheepishly, knowing that he had trespassed on holy ground, but he found no condemnation written on the face of the escort — only understanding. Turning his gaze back to the portraits all around him, Kent struggled to get a handle on exactly what it was that he was looking at. It was not a long-lived battle. A moment later he tipped his king and turned away, no closer to understanding anything.

The procession of portraits continued as he resumed following the escort down the hall. Some were clad in the garb of peasants. Others wore matronly robes. Still others were outfitted for battle. They were all fascinating. A tiny Mongolian woman stood larger than life on the wall to the right. Several steps further on was the image of an ancient and strikingly plump Persian, followed immediately by a figure who wore an arrangement of feathered trappings the likes of which One had never seen. Drawn from every tribe and nation under the sun, the mighty company led him down the hall. Explorers, bankers, mothers, kings; they were all there to watch him pass. None was absent. They looked on him with compassion; they glared at him in challenge; they surrounded him with wisdom. He was a child in their midst.

In the end it was too much, and One arrived at the door completely spent.

He reached for the doorknob, exceedingly grateful for something to hold onto. Had it not been for his forward momentum and the steadying presence of the escort, he would surely have been swept back out onto the street by the immensity of the company gathered in the hall.

The doorknob now his momentary touchstone, he braced himself to twist it and fling the flimsy door out of the way. However, just as he was about to pass through and end the daunting journey through the hallway, he looked up and collided with a force too massive to ignore.

One's knees buckled and his legs went to rubber as he dangled there, clutching the doorknob like the edge of a cliff.

Directly above the door was one last portrait.

Magnificent in color, striking in splendor, immeasurable in every way, it towered far higher than the ceiling should have allowed. Sprawling like a newborn calf, One fought to regain his balance, but he could not tear his eyes from the portrait above the door. It was glorious.

Overwhelmed, Kent stared up, fully transfixed by the greatness of the One upon the wall. In all his life, he had never seen anything so perfect.

It was a portrait of himself.

8

The Mailman's Route

"I guess it's better that you aren't around anymore."

It shouldn't have surprised him. He'd been expecting it for months. But when the moment finally arrived, Eric felt like he'd been plunged into a tub full of ice water.

"You're going to keep doing whatever you want to do. You've proven that." The words were flat and emotionless – facts were being laid out. "Everyone keeps throwing second chances at you, but you are either unwilling or unable to change. It's sad, you know? Getting to the point where it's better to leave someone behind? But that's where we are. We're done letting you hurt us."

"So you're quitting on me, too, huh?" Eric mumbled as if he didn't care.

"Don't...!" Her voice was hard, and it grew harder as the rage took hold. "Don't you dare put this on me! Or on anybody else! You own this. This is yours. For as long as you've been here you've been thinking that your messes wouldn't catch up to you, or that you don't care if they do, or that you'll deal with them later. Well... it's later." The small shoulders shrugged once, cutting him off as she turned away. She would waste no more time or tears. The long dark coat she always wore swayed back and forth as she marched down the driveway and disappeared up the street.

Eric heard the rapping of her heels long after he lost sight of that coat.

Ka-lak ka-lack ka-lak ka-lack...

He heard them all that night.

Ka-lak ka-lack ka-lak ka-lack...

It was the sound of being walked out on.

It wasn't the first time he'd heard that sound, but for some reason this time it hurt a lot more – a lot more than he thought it would; a lot more than he would ever admit.

When Eric woke up he was alone. The last person in his life to try to care had finally had enough. His family had released him years ago, and anyone that could be described as a friend had written him off long before that. There was only one who stuck around, one who scraped and fought and tried to make it work. Now she was gone, too. He'd beaten them all.

Eric didn't get up quickly. He stayed there in bed and had a cigarette. Then he lit another. He fell asleep again just for a bit, hoping to not wake up, but sleep was too fragile to shield him for long. It was broken around lunchtime by the growling in his stomach, and he pulled the sheets to one side and swung his feet to the floor. A fog of depression clung to him as he made his way slowly to the ancient refrigerator. He stood staring for several minutes at the half-dozen items inside, hating all of it. He resented having to feed himself; having to provide fuel for the body that held him here in this god-forsaken trailer.

With an angry jerk, Eric tore the milk from the cold and slammed the jug on the table. He didn't care if it spilled – so it didn't. He ate a bowl of cereal without tasting it, then left it all on the table and crawled back into bed. There was no point in answering his phone, so when it rang he hung up without looking. It could only be two places now, and he didn't want to deal with either one. His stomach burned. Anxiety squeezed his skull. There was no energy to move.

He stayed there for days... until the food ran out and the phone stopped ringing.

A loud knocking on the thin aluminum door jolted Eric from his stupor. Lying perfectly still, he growled silently, willing them to leave.

They knocked again.

Eric slammed his fist into the bed and got up. He didn't feel like dealing with anyone, but he didn't want to hear the knocking again either. Sadly, he moved too slowly to prevent the latter and too quickly to avoid the former.

The infernal banging came a third time.

Eric whipped the trailer door open and stood staring at a man wearing knee-high socks and carrying a large mailbag.

"What do you want?" he barked.

The mailman smiled and nodded. "Delivery, sir."

Eric squinted, confused. "What?"

"I've got a letter for you, sir."

"You apparently also have vision problems," Eric snapped. "The mailbox is out front!"

"I'm afraid it's not going to fit," the mailman replied.

"Not going to fit? How big is this letter?"

The mailman held up a standard size envelope.

"Can't fit that in a mailbox?" Eric pointed at the letter demandingly, incensed that he had gotten up for something so utterly stupid. "Not much of a mailman, are you?"

The man holding the letter wore a disarmingly genuine smile. "Sorry sir, but I'm no miracle worker." He turned and motioned back behind him to where a thick stack of envelopes erupted from the front of the mailbox, threatening to fall to the ground at any moment.

"Oh. Yeah..." Eric muttered.

"Can I bring you the rest of the mail from the box?" the mailman offered brightly as he handed over the letter.

"Sure," Eric allowed. "Just put it right here." He stepped forward and dropped the letter into a trash can just inside the door. It was already filled with a pile of unread paper.

"You got it!" The mailman left without another word, only to return seconds later with a thick stack of envelopes cradled underneath his arm. He added the stack to the growing mountain, gave a quick nod, and turned to go.

Then, all at once, just before Eric was able to slam the door, the mailman paused and turned back. "Say, do you play checkers?"

The battle had begun.

"Do I play checkers?" Eric's lip curled in disgust.

Unseen troops raced into position.

"Yeah," the mailman confirmed. "I carry a board in my mailbag just in case one of the old ladies on my route wants to play."

The air went deadly quiet. Eric flashed a tight smile and hoped, his rage boiling beneath the surface. Just one wrong word is all he needed. "Did you seriously just call me an old lady...?"

"No. I just, um... That came out wrong," sputtered the mailman. "All I mean..."

Eric's expression was one of utter disdain.

"He thinks you are an idiot."

The voice was a roar. Echoing up from somewhere between the mailman's neck and his shoulders, the roar was deafening, suffocating, oppressive. It made the trailer feel even smaller than it was, pressing in on all sides and demanding his retreat.

But the mailman was not a new thief.

"Here's the thing..." explained the mailman, refusing to back down. "There are a few older ladies I've delivered to for years who are pretty lonely, so I try to drop in on them once in a while for a game of checkers. They seem to really enjoy the company." He tried to smile despite the derision smoldering in Eric's eyes. "But I would love, just once, to sit with a guy my age, you know? So here's the deal. I'm on my route and I have a few minutes to kill. Let's play some checkers. One game. What do you think?"

Eric smirked for a moment. His guards screamed at him not to do anything that would betray the irrational excitement he felt at the idea of playing a game. He hadn't played checkers since... he couldn't remember the last time he had played checkers. "I don't think so, man."

The mailman wrestled for an instant. He felt exposed and vulnerable. A strong desire to retreat swept through his bones.

This is where the heist would either fly or fail.

The mailman looked Eric in the eye. "Why not?" he asked candidly. "You got something better to do?"

A long silence did the talking for Eric. He had nothing better to do. He had nothing to do at all.

The mailman smiled and walked past Eric into the trailer, pulling a thin wooden board from his mailbag and retrieving a set of checkers from his jacket pocket.

Not knowing why, Eric followed and sat down.

As the mailman set the checkers in place upon the board, his thieves' eyes snapped open and the unseen came into view. This was more than just a run-down trailer. It was a prison camp. The target was being held in a remote outpost, miles away from the rest of the world. Shadowy figures rode high in the three guard towers of the triangular compound, their weapons on hair triggers, and somewhere in the middle of them was the vault. The mailman saw it all; the hidden barriers appearing like barbed wire fences in the mind of the thief.

"Hey! Who's out there?" one of the guards barked into the darkness.

The mailman crouched just out of sight, excitedly hiding within the cover of the trees. This part terrified him. He looked at the captive man sitting on the other side of the table and focused on the goal. This man mattered. His freedom was the point of the entire operation. No matter what else happened today, the mailman knew one thing: he would be walking out of here with as much as he could carry.

A shot rang out, followed by a flurry of blasting as the guards unloaded blindly at the tree line. The mailman laughed to himself. He could sense the fear behind their noise and thunder. Their hold was a tenuous one and they knew it. The mailman waited for the first shots to fly overhead, shrugging off the insults the guards sent spraying from Eric's mouth. Then he popped a smoke canister and sped from the trees, flanking the first guard tower and diving underneath to wait out the second volley. The long burst that followed finally slowed and subsided to a few individual pops here and there. The guards shouted back and forth, nowhere near as strong as they tried to sound.

Checkers moved diagonally across the board, pushed forward from both sides.

Spotlights swept the trees.

With the guards' weapons still trained on the forest, the mailman carefully inspected the fence. It was tall, but poorly built, and there were several large gaps in the mesh.

A voice crackled on his radio. "Careful. Watch for ambush."

It was a valid warning. He had rushed into such gaps before, only to get himself pinned down by enemy fire. A full-scale alarm at this point would destroy any chance of success. Still, he could not hold his position forever. There were only so many moments before the camp would be swept by a full decimation patrol, and those patrols always had the same order.

The mailman made a dash for the nearest large gap in the fence. It was wider than expected, and he saw evidence that it had once been a main gate. Largely wired shut, it appeared as if it was still being secretly maintained around the edges. A supporting pole remained intact, and the interior frame had never been fully removed.

He crept forward delicately, senses straining. Every sound and motion mattered now. They were in the thick of it.

"King me."

The mailman stepped carefully. He did not force his way through or come in with guns blazing. He simply followed the gap in the fence, and a moment later he was in.

Once inside, there was almost no resistance. A random shot would ring out from time to time, but none came close enough to do any damage.

With growing confidence, the mailman began to load his pack with sections of the prisoner's chains. He took his time. Each link of chain he stole was deeply stained, and there was a sorrowful groan released by the prisoner with each heavy piece that tumbled into his pack, but in the end his weapons proved more powerful than those of the guards. Each kind word, every genuine smile, the soft stream of patient questions; they all lightened the crushing load just a bit, and the mailman did what he came to do. He stole some of the pain.

When he left an hour later the compound was still standing, but Eric had tasted fresh air for the first time in months, and the cloth bag that once held only checkers was bulging with dark coins.

μ̄

μ̄

9

Waltzing with the Id

One had never – not on his best day – looked as good as he did in the portrait above the door. He wanted desperately to take the whole thing outside, frame and all, and hang it up on every billboard beside every road in the world so that every person everywhere would see him just like this.

It was more than just the lighting. Or the angle. Or the fact that it captured him in his prime. The man in the portrait was complete! Every ounce of potential had been realized, each talent maximized.

Kent stared up at himself in awe.

It was not easy to exhaust the escort's patience, so when the weathered one gently cleared her throat One flinched. He blinked several times in confusion, wondering why his neck was so stiff and why he felt so hungry. Then he looked back and found that the drawn shades behind him no longer blazed at the edges.

One spun around in alarm, looking to the escort for some kind of reassurance. Surely he hadn't stood here all day!

The escort said nothing.

The mortifying reality could not be denied – night had fallen.

"I'm sorry," mumbled Number One. He felt ridiculous.

A sad and understanding nod came from the escort.

"Is it too late?" he asked fearfully.

"For what?" the steady one asked.

"To go in?"

"No," she said softly, "it's not too late. Not yet."

One turned back to the door, struggling to keep his eyes down. He knew that it would be wrong to sneak another look, but the draw of the portrait was overwhelming. He seized the doorknob, fully intending to hurry by, but one glance and was hooked again. He could look all day. The One in that portrait was a truly great man!

The escort did not stand by this time. She moved in quickly, and One felt a surprisingly strong hand on his own. It squeezed and twisted and the door before him swung open. Greatly relieved, One pulled his eyes down and stepped through.

The door closed quietly behind him.

On the wall to One's left was the mirror.

Hanging on the wall exactly where it had before, the mirror now served as an anchor, for it was the only part of the room that was the same. Like the hallway outside, this inner room had transformed dramatically since his initial visit.

The old plastic-covered bank of fluorescent bulbs overhead was gone, replaced by high hanging lamps encased in globes of emerald glass. The far wall had retreated two hundred feet, and the resulting space was filled with small round restaurant-style tables. A long bar with stools stretched the length of the wall to his right.

Conversation filled the air as people milled about the room, visiting one another at the tables and sliding into deep booths against the back wall. Several faces looked up and smiled as he entered, and One waved mechanically in response.

"Welcome back."

Startled, One whipped toward the mirror. A million questions swirled in his brain, but he was unable to assemble the pieces of a single one.

"Have you completed your assignment?" asked the voice behind the glass.

One blinked and licked his lips, still trying to get his bearings. "I'm not exactly sure what my assignment is," he answered.

"Did you read the assignment?" the voice asked.

"I did." Number One noticed his reflection nodding in the mirror and self-consciously slipped his hands into his pockets. "I'm just not sure I understand it. It seems like it's someone's personal journal."

"Whose journal?"

"Don't you know whose journal you gave me?" Kent challenged.

There was a short pause.

"It is not for you to question what we know." The voice behind the mirror did not sound angry, but it was extremely firm. One felt the rebuke in his bones. "Whose journal is it?"

"A mailman?" One replied.

"Yes. The mailman is your assignment."

"I don't know any mailmen." It was a reasonable comment. It was also ignored.

"Do you have anything to turn in?" asked the voice behind the mirror.

One reached instinctively into his pockets. Car keys. Phone. Coins. The dark coins slid over one another at his touch, and he wrapped his fingers around them. Drawing them out, he held the coins toward the mirror. They felt exceptionally cold and heavy in this place.

"Who are those for?"

"What do you mean?" Kent asked.

"The coins you hold are extremely valuable. They are in your hand, therefore they are yours. What do you want to do with them?"

"Do I have a choice?"

"Yes."

"What options do I have?" he inquired.

"They can be kept. They can be used to buy certain things. And they can be turned in."

"What can I buy?"

"That depends. Who are they for?"

One paused. There was a tugging inside. It was gentle but urgent. The moment approached, then was present, then began to pass by. He decided to go with it.

"The Sweet Thief." The answer was out before he knew what he meant, but it felt right.

"Are you sure?"

"Yes. These coins are for the Sweet Thief."

The words had no sooner left his lips than there was a lightening in the room. Heads all around the den looked up from food and games and conversation as a trumpet blast echoed from all four walls. The crowd raised their fists and cheered as the coins in Kent's hand blew into the mirror like smoke.

"Well done." The voice sounded pleased, almost proud. "You are now Number Two."

10

Den of Thieves

A thin wine-colored carpet covered most of the floor. The areas that weren't carpeted, including the open space just in front of the bar, were checkerboard tile; black and white. An assortment of tables and booths were scattered throughout the room, and with the lamps glowing dimly with subdued tones of garnet, ruby, and an occasional splash of emerald, Number Two felt like he had stepped into the strange hybrid offspring of a casino and an all-night pancake house.

There were no windows in the place, and all of the lines and corners were soft, as if the entire scene was an unfinished sketch – partially erased and smudged so many times that it appeared to have no real edges. The overall effect was easy on the eyes, but Number Two wasn't sure what to make of the faces peering at him from the tables. As was becoming the norm with this place, he had expected more.

These people – he could only assume they were other thieves – didn't look the part at all. They were altogether ordinary; not the sure-footed cat burglars that he secretly hoped to find gathered here. There were no ninja assassins or world-savvy superspies within their ranks. They were just average, unimpressive, run-of-the-mill folks. As they looked up at him from the room's fleet of tables, he doubted that even one of them had any more going on than he did. Kent's heart sank. This was not the powerful company he was hoping to find. This was just a bunch of nobodies sitting around chatting.

He turned halfway back toward the door, fully intending to leave, when suddenly his view was obscured by a figure in his face. The person was so close that Kent had to lean back just to see him, and even then it was hard to focus. Dark spiral curls and fiery red cheeks all but engulfed every other feature he had.

"I haven't seen you here before! I would know if I had. I have a great memory for faces. You're new aren't you?"

"Uh, yeah." Cringing uncomfortably, Kent tried to disengage, but the man shuffled quickly around to stay in front of him.

"That's great!" The effusive invader stuck out a hand and smiled far too forcefully. "I'm William."

Kent felt trapped. Not sure what to do, he glanced around and found a group of thieves watching from a table nearby. The four of them wore expressions of warning, sympathy, apology and amusement, in that order.

Despite their silent counsel, Two gave in and shook William's hand.

He immediately regretted his decision.

Clearly delighted to be shaking the newcomer's hand, William showed no interest in ever giving it back. It seemed as if he found Kent's reception and subsequent indoctrination into the den to be the entire purpose for his own existence and that, moreover, the mission was one that needed to be fully accomplished within the hour.

With manufactured interest, ruddy cheeked William began asking prying questions that seemed specifically designed to make Kent's personal space his own permanent sitting room. It was so unnatural, so forced, that Two began to squirm, awkwardly trying to reclaim his abducted limb.

He must have looked pitiful, because one of the women at the table finally rose and came to his aid, gracefully taking the octopus by one of his clingy arms. "Excuse me, William, but can I ask a quick favor?" she said as she stepped between them. "You are probably the only one who can help."

Two never heard what the favor was, but as William was led deftly away, he knew that he had just been done a huge one.

The three thieves who were still at the table had put their conversation on hold only long enough to witness Kent's deliverance. Now they dove back in, one of them motioning for Two to come over and sit down.

"So what really knocked me off course," explained the lone remaining woman, "was how well-guarded my last two assignments were. Totally not what I expected." She was speaking to both men seated with her, though she was glancing more to the person on her right than her left.

The man to her right nodded supportively, though his accompanying grin was not an altogether happy one. A faint hint of sorrow tinted the edges of his eyes. There were two very distinctive scars on the man's face that seemed to line up with his smile; a pained smile that was allowed to slowly melt away. Exactly what had caused the fascinating scars was unclear, but Two forced himself to look away before he got caught staring.

"This last one, for instance," the woman continued, leaning in intently, "was just a child. It almost seemed like overkill to steal from one so small. I didn't bother preparing much at all, expecting to simply walk in and take what I wanted."

The scarred one chuckled, but from his expression — and the fact that he was staring through the floor — it was clear that he was laughing in tragic agreement at some memory of his own.

"It was one of the most vicious experiences of my life."

Again the scarred man nodded absently, unconsciously tracing a line on his cheek with a gloved hand.

"So how do you know?" She did not ask the question merely to bait conversation. The young woman was searching for answers, hunting for wisdom. Kent thought she was pretty. Very pretty. She was also intensely focused on getting an answer to her question.

The scarred one shook his head and frowned. "I'm not sure we can."

His pupil frowned thoughtfully. Then she sighed, drew her mouth to one side, and nodded. Disappointing as the answer was, it was the one she was expecting. More importantly, it was the truth.

Two was star-struck. Clearly the wisdom of the scarred thief was not for show, as he was not willing to make up answers to dress himself in sage's robes. And the woman was willing to assume a student's pose. Kent was impressed on both counts, and he looked at the thieves at the table with a fresh perspective. While they had initially appeared unimpressive, their clever disguises were now transparent, and Two saw that these were the kinds of thieves he should have expected all along.

The third person sitting at the table – the one who had motioned him over – now glanced up and lifted several fingers in his direction. Two wasn't sure if there was any specific significance to the greeting, but it seemed friendly enough. The man's meaning might have been easier to interpret were his face not half-covered, but he had been listening to the conversation with his chin and mouth buried in the palm of his other hand and he did not seem overly anxious to change anything about it. He rotated his head on its perch and gave Two a long blink, as if bowing to him with his eyes – a pair of bright green gems that gleamed with hidden knowledge. The rest of his features were almost cartoonish, with a tiny upturned pug nose, bright gray hair, and barely any ears at all. "Jim," he said in brief introduction, then pointed to his right. "Adelle. Sam."

"Samuel," Sam corrected.

Two smiled a hello to each of them, began to introduce himself, and then paused as if he was confused about how to proceed.

Jim caught on instantly. "It's OK. Numbers and names both work at our table. Samuel likes it better that way." A complex flurry of glances shot back and forth.

"That's it!" Samuel stood up in mock outrage. "Waiter, we're going to need a large pitcher of water and a branding iron over here." He glared at Jim and raised a hand into the air, motioning as if to summon the waiter over. It was all in fun, of course. There was no waiter. There was no branding iron either.

Samuel sat back down and all three looked over at their guest.

"My name is Kent Hentrick," he said. "I am Number Two."

Jim pretended to stifle a chuckle that he had stifled far too many times, and Samuel sighed in exasperation as the green-eyed thief slapped the table and breathlessly mouthed the words, "Number Two!"

"Good, very good, can we move on?" Samuel silently apologized to Kent as he jerked a thumb over at Jim and shook his head.

The mock hilarity faded into comfortable grins all around, and Adelle stuck out her hand. "Welcome, Two. Glad to have you with us."

Kent stood up halfway and shook her hand, then did the same with the others. He was glad for their acceptance, but knowing all too well how easily a loose tongue can ruin a first impression, he sternly ordered his mouth to stay closed as he sat back down. It obeyed, but only for a moment.

"How do you like the den?" Jim asked.

"I'm not sure yet," Two answered honestly. "Just got here." He added a wry smile and was rewarded with three approving grins. Bolstered by their response, he decided to try to relight the conversation. "What were you talking about when I came in?"

They all regarded him with mild surprise at the bold question, and he quickly tried to make amends. "Sorry. Is it out of line for me to ask that? I'm afraid I haven't had time to learn thief etiquette."

"Thief etiquette?" Jim erupted incredulously.

"Oxymoron," Adelle muttered.

"Don't call Sam names," Jim returned.

The banter was fast and casual, passed around like a shared glass of wine. They all sipped without making too much of it, which only made it that much better.

The taste still on their lips, Samuel raised his eyebrows in Adelle's direction. The choice was hers.

The young woman regarded Number Two for a moment, then led off with a question. "How much do you know about assignments?"

Here it was. Kent sat up straight. Time for joking was over. This is why he walked over in the first place.

"Well, I'm just beginning, obviously."

The three looked at him, waiting. Their demeanor made it clear that stalling would not be entertained.

"To be honest, I'm really not sure what to make of my assignment. It's not very clear what I am supposed to do."

Again they waited, offering nothing but ears. If they were impressed by his humble confession, they didn't show it. They just sat there looking at him; clearly willing to accept whatever he decided to share.

Two went silent, unsure of whether he should tell them anything else. They were thieves, after all. Could they be trusted? He didn't know. Fear pressed in heavily, and Kent was aware that by offering nothing else he would be forcing them to take over his part of the conversation. The decision hung in the air for one long moment – the chance to resist that fear and speak; to face the risk and step out into open space.

He missed it.

Silence claimed the table, and one by one the three looked away.

"Well," Adelle resurrected things at last, "there are many different types of assignments. I'm not sure which kind you have, or how you earned the tokens you just turned in, so I don't know how much of this you will understand." She glanced at Samuel and again he shrugged permissively.

"My latest assignments have involved guards that were much stronger than I expected. Samuel has been here at our table the longest, so I was asking him about that." She trailed off, unsure of whether or not the newcomer was tracking with her.

Two was not only tracking, but his curiosity overwhelmed his caution and he blurted out, "I don't think my first target was guarded at all. In fact, she was the one who extended the invitation!"

Samuel again nodded to Adelle. This was now as much a quiz for her as a lesson for Two.

"Some targets aren't guarded," she began. "But that doesn't mean there are no guards."

The puzzled look on Two's face spurred her on.

"Part of you didn't want to steal from her, right? Too tired? Too much to do?"

Suddenly Kent saw them. Adelle's words flipped on the light and they stood out in his memory plain as day. They *had* been there! So familiar as to be invisible, camouflaged within his own skin, the guards were there from the beginning.

Adelle verbalized what he was seeing, "Guards are guards, even if they are hiding within the thief."

Number Two could almost see the guards attempting to steer him away from the old lady, trying to prevent him from taking the time to have lunch with her. The walls of these particular guards, though, were not built on her side. They were built on his!

Two looked down at his chest with a sickening new awareness. His own body... his own mind... the guards were already there! It was the first time the thought had occurred to him, but it was undeniably true. He was compromised from the very beginning! Feeling violated, he resolved then and there that he would never fail to see the guards again. From now on he would be vigilant! Yet even as he declared his resolution he heard them laughing. They would be back, and in greater numbers. They would wear him down.

Adelle looked to Samuel and he smiled, evidently pleased with the answer she had given.

Then the scarred one turned his attention to the brand new thief at their table. "Those guards," Samuel said quietly, "the ones inside of me... they have come to be the most formidable guards I ever face." The words were not loud or overbearing. They did not need to be.

They were true.

11

Poisons and Packages

The sidewalk feels old today, I'm not sure why. It's as if there is a thin layer of mildew on the world. I'm having a hard time finding places to look where things aren't in some state of decay. Dilapidated houses, cars forever up on blocks, the half-eaten squirrel carcass pressed up against the curb – everything is breaking down.

The sidewalk cracks don't feel much like music lately. They feel like broken bones. The shattered spine of some old forgotten dinosaur.

I hate to be so negative, but the route has grown long; far longer than I bargained for. My feet are tired. The bag is heavy. Even the songs in my pocket feel weighed down.

Few things are as sad as stale music, especially when the recording is crystal clear. It's like catching old age in a jar.

The problem is I know it's going nowhere – this world that we're in. There are no new letters in the mail. It's all the same old stack, just reshuffled and sent around one more time. All that changes are the names, and every one of them already is on the way out before they read a word.

I'd rather be stealing now. I'd rather be stealing all the time. It's the only thing that matters. Paper feels heavy by comparison. It's a terrible chore to carry loads that don't last, to bear irrelevance from here to there, only to turn around and bring it back. I can almost feel my life draining out, like bathwater from the tub.

There is a sign that hangs just inside the den's front door. I have no idea how many times I've read it, but I can picture it clearly in my mind, right down to the grain of the wood and the chips in the paint. Its words echo with every crack-filled step I take.

**"A few will spend their days etching eternity.
The rest are merely scribbling on the wind."**

Those words haunt me now. There is no longer any contentment in things that do not last. The farmer breaking his back to fatten future corpses... The doctor wracking his brain to wrestle from death a brief delay ... Why the struggle? In the end it ends the same. What good is all my work once the dirt is tossed on — once rains have rubbed each letter from the stone?

It's all meaningless. All but the heist.

So I pull my cap down grudgingly and walk my route a ruined man. Sweat never seemed so cheap, labor so overpriced. I see the cost of living here, and cannot justify it.

That is why I steal. It's the only thing that feels permanent now. What I steal they can't have back. There is no erasing that work. I see the coins I've taken. I witness the lightening of the load.

I can't unsee that, and there's no way I can go back. The world is different now.

I'm heading to the clinic again in the morning. Wish me luck.

Number Two scowled as he looked at the page.

The escort had delivered it to him at the table in the den. As she approached, his heart had leapt at the sight of the manila envelope in her hands. Surely this time he would find some answers about exactly what he was supposed to be doing.

No such luck.

It was just more of the mailman's ramblings.

Two excused himself from the table and stalked toward the bar, shaking his head in frustration. How was he supposed to complete his assignment with no instructions, no address, and no name? And what was the point of giving him this person's journal?

Number Two slumped down on a barstool and carefully examined the envelope. He had seen enough spy movies to suspect that there could be hidden messages involved, especially given the string of mysterious clues that had led him to the den in the first place. But as he turned the envelope upside down and inside out, it was clear that it contained nothing beyond the two handwritten pages he had already found.

Exasperated, he unfolded the second page – apparently a later entry in the journal.

I've been a fool. Drawn down an endless sidewalk to nowhere...

They did not hide the cost when they taught me how to fill my bag and haul it out. They told me it would hurt. But they also assured me that it mattered, and that I wouldn't be alone. Liars! I don't even know who I am writing to anymore.

The bag is frightfully heavy now. Not the mailbag. That one remains the same. It's my checkers bag that weighs me down – that and others like it. I can't carry any more, and I don't know what to do with it all now that they didn't show up...

How many hours did I spend listening to people cry about their problems? How many of their worries did I take up as my own? How much did I sacrifice just to lighten others' loads? I cannot count it all.

And for what? For the den to abandon me and leave me to die...

I don't know how much more I have in me. The music has gone flat. Monotonous rhythms and tedious songs are all I hear, and there is no room for checkers in my bag. I've grown to hate the game.

Something's got to give.

μ̄ μ̄

Two slammed the folded paper down on the bar and whirled around, resolved that he would not leave this place again without getting a few answers. But there was no one around to hear his questions. The den was deserted. The dim lights had gone dimmer still, and the tables, which only a moment before had been crawling with thieves, were now completely empty. A lone barkeep was the only other person left, wiping the tables and sweeping the floor as he moved slowly through the room. He paused momentarily and looked over, apparently just to let Two know that he was there.

"Where is everyone?" Kent barked, his tone far more forceful than he intended. Still annoyed by the unhelpful journal, he was also unnerved to find himself in a room that had been so swiftly abandoned. It felt as if there was an evacuation and he alone had missed the alarm.

The barkeep leaned his broom against a table and instantly began to perform a strange medley of tics and twitches. Passing both hands over his balding scalp, he folded his arms on top of his belly, stroking his forearms with his fingertips. He swallowed hard, blinked once for a really long time, and then wriggled his nose and upper lip. An instant later he was pinching an earlobe with one hand while tugging the side of his belt with the other. He went through all these motions again, in such quick succession that it would have been comical to watch if he weren't so clearly discomfited by Kent's question. When he spoke, it was with a profound stammer, and it took some effort for him to get the words out. "They usually c-c-clear out p-p-pretty quick… w-when it's time to go."

"No kidding." Two looked around again. "It's like everyone just disappeared."

"W-w-well… you *are* thieves," the man said. Had Jim, Adelle, or Samuel made the same remark, there would have been a significant pause tagged onto the end. There was no such witty emphasis here. The man was dealing in facts and nothing else.

"What about the office?" Kent probed, glancing in the general direction of the mirror. "Anybody back there?"

The man shook his head and reclaimed his broom. "I always lock up on m-m-my own. Won't be anyone round here for a f-f-few days."

"A few days?"

68

A slow nod and averted eyes were all the barkeep offered in response, but Two was tired of waiting for answers. If this was the only person left in the place, he was going to tell Kent all he knew.

"What about you? Are you a thief?" demanded Number Two.

"I just take c-c-care of the place." The man was sweeping again.

"But they don't let just anyone in here," Two pointed out.

The barkeep's big dopey eyes shot up, glaring at him seriously. He stood up straighter, his voice grew louder, and his stammer disappeared. "Oh no! Nobody else gets in here! Nobody." His knuckles went white around the broom handle, and he swung his massive head first to one side, then to the other.

Two felt bad for setting him off.

"Of course... You're right," Kent assured him. "No one else is here. I just thought maybe you were a thief, too."

"I just take c-c-care of the place," the barkeep mumbled, beginning to sweep again.

Though he was glad to see the man calm back down, Two was far from satisfied. He decided to try a different strategy. "I bet you hear all kinds of things."

One huge eyebrow moved toward the ceiling. "Whatchu mean?"

"There are people talking in here all the time. You must hear a lot of stories."

"I don't p-p-peek," he stated adamantly. "That's rude."

Number Two sighed. He looked away from the barkeep and scanned the rest of the darkened room. There was no one else.

"But you are friendly," he tried again. "Surely people talk to you about things."

"I like it when p-p-people tell me things."

"What kinds of things do people tell you?"

"I don't remember... b-b-but I like them."

"You don't remember anything that people tell you?"

The barkeep thought for a moment. Then his eyes lit up. "I remember ab-b-bout them sailboats. I wouldn't forget that!"

"No. I guess not. Sailboats are wonderful things."

Something in the man's expression suddenly changed. He was seeing them. Huge sails, brightly colored and full of wind, drifted past his eyes as an entire fleet of ships headed out; away from safe harbor and into danger. Terrible storms awaited them and some would not return, but they sailed out anyway into the full host of fortune. Daring the monsters of the deep and pushing at the edges of maps, the sailors mounted their huge chariots and rode the waves. The barkeep was with them. He was seeing their faces and smelling the salt air — never mind that he had never set foot on the shore himself.

No, he would never forget them sailboats. To him they were the greatest things in the world, and as real as the table under the touch of his rag.

"I don't suppose you know who I could ask about my assignment, do you?" Kent interrupted.

The question startled the man out of his reverie, and his eyes went dull once more. "What?"

"Is there anyone I can ask about my assignment?"

A slight scowl of consternation leapt to the man's face, revealing how obvious his answer was going to be. "You can ask anyone you want."

Two shook his head. They were not speaking the same language. "OK. Can I ask *you* something about my assignment?"

The man looked up in surprise. "Me?"

"Sure. Why not?" Two said brightly.

What could it hurt? Worst-case scenario, the barkeep wouldn't know a thing and he would have to come back in a few days and ask someone else — exactly the situation he was in now. There was nothing to lose. Expecting nothing, he gave it a shot. "Do you know anything about the mailman?"

The barkeep jerked as if he'd just been sucker-punched and turned to glare at Kent with surprising clarity. "Who did you say?"

Two tensed and balanced his weight on his feet. "The mailman."

Eyes flashed. Tears fell. The broom shook. Echoing sobs filled the room, followed by peals of remembered laughter and instants of nearly catatonic staring. The storm went through this entire cycle twice before the barkeep finally spoke.

"He was nice to me." The words were choked out between heaving sighs. "So sad what he d-d-did." Waves of powerful emotions flooded the broom bearer's face. Then he gave up the fight and dropped his head.

"You know him?!" Two could not hide the shock in his voice.

The man did not answer the question, only looked up piteously, his droopy bulldog eyes begging for things he did not know how to say.

"Who is he?" cried the thief, leaning forward in desperate excitement.

"You help him, OK? I've been asking a long time. You b-b-b-bring him back, OK?"

"What do you mean?" Kent begged. "Who is he?"

Again the man buried his face and shook for a while. When he was worn out he wiped a wet hand under his nose and took up his broom and his rag to leave.

"I don't understand," Number Two wailed. "Who is he?" Kent didn't want to drive the man into further sadness, but he needed the answers hiding within this strange mountain. If it meant learning something useful about his assignment, he was willing to tunnel in, drill, and mine. He would resort to dynamite if that's what it took. "Who is the mailman?!"

The barkeep turned one last time and fixed him with a piercing gaze. "You think this is b-b-by accident? This is big. B-b-bigger than you!" Then he shuffled away, his broom in one hand and his rag, soaked and heavy, in the other.

The words he had spoken remained in the room.

Number Two felt as if an enormous weight had been lifted off his chest. The barkeep was right! This whole thing was bigger than him. Much bigger! It was no accident that he was here, and whoever had gone to all the trouble of getting him here wouldn't leave it like this. Two let the swirling slow and settle around him. There would be time. There would be more clues. There was peace in that. He would simply keep his eyes open and take advantage of whatever came along.

Greatly relieved, Two slid the journal pages back into the envelope and tucked it under his arm. This wasn't an accident. The path was still unfolding up ahead. In the grand scheme of things, there was no need for him to freak out. The whole thing was much bigger than he was, there was time for it all to happen, and that barkeep was a sweet thief after all.

12

Puzzle Pieces

Number Two didn't make to-do lists or outlines. Leaving occasional notes for himself on the refrigerator door was as close as he got to having a structured organizational system. Those tools just did not feel right in his hands.

The lone exception lay before him on the coffee table in his living room. For some reason, this one thing grabbed his brain like nothing else ever had. He saw the pieces behind his eyelids. They swam in and out of his dreams. He caught himself trying to put them together as he drove, as he sipped his morning coffee, and as he stood in the shower each night.

The first was a thin silver chain, broken at the clasp. He had placed the chain at the top of the table, dead center.

To the left of the chain, about six inches away, was an extremely old photograph. The people in the picture looked as if they were from his great-grandparents' generation. It was striking to look at them and know that they were all gone. The earth could be turned inside out, and not one of them would be found alive. That was an odd thing to consider while looking in their eyes.

On the other side of the chain was a hospital wristband, clipped two holes in. He'd tried several times to read the name on the band, but most of the letters had been blacked-out with a marker. At least one of them looked like it might be an "m," or maybe an "n," but he wasn't sure.

In the bottom right corner of the table lay an empty bullet casing.

To the left of the casing was a wedding invitation, all the names and dates removed by a pair of scissors.

Still further left was a small silk sachet filled with lead pellets.

Above the sachet was a tiny vial of water; the glass etched with the mark that he now seemed to see everywhere he went.

To the right of the vial, in the very center of the table, was the yellowed note with the address that was turning his understanding of the world upside down.

And in the space to the right of the note was just that – an empty space. It wasn't because he was still waiting for a clue. No, the seventh envelope had contained nothing at all.

Nine spaces. Nine clues. Hundreds of questions. Precious few answers.

Two glanced below the table without meaning to. He still had the stack of envelopes in which the clues had arrived. Identical in size and shape, all the same shade of standard yellow-brown, they were each addressed to him, his name pecked out on some ancient typewriter.

Not knowing what they were, he'd actually thrown the first two out with their contents, but he'd gone and dug them from the trash when he received the third. Curiosity made him do it.

There were nine in all.

Nine packages arriving in three waves of three consecutive days, each wave falling three weeks after the last. Kent didn't see the order of the pattern until he wrote down all the postmark dates and plotted them on a calendar. But once he did the picture emerged before his eyes like some kind of magic trick. He was amazed. He even felt strangely honored that he was the one being allowed to play the game. Someone had put a lot of thought into this.

Kent quickly noticed, once he had all the dates written down, that one day out of each wave fell on a Sunday. That anomaly, in conjunction with the journal, led him to lie in wait near his mailbox, thinking that he would ambush his assignment the next time the mail was delivered. But the mailman who delivered to his apartment turned out to be a woman, and while she was friendly enough, willing to stop and chat with him for a moment, she responded to one of his strange questions by admitting that she could not whistle.

It was another dead end.

Kent headed back to stare at his coffee table.

According to the calendar, the first clue was stamped on the autumnal equinox. It was now almost Thanksgiving. That meant that the chase was officially two months old, though Kent knew that his journey toward the Sweet Thief had been going on under the surface much longer than that.

It had never been this clear before, though. There were clues on the table. There were things going on!

In between the pieces on the table were small bits of paper that he had written himself, notes and ideas and questions scribbled as he went. He saw in them an evolution, an organic connection, and even though the puzzle was still in pieces, there was an undeniable force at work that was pulling the pieces closer. It was not random. Too many unrelated events were lining up for him to write it all off as chance.

So he kept digging, unwilling to accept or deny anything without knowing more.

That had been his mindset throughout the first month, defending the entire irrational search on the basis of his own need to see what was there. The second month was easier to justify, as it was based much more on his first-hand experience. After all, the things he'd seen for himself were the easiest things to believe.

Now, however, it seemed that even personal experience was not invulnerable to doubt. Already he could feel time beginning to rebury what he'd found; eating away at the freshness and erasing the details. If he was not careful, the whole thing might soon become nothing more than his own personal mythology. So he rushed to write it down, date it, stamp it. Perhaps then it would stay real.

Number Two grabbed a pencil and furiously captured all he could remember of the conversation with the thieves in the den, then read through the mailman's journals again, underlining phrases that jumped out at him. He stared at the pages and the clues and the scribblings until his dinner went cold, still sitting in the microwave. Was he any closer to the mailman now than he was before? Maybe. Maybe not. One thing was sure. This was his life. For better or for worse, he was married to this path – this story that was evidently being written long before he knew he had a part in it. He read it all again, turned over each piece, stared at the ceiling, searched his soul.

Kent did not last long. Punished mercilessly by his neck the week before after falling asleep awkwardly on the couch, he had promised himself not to make that mistake again as long as he lived. With a resigned sigh he pushed himself to his feet, ate dinner without tasting a thing, and stumbled through the shower into bed.

His body slept.

His mind did not. The nine pieces swirled in his dreams all night, while the mailman walked his route through the places Kent knew best.

13

Back to Work

Kent was not sure what to expect as he drove in to the warehouse Monday morning. With the early glare reflecting off his sunglasses, he weaved expertly between the other commuters, wondering the whole time what it was going to be like when he clocked in. He had seen too much over the past three days to pretend that everything would be the same. But would the others be able to tell? Maybe they already knew. Maybe they were watching him.

Number Two pulled in and parked in his usual spot, feeling like the new kid on the first day of school. He took a deep breath, blew it out, and leaned over to peer up at the warehouse through the window on the passenger side.

The building looked normal. Its pale walls were their usual shade of drab, and the heavy green door looked exactly like it had last week, complete with the patchwork of rust creeping across from east to west.

Two got out of the car and headed toward the door. He strode across the parking lot and marched up the ramp, but just as he grabbed the handle he noticed that his jaw was aching.

How long had he been clenching his teeth?

Two opened and closed his mouth several times, trying to loosen the muscles in his face and neck. Then he pulled the door open and stepped inside.

As usual, it was the smell of propane exhaust from the forklift that hit him first. For several minutes that was all he could smell. Then slowly he became aware of the gentler aromas of concrete flooring and iron racks. The potent odor of tile adhesive was stronger than them all, but it was trapped in thousands of tubs, stacked on pallets and stored on huge racks throughout the warehouse, and he could only detect a hint of it.

It all smelled very familiar, and while part of him found that greatly comforting, he also found it strange. How could things be the same today as they were last week? How was the world not completely different?

Kent glanced over to the wall beside the large bay doors and saw the stacks of empty pallets, a few jacks waiting nearby to push them around once they were loaded. There were several rolls of plastic there as well, leaning against the wall until the time came to wrap filled orders for shipment.

Beyond the loading dock were all the different racks of product. Tubs of three different sizes in each of four different colors filled the majority of the warehouse, forming long aisles in between the enormous steel shelves that stretched all the way back to the end of the warehouse. Everything was in its place. Nothing had changed.

Kent swung his arms in wide circles and clapped his hands twice.

Time to get to work…

He walked briskly across the wide concrete slab to the interior office, waving to a few other workers as he went. As with most businesses, the warehouse had its own set of systems and schedules, and they generally resulted in things running fairly smoothly. Number Two hoped that this would be one of those smooth, play-by-the-rules kind of days. Slowly opening the office door, he was relieved to find no one inside.

Against the near wall hung an angled metal rack. Two stepped over and snatched a thick stack of shipping manifests from the third basket. He began thumbing through them, checking to make sure that everything was in order. Not wanting to linger in the office a second longer than necessary, he made a hasty exit and finished looking over the orders back out on the floor. It was a full delivery schedule, but not nearly as bad as he thought it might be given his missed shift on Friday. Many of the late orders could be doubled up with the ones going out today, so that if he packed the truck tight enough and managed to squeeze in an extra half of a run, he could be largely caught up in one shift. He smiled to himself. Back to normal. After the weekend he'd had, that sounded nice.

Two wound his way through stacks of pallets and aisles of glue, quickly tagging the different products and quantities he needed to have loaded on his truck. Then he went to the dock manager, got signed off, and pulled his rig out into the yard to fuel up. By the time he returned fifteen minutes later, his load was already half assembled and wrapped in plastic. He backed in carefully, leapt from the cab, and walked around to the rear of the truck, throwing open the latch and raising the door.

"Missed you last week, Chieftain."

"Yeah, thanks Nelson. Crazy day."

"Aren't they all?" The dockworker spun his jack around easily and ran the forks under a loaded pallet.

Though consciously trying not to see anything strange, Two could not help but notice that Nelson was carrying a ton of damage. Dimples, like the ones made by bullets on steel, covered Nelson like huge chicken pox.

Working nearby, busy wrapping the next pallet, a young dock assistant wasn't much better off. There was some sort of creature attached to the back of his neck by a handful of short suction-cupped arms, two of which stretched around each side of his head and latched on at the corners of his eyes. As the men loaded the truck the blob-like creature would periodically start throbbing and pulsing, gorging on the boy for long stretches before settling back down.

Two blinked and shook his head, trying to shake the images away.

"You OK, Chieftain?"

"Yeah. I'm good. Just trying to get myself together."

The dimpled one grunted appreciatively. "Must have been some weekend."

"You have no idea..." Two replied. He focused on the upcoming drive and the images faded out, but as soon as he realized that they were gone they appeared again. How was he ever going to function normally?

"You hitting Sarlacc first?" Nelson asked, checking his clipboard to make sure they were loading the pallets in the right order.

"Yeah," Kent nodded. The name of the customer was really Sarland's, but the dock workers had renamed them all, and the dock names were almost as official as the ones on the invoices.

"Good luck getting out of there in less than a thousand years," Nelson murmured in what they all agreed was a pretty spot-on Calrissian.

It was one of the ten standard jokes that the dock crew had on hand, and even though it wasn't that funny, they all grinned approvingly as they rolled the next set of pallets from the dock onto the truck.

In less than an hour the day's first shipment was packed in tight.

"Thanks guys," Kent called out as the trailer door crashed down.

"Drive safe," Nelson shouted back.

The dock assistant gave a quick nod and walked away, the creature on his neck gorging as he went.

Kent walked outside and hopped up in the cab. After noting the time in his logbook, he pulled out from the back lot and spun the wheel to the right. The morning's run was as smooth as any he had ever had. Traffic was unusually light, his stops went flawlessly, and not one person even mentioned his absence three days earlier. Even Sarlacc had a loose grip.

The afternoon run was even better.

Almost miraculously, Number Two was completely caught up in one shift, and he parked his empty truck at precisely the same time he would have on a normal day. He couldn't believe it. Whistling to himself, he walked to the office to turn in his invoices.

"I see you decided to show up today…" Mrs. Sullivan was apparently angry again.

"Yes, ma'am. And I was able to get caught up."

"I'm glad to hear that," she sniped. "It's only your job, after all. Nothing important."

The sarcasm bit in deep and multiple rounds of hot ammunition leapt up in Kent's mind for a return volley, but Number Two never fired. He was fixated on her wounds; too appalled at her injuries to want to hurt her any worse.

Deep and just a few hours old, there were long, jagged slices in the skin on Mrs. Sullivan's hips and thighs. The area under her chin was torn as well. Everywhere she saw flaws there were wounds. She was careful to keep them hidden from the world, but Number Two was no longer looking with worldly eyes. He could see the gashes from across the room. Suddenly the darts her guards threw at him as he walked in became clear for what they were. He brushed them off and smiled.

"Why are you looking at me that way?" Mrs. Sullivan snapped.

"Because I think you are OK." Two leaned back into the calmness of his own words. The kindness, once he let himself settle into it, was sublimely comfortable. The guards' darts lost their sting.

"What?"

"I've worked for quite a few people," shared Two, "and as far as bosses go, you're really good."

The wounds did not close up, but the screaming sound of inferno in the room died down. Her guards were not pleased. They raised hands full of darts.

"I never took you for the brown-nosing type, Mr. Hentrick," she snapped, "but let me make this perfectly clear... Flattery does not excuse negligence."

"No," Kent agreed. He looked at the darts and they fluttered to the ground like toys. "And it shouldn't. That's one of the reasons I think you're OK. You hold the line." Two handed her his invoice copies respectfully and walked out. He felt good. More than that, he felt purpose! A plan formed before his eyes even as he walked across the warehouse floor. For the next two weeks, he would make it a point to compliment Mrs. Sullivan once every day.

You can't do that.

Four little words...

Suddenly the warehouse erupted in bursts of gunfire. Blinding sheets of gray smoke blew in through the bay doors and the ceiling flashed ominously with the light of distant shelling. Two dropped and crawled beneath the line of fire toward the nearest stack of pallets, choking on the thick smell of sulfur as bullets pinged off the steel racks above his head and ripped through tubs of glue.

As the smoke rose like a furnace and pallets exploded into splinters all around, the warehouse disappeared. Glue ran out from the mangled tubs onto the floor and turned the concrete slab into a swamp. The guards moved in around the perimeter. Two could see them stalking closer through the smoke, but with the muck sucking at his calves and ankles he couldn't move. The glue jumped all around with splats and splashes as the guards opened fire and sprayed the swamp.

Two felt his pulse racing. He was vulnerable out in the open like this. He needed to find cover, but the glue was too thick and the guards were too fast. They advanced and quickly flanked him, keeping him pinned down with suppressive fire while they loaded larger weapons. Only one way was still clear: full retreat.

The terms were simple. All he had to do was take back the plan and the guards would lower their weapons. Forget Mrs. Sullivan. Scrap the idea. No one would know, and no one would get hurt. There would be no comments about him sucking up to the boss. He wouldn't be charged with harassment or inappropriate behavior. He wouldn't have to worry about Mrs. Sullivan getting the wrong idea about his feelings toward her. All he had to do was come in to work, do his job, and go home. That's what he was being paid to do, after all. It wasn't his business to care about anything else…

The swamp bubbled and hissed as mortar rounds dropped in through the smoke.

Number Two thought it over. There were a thousand reasons to simply back up and disengage and only one to keep on fighting.

He would start tomorrow.

Two of the guards gurgled as they fell back into the glue. The rest roared in outrage and fired recklessly into the opposite wall, unable to find him in the blinding light of the flash grenades he tossed out.

The more that Number Two focused on Mrs. Sullivan and her wounds, the less he thought about the guards. And the less he thought about the guards, the more of them were sucked down into the swamp.

They did attempt several attacks over the next two weeks, but for all the aggression of their initial charge the guards ultimately proved to be of little substance.

"People are whispering in the warehouse. They are talking about how you are making advances toward the boss."

"She must think you are after something. Remember what she said earlier…"

"Who do you think you are? You are a driver! You drive a delivery truck full of glue. Stick to what you know."

"Ever hear of harassment? Better keep your distance."

Kent ignored the guards' attacks and pressed on, delivering one compliment every day. A few of the compliments fell flat, and one earned him an all-out rebuke when he found Mrs. Sullivan in a particularly hostile mood. Each time the guards leapt up to laugh at him, but he met them head on. He was waging war. He didn't expect it to be comfortable.

The guards swung at him in flurries, often at night in his thoughts and always just before he went in to see her, but the more he battled the more readily they gave ground, and at the end of two weeks Mrs. Sullivan had received ten kind words just from him. Ultimately the guards could not stop him, and after every shift he reported to Mrs. Sullivan's office with more than just receipts and invoices. Kent broke through the walls and endured the sting of the darts to bring a tiny light into the room, and for a few moments each day the guards were pressed back into the shadows, forced to watch helplessly as their prisoner strolled around in freedom. They spit and cursed, but the darts soon stopped flying.

They hated him.

They hated his visits.

They hated the loss of every dark invoice-stamped coin that slipped away in his pockets.

Finally the guards called it in.

"What's his name?" asked the operator.

"His name is Kent Hentrick. Do you need the address?"

"Oh no," the operator assured the guards. "We know exactly who that is. We've been monitoring him for quite some time."

14

Talking Shop

"Who are they for?"

There was no hesitation this time. "The Sweet Thief!"

As the invoice-stamped coins evaporated from Kent's outstretched hand the den went absolutely bonkers with cheering. The walls felt as if they might explode outward for the energy that surged through the room, and Number Three rode over to the familiar table on a wave of euphoria.

"Kent! Welcome back." Adelle's eyes were shining.

"Another successful mission? Outstanding!" Samuel beamed at him.

"You're two for two, my man!" Jim cheered.

"Actually," Kent drew himself up ostentatiously and placed a hand upon his chest, "I am now Number Three!" He declared his new station with such self-importance that the table cracked up.

"Oh, of course! How thoughtless of me!" Jim played along, "I grovel for pardon, your Trifold Eminence."

"Pardon granted," Three returned, then added gravely, "this time…"

"Forever in your debt," whispered Jim, solemnly bowing his head.

Kent sat down to their eye-rolling applause and accepted a plate of food that was pushed in his direction. "Oooo. What are we having?"

"We got the sampler platter," Adelle replied.

"Which means," Jim added, "that since you got here last, you mostly get what we liked least."

"That's only fair," Three shrugged, reaching out to try something that he immediately discovered tasted nothing like chicken.

"Good, huh?" Jim prodded.

"I think so," Three answered, still chewing. "Give me a minute." After a short gustatory pause he confirmed, "Yeah, it's really good. Did you get this from the bar?"

"Sam did," Jim nodded.

As Kent went in for another taste Adelle reached out and lightly patted the table in front of Jim, "So you were saying?" she coaxed.

"Hmmm..." the green-eyed thief tugged at his earlobe. "I think I was talking about how it boggles my mind that he willingly attaches his name to the den – that whatever we do gets pinned on him."

Adelle did not try to act like the whole idea wasn't puzzling. "It does seem like a reckless thing to do with his reputation. I wonder why..."

Three pairs of eyes shifted toward the same side of the table.

"Don't look at me," Samuel said, raising his hands as if to ward them off. "I don't get it either."

Kent had no idea what they were talking about, but it seemed that they had reached a dead end in the conversation anyway, so after allowing enough time to make sure he was not intruding, he pointed an onion ring at them and spoke up. "I have a few questions."

"I'll bet you do," Jim said.

The experienced thieves all went silent, yielding the floor to the newcomer.

"First of all..." Three glanced around the room and pointed out the significant number of vacancies, "why are there so many empty seats?"

"Stealin ain't easy..." Jim drawled, leaning back and lacing his fingers behind his head.

Adelle smirked at Jim's antics and explained, "Many people who could be amazing thieves are too afraid of losing what they have."

"So their seats go empty?" Kent surmised.

"Yes."

"OK, next question." Number Three was now all business.

"Whoa! Easy, rookie…" Jim teased. "Just how many questions do you have?"

"All of them," Three shot back.

"Yeah, that sounds about right," Jim acquiesced. "Fire away."

"Do we choose our targets or do our targets choose us?" Kent asked.

"Ooh-hoo!" Samuel hooted in delight from the other side of the table. "Now that's a question!"

"And the answer is?" Kent demanded, focused like a laser beam.

Samuel pointed past Adelle to the thief directly across from him.

"Both and, my man!" Jim crowed. "Both and."

"I don't get it," Three replied.

"I'm afraid you're going to run into more and more of that," Samuel interjected. "Hard and fast answers aren't really how things work around here. A lot of times we ask questions looking for a yes or no answer and we get both."

"And more questions," Adelle added.

"That sounds frustrating," Three observed.

"It can be," Adelle replied, "but it helps a little once you understand why."

"Alright then… Why?" Kent pressed.

"I'm not sure it will make sense to you right now," she replied.

"Try me."

Adelle looked at Samuel, who gave a quick nod.

"OK, let's say your Grandma wants to spend time with you, so she invites you over to bake chocolate chip cookies."

"You're right," Three smiled. "This isn't making sense."

"Stay with me, Kent. Now you love Grandma's cookies so you go over and bake with her for an hour every weekend and it's wonderful."

Jim rubbed his belly and licked his lips with over-the-top enthusiasm, drawing a quiet chuckle from Sam.

"Zip it you two!" Adelle scolded, laughing as they both instantly froze in place, lips dramatically sealed. "Now one day," she continued, "Grandma gives you a copy of her cookbook because she knows how much you love her cookies." Adelle paused, wondering if Kent might be catching on. "Do you see a problem with our story yet?"

"Nothing glaring," Three shrugged. "I'm assuming this isn't where I steal Grandma's recipe and publish it myself for a small fortune?"

"What?" Adelle gasped, horrified. "No, I hadn't even thought of that!"

Sam burst out in a laugh, while Jim nodded at Kent in cold approval.

Three winked at both of them before turning back to Adelle. "Sorry. You were saying there was a problem?"

Adelle scowled playfully. "Actually, Number Three," she scolded, fixing Kent with a glare that he found extremely attractive, "what often happens is that now that we have the cookies we stop going over to see Grandma."

Jim and Samuel looked down guiltily.

Three felt it too.

"We are like that, aren't we?" Kent reflected.

"Yes, we are." Samuel's voice sounded strange.

"And we would certainly do the same thing here," Adelle continued. "So the answers we get are designed with too many layers for us to simply run off alone and never come back. They require connection, and that's the whole point."

Alarm bells went off in Three's head. "So truth isn't constant for you?"

"No. Truth is constant," she replied.

"Then the answers must always be the same."

"No," Adelle frowned. "They're not."

"Then there can be no absolute truth," Kent reasoned.

"But there is."

"Which one is it?"

Jim chuckled. "Both and, my man. There's no way around it."

"That makes zero sense," cried Number Three.

"That's where we started, remember?" said Adelle.

"The point is," Samuel clarified, "we have to stay plugged in. Our strength does not ultimately come from us. So while being industrious and self-reliant are sometimes positive qualities, they can be twisted just like everything else when taken too far. Absolute self-reliance is more than dangerous. It's deadly. We have to stay plugged in."

Kent shook his head. "If I wasn't already sure that you three were pretty smart – and if there weren't so many weird things going on in the world – I would say you're all nuts."

"Me too," Jim agreed.

"Any more questions?" Adelle asked. Then she spun her shoulders toward Samuel and murmured excitedly, "It's fun being on this side of the conversation for once."

Samuel grinned at her and then turned to Kent. "You had asked earlier about choosing targets," he said calmly. "That's a vital question." As the scarred thief continued, his tone grew more deliberate, "All of the pain in the world... Just think about that for a moment. The pain of the entire world is an immense, unimaginable weight. Even the pain a single person experiences in their lifetime is crushing. Multiply that by all of the people on the planet and it's a lot."

"Too much," Jim whispered.

"Right," Samuel nodded. "None of us could bear all of it, even if we wanted to. There is simply too much. But that's where our mission begins. We aren't made to carry it all, just some. If we try to bear all the pain alone we get crushed. But if I carry my part of the load and you carry your part, together we can carry quite a bit."

"Like ants," Kent observed.

Adelle laughed out loud.

"Sure," Samuel nodded. "Like ants. That's a good example."

"And convicting," added Adelle. "Bugs have it figured out better than we do."

"Hmmm..." Kent murmured as he considered the comparison.

"On the other hand," Samuel warned, "it's also dangerous to assume the colony will carry the load without you. If you refuse to get in the battle, those beside you end up having to bear more than their share and some of the burden gets dropped. So it's important that you actually choose a target. Failure to choose is failure to steal, and there are few things worse for a thief than to be caught empty-handed."

"But how do you choose?" Three interrupted.

Jim slapped his forehead in mock exasperation. "Oi! Let him get there! You're like kids in a car."

Samuel went on as if Jim hadn't said a word. "There are a few things to consider. First of all, not everyone can be stolen from. Some people are determined to keep their pain; convinced that they deserve it, or that they can handle it alone. Others are so afraid of letting anyone get close enough to see their wounds that they actually join forces with their guards. Trying to steal from them, if you aren't wise about it, will only drain you and get you captured – or worse."

"So we *do* choose our targets," Number Three concluded.

Samuel waved Jim off this time. "Yes and no."

Jim whined from across the table.

"Oh, alright," Samuel relented. "Both and."

Jim nodded, satisfied.

"Meaning what, exactly?" asked Kent.

"Meaning there are some targets you are made for and others that you are free to add at your own discretion."

"But the ones we are made for…" Kent asked, trying to get it all straight in his head. "… they are the ones that matter most?"

"Matter…" Samuel paused, "is probably the wrong word. All the targets matter. But some targets will be more open to being stolen from by you than by anybody else. If you don't steal from them, there is a chance that no one else will. So while every target matters, some need you more than others. And some targets will need other thieves more than they need you."

Kent nodded slowly. That part made sense. "Are there some people who don't need to be stolen from at all?"

"I don't think so…" replied Samuel. "Every person I ever met was carrying something, myself included. Nobody gets out of here without getting banged up in one way or another."

"I know that I have been stolen from many, many times." Adelle admitted. "And while I often resisted the stealing, I have come to treasure those who were brave enough to face my guards and stand beside me. My thieves have been my truest friends – even the ones I never met."

For a moment no one said a word. They were all busy remembering the people who had been there for them over the years, each of them strolling down the hall of portraits in their hearts — sweet visions of their own personal saints.

Finally Samuel broke the silence, "Follow this path long enough and you will learn that the pain we steal eventually becomes a treasure. The coins are a symbol of that."

Kent nodded easily. "Right. So the age-old question about whether pain is good or bad…"

Adelle and Samuel simultaneously turned toward Jim, and he gave them a look of feigned surprise, as if he had no idea what they wanted. He did not bother repeating the line. Everyone had already heard it in their heads.

Samuel continued solemnly. "Now there are those who love stealing pain for the pain itself. They love the feel of it. They actually get pleasure out of hurting themselves. That is not us. If the enjoyment of pain is your thing, you should head for the door now. That's not what we're about. We do not steal for the pain itself, but for the freedom of our targets."

"That makes sense," Three smiled at the veterans gratefully.

"One more thing," Samuel added. "I have already shared this many times with Jim and Adelle. It may be obvious to you as well, but I feel it is important enough to point out… When it comes to stealing, the skilled thief can take away one more thing."

Three stared eagerly.

"Strength, Kent." Samuel's normally calm demeanor moved aside for a moment and his eyes flashed. "Learn from the struggle! Let it make you appreciate things. It can help you grow as a thief."

Three considered the idea. "How?"

"Thieves often become particularly good at stealing the very same type of pain they suffered themselves," Samuel explained. "The reason for that is pretty obvious, but I think about it like this… You have already won some coins, so you've probably discovered that the power to steal pain is rooted in compassion. Would you agree?"

"Yes," Kent replied. "Completely."

"That word. Compassion. It basically means 'feel' and 'with.'" Samuel nodded at Kent significantly.

On the other side of the table Jim raised his hand as if he was in school. However he didn't wait to be called on before jumping in, "What

Samuel is trying to say – in his own special, painfully didactic way – is that those who have been hurt by something often understand that pain better than someone who has never been there."

"For instance…" Adelle cut Jim off, nearly beside herself with enthusiasm, "a person who has been bitten by a bear can understand the pain of someone being mauled far better than someone who has only read about bears in books."

"What?!!" Jim bellowed, laughing. "Bitten by a bear? Really?"

Adelle suddenly realized what she had said and her cheeks went bright red. "Hey! It's all I could think of."

"Being bitten by a bear is all you could think of?" Jim sputtered in disbelief. "What kind of world do you live in, Adelle?"

Adelle searched for something witty to say, found nothing, and stuck out her tongue instead, slapping playfully at Jim's shoulders until he cowered in surrender.

Three tried to salvage the point of Adelle's illustration. "So people who wrestled through their parents getting divorced can relate better to someone who is dealing with the same thing now?"

"Sometimes," Adelle nodded. "At least about the divorce part. But more important is that when you've tasted the same pain as someone else you are less likely to see them as a problem and more likely to see them as a person."

Samuel leaned in across the table. "It's true, Kent. Your wounds can be useful." Then he added carefully, "Once you heal, of course."

Number Three went silent, browsing through his collection of scars, trying to imagine how any of that ugliness could ever turn into something good. He didn't see it. He didn't see how his darkest experiences could become anything valuable. Finally he spoke – a confession to no one in particular. "I've always worried that I would make one huge mistake and ruin my entire life."

Samuel spoke a moment later. "That's funny. I've always hoped that I would do one great thing that would make the rest of it right."

Jim nodded along, staring off into space. "Both and."

15

Thieves' Tools

Number Three was in a near-meditative state of reflection – racing to collect the gold flecks of wisdom falling from their conversation – when all at once Adelle's mood changed. For no apparent reason, she became very sullen and restless and seemed unable to shake it.

"What is it?" Samuel asked at last.

Concern scrawled deeply upon her features, Adelle glanced toward Kent and then looked back to Samuel, silently asking for guidance.

"Tell him." The scarred face was set.

"Are you sure?" she asked.

Samuel nodded.

"Kent," Adelle began gently. "You are about to be tested."

There was no hint of playfulness, no light-hearted joking this time. Adelle was dead serious.

Kent bristled at the warning; not because he was afraid, but because it felt like Adelle was offering up a mystic prediction about the future. He didn't buy into that. Palm readers, psychics, and astrologers all made him pity the human race, and he wasn't about to accept that nonsense here.

"Tested?" he challenged.

Adelle nodded.

"How do you know?"

"I can smell it coming," Adelle said gravely.

Of all the expressions Adelle could have used, none could have annoyed Kent more. It had always evoked images in his mind of hot garbage, and immediately added to the revulsion he felt at someone trying to pretend to be a fortune-teller.

"Do you think you could pick a different expression?" grumbled Number Three.

"What?" Adelle blinked, confused by the request.

"A different expression," Kent repeated. "You know... 'I've got a feeling' or 'my spider sense is tingling.' Something other than 'I smell it coming.'"

"Are you serious?" asked Adelle.

"Yes," Kent said flatly. "I hate that saying."

Across the table, Jim snickered.

"You don't understand," Samuel spoke up beside him. "She does smell it coming."

Three groaned in displeasure. "Great, you too?"

"Kent!" Samuel snapped. His forceful tone took the new thief by the ears. "You are hearing but you aren't listening! Adelle is not using an expression."

Now it was Kent's turn to look confused.

Samuel continued, "You see images of strange figures when the guards are holding a person captive, right?"

Kent nodded.

"Well, not all of us can see them that way. Some of us hear them. Some feel them." Samuel paused. "Adelle happens to smell them."

Kent looked at him as though his head was on backward.

"You don't get it?" Samuel remarked. "That's fine. All that matters is that Adelle sensed something moving in and she chose to let you know. It was uncomfortable for her to share, but she did it anyway because she cares. Do with that what you will." Samuel eased back in his seat.

Kent scowled doubtfully as he glanced toward Adelle, only to find her staring down at a spot on the table, trying hard not to meet his eyes.

"You smell them?" Three asked.

"I do…" she answered, but said no more than that.

Three was still grappling with the concept of someone smelling the guards when Jim leaned across the table, his green eyes sparking. "You know, Kent," he added cryptically, "there are some thieves who supposedly can't sense the guards at all."

Number Three frowned. "Then how do they…?"

"Trust," Samuel interrupted. "That's all they have. It's rare, but very powerful. They are special. Purists."

Kent eyed Samuel suspiciously.

"No, not me." Samuel shook his head. "I see them much like you do."

Kent shifted his gaze to Jim, who also waived him off. "No, I see them too, although I am able to distinguish differences in the strength of their shadows."

"Differences in the darkness?"

"Yeah. Weak ones are wispy, like the highest clouds. The strong, deeply entrenched ones get closer and closer to being solid."

"That would be helpful," Three mused. "You could tell the strong guards from the weak ones before you even got started."

Jim leaned back and smiled proudly in agreement. It was indeed a great skill to have.

"Careful Jim," Sam warned from across the table. "Don't feed your own."

Jim nodded and sat back up immediately.

"Don't get too caught up in the mechanics, Kent," Samuel warned. "What we see and don't see is just the backdrop of what is really going on. The heart is what's important."

Kent didn't understand, and he told Samuel as much.

"Your skills as a thief – your talent and strength and knowledge – they are all good," said Samuel, nodding as he spoke. "But if you forget what they are for, if you start to worship those things for themselves, they will puff you up and make you vulnerable to a whole host of the worst kind of guards. Tradition can be valuable, but when ritual replaces compassion, assignments go undone."

"So don't take notes?" Kent asked lightly.

"Take notes?" Samuel smiled. "Sure. You can take notes. Just don't let them turn into guards…"

Kent looked down at his hands, overwhelmed again at the complexity and magnitude of the whole thing. How could he fight an enemy that was able to attack him from the inside out?

"I know it's a lot all at once." The calm and warmth in Adelle's voice eased the panic that was starting to creep in. "Just remember, you were invited to be here. You aren't alone, and you don't have to do it all by yourself. You just have to carry your piece."

Kent took a deep breath, not even aware of how brilliantly Adelle had just pillaged his guards. Feeling someone at his left shoulder, he glanced to the side and nearly fell out of his chair. The escort from the hallway was standing beside him.

"Do we need to go?" he asked, concerned.

"We have a few minutes," the escort replied.

Everyone at the table stood as the escort pulled up another chair. She was seated and the thieves sat back down. Opening her hand, the escort extended it to Adelle, palm up, inviting her to speak. The thief lit up in response.

"I used to get distracted by my gifts," Adelle began. "The smells are so vibrant, and the memories they dredge up are so powerful… I would often wander off target. It turns out that I was giving them too much attention. Tools should not be treated with more significance than tools deserve."

The escort approved.

"So what do you treat with significance now?" Kent asked.

"We have to find a balance. Cookie cutter formulas don't work. What might be required this time could be totally different next time, even if the situation looks the same."

"I suppose there is a reason for that?" Three asked.

Jim smirked as the other two looked at him. "Gotta stay plugged in," he obliged happily.

Adelle grinned and continued, "The best defense against it becoming either an empty habit or an unhealthy obsession is to always come back to the main thing. The Sweet Thief."

Jim, Adelle, and Samuel all smiled at the mention of that name.

The escort stood up smoothly and gently cleared her throat. "It's time. We need to get going."

Kent delayed, wanting to drink in more of the conversation. "Who is the Sweet Thief?" he pleaded.

"The Sweet Thief?" Samuel looked past the table with wide and longing eyes. "There is no one greater. No one is more worthy of every good word and every thief's constant emulation." Then Samuel looked straight at Kent. "The more challenging question, however, is why you or I would want to be like him. To share in the celebrity? To be as famous and well-loved? The goal must grow beyond that. Otherwise the heart will not endure the cost. Glory and praise from people is not enough to warrant the burden you will bear."

Once more the escort leaned in close. "Number Three," she whispered, "it is time for us to go." Then she walked away, winding her way briskly through the tables and gliding past the mirror toward the exit.

Adelle looked at Kent. "What are you waiting for?"

"I've been longing for this for so long," Kent replied. "Now that I've finally found this place I want to know more. I don't want to – "

"Go!" all three cried at once.

Jim added resolutely, "Kent, my man. This is a tough one, but the sooner you learn this lesson, the better. The den is not where we live."

Adelle jumped in, "When the escort invites, don't wait. Every time I ignored the escort I missed out, and every time I followed, even when the road was brutally tough, I ended up in the best places."

"Kent," Samuel interjected. There was both warmth and admonition in his voice. "You should go."

It was the last call, and Kent took it.

He caught up to the escort just as she took hold of the door.

16

Mail Bombs

The letter arrived on a Tuesday.

Sorted into a post office box, it sat unread for days, inconspicuously sandwiched in among a stack of others.

Why was it delivered? So much pain could have been avoided if it had just been lost; if the stamp had peeled away; if the malicious envelope had been allowed to fall from the bundle unseen...

Alas, the carriers were faithful.

A key, a quarter turn, and the plague arrived, wicked words slithering from the envelope like ink-black serpents. Deadly silent and full of venom, they sped from page to eye to heart, and there began to breed. No one knew. How could they? Only the writer and the reader ever saw them. That is the danger with secrets. It's hard to tell how much is true. Make the words painful enough, embarrassing enough, dangerous enough – and they never get out into the open; out where they can be exposed and killed.

The mailman was counting on that.

"Things have gotten worse," the escort announced. "We have to move quickly."

"I thought you said we had a few minutes," Kent pointed out.

"We did." The escort opened the door and stepped from the den into the hall.

Kent followed immediately, but as he closed the door behind him and turned to face the hall, Number Three pulled up in alarm.

His portrait had been moved!

Still spectacular in size, the glorious image of Kent Hentrick was no longer above the door. At some point while he was inside someone had taken it down and rehung it on the right side of the hall.

Number Three spun around, scowling as he looked up to find out who had usurped his place of honor. Sure enough, a new portrait was there above the door, crowning the entrance to the den.

The canvas of the invading portrait was old and faded; tattered around the edges and terribly plain. It was nothing compared to his. Kent didn't understand why such a shabby thing would be hung in such a high place. There was nothing attractive about it. In fact, the portrait had only one remarkable feature – it was impossible to tell who it was.

It wasn't a portrait of no one. There was definitely someone there. But though he squinted with effort, Kent couldn't seem to be able to focus in on the one depicted on the canvas. The length of the hair, the color of the eyes, the pigmentation of the skin… he could see none of it.

Number Three looked down from the portrait just in time to hear the door close softly at the other end of the hallway. The escort had gone. Stunned that she had actually left him behind, Kent stood alone in the silence, struck by the realization that he did not have to follow.

He could linger a while, take some time to look at some of the amazing portraits – especially the one of himself. But he also recalled the words the other thieves had shared: the escort had the best path. Kent made his decision and sprinted down the hall, charging outside into the steady light of mid-morning.

Warm air swirled around him as Number Three leapt down the steps in front of 2212 and ran after the escort. Loping along the sidewalk, he caught up fast and drew up panting beside her, his forehead beginning to glisten with beads of sweat. It was uncommonly hot outside for being this late in the fall. The air felt heavy.

The escort did not say a word; just glanced over and smiled her peaceful smile.

That was enough.

Kent matched her pace, even if he was unable to match her peace. He was still wound up thinking about his portrait, wanting to know why it had been moved down from its place above the door. Five or six times he started to ask the escort what that was all about, but each time he stopped, ashamed of his motives. He knew it was petty.

Finally he managed to ask without asking, observing as casually as he could, "I've noticed that the portraits in the hallway – people seem to be moving them."

"No," the escort said firmly, "the portraits do not change."

"Well someone moved mine," Kent grumbled. His words were lost in blazing sunshine as they turned a corner and began heading due east. Three shielded his eyes with his hand.

As they made their way up a gentle incline, thoughts of portraits gradually gave way to curiosity, for it occurred to Kent that this was the first time the escort had ever gone with him outside. Where was she leading him?

Kent was about to ask exactly that, but the escort was faster. "What have you learned about your assignment?" she asked.

"Everything?"

"Yes."

"He is a mailman," Three stated plainly. "And at least for a while he was a thief. From his journals, however, it seems that he has had a change of heart and is now angry, though I'm not exactly sure why."

"Anything else?"

"I asked around the den. Quite a few thieves seem to have heard of him, though they are strongly divided as to where they think his loyalties lie. Several claim that he is responsible for a baffling number of thefts, and more than a dozen shared that the mailman played a central role in them being with us. Others call him a traitor, and the things they say he's done make me wonder why we are going after him at all."

"Good," nodded the escort. "You have done some homework."

"Do you have another packet for me?" Three inquired.

"There will likely be no more packets," the escort replied. "The mailman is no longer checking in. He has ceased correspondence."

"What does that mean?"

"It means we need to change tactics."

Three and the escort crested a small hill and found themselves looking down on a landscape of fresh-paved streets and empty lots. The raw face of a brand new housing development stared back at them. Several of the lots had been cleared so recently that there was nothing to find on site but bulldozer tracks and half-buried branches. There were even a few lots here and there that were still owned by the trees. Not many, though. Most were crowded with new construction.

The pungent aroma of clay and standing water shared the air with that of plywood and sawdust, as all along the street the shells of houses were in different stages of development. A veritable armada of pickup trucks lined the unfinished curbs and dirt driveways, many displaying the names of different contractors and subcontractors.

Smith and Sons Construction Corp; Apex Plumbing; Johnson Electric; FCC Windows and Doors; if there was a job to be done, there was a truck there to do it, and those trucks not marked with company names were given away by the tools stuffed into the cabs and beds. These were work vehicles. They were here to get things done.

Three and the escort made their way down into the infant subdivision, passing a dozen lots before reaching one where the crew was right in the middle of digging a foundation.

The escort turned in at the driveway and walked directly up to the foreman. "Here he is."

"Can he dig?" the foreman asked.

"Find out," she replied.

The escort turned to Three and put a hand on his shoulder. Lowering her voice, she said, "Stay here and find out what you can until I come back."

"What am I supposed to do?" Kent asked.

"Work." Without another word she turned and headed back in the direction they had come.

Three didn't understand. "Work? I already have a job!"

The escort kept walking.

Yet again, this path made no sense. When Kent called in and took the day off from work, he didn't think it was just to go work somewhere else. It made him kind of angry. He was looking for answers about his assignment; not a career change.

The foreman looked over to Number Three and pointed toward a truck parked out front. "Gloves and shovel are in there. You're in the trench with the other guys."

Partly out of curiosity, but mainly because he had no clue what else to do, Three did as he was told. He went to the truck, found a pair of gloves and a shovel, and five minutes later he was digging away, clearing out whatever the backhoe's bucket left behind.

"Get any interesting mail lately?"

Kent instantly forgot about being angry.

With his shovel paused mid-scoop, Number Three glanced over to the pair of mud-caked boots beside him in the trench, and seven feet directly above the boots he discovered the source of the cavernous voice.

If this was the mailman, there would be no stealing of anything.

A five day beard framed the dark brown face, and sweat ran in streams from the top of his bald head down onto shoulders that were roughly the same size as the truck out front where Kent had gotten the gloves and the shovel. Considering his swollen arms and massive chest, Three wondered why this man didn't simply carry a house over and drop it in place.

"Maybe," Three responded at last, projecting far more confidence than he felt. "You send me something?"

"Oh, not me." The huge man kept digging, careful to keep his voice low enough so that no one else heard.

Number Three followed his lead, scraping out the trench while he spoke. "Do you know what they mean?"

"I ain't sure what 'they' you talking about, but obviously you found your way to the den."

"Yeah," Kent nodded. "What I don't know is why I'm here. You clearly know I got something in the mail but you can't tell me what it is? Come on, man!" Kent cried under his breath. "What is this about?"

"Simmer down. You'll get there..." the hulk assured him. "But that ain't why you here today."

"Why am I here today?" Kent pressed.

The huge man tossed a shovel-full of sand and clay up out of the trench, and when he put the blade of his shovel back down he subtly inched a step closer. "I was with him," he whispered, "…the mailman. I was with him when it all went bad."

Kent's eyes widened with excitement "Where is he?"

"Oh, that'd be easy enough to find out. I could tell you his name right now. But that ain't what you need… Trust me. You run in there against this dude, he'll put you in a hole deeper than the one you in now."

"So he *is* evil…" Kent murmured, mostly to himself.

The huge man frowned and raised an eyebrow. "I guess that depends on what you mean. He's dangerous, no doubt about that. But so are a lot of things." Another shovel-full went flying. "Thing is, he's a man. A complicated man, but still a man. Just like you and me. So yeah, there's evil in there. But that's not everything. That's just what he's choosing to live in lately."

"So what do I need to know?" Kent asked.

"What would you want a person to know?" the huge man replied.

"You mean if they were coming to save me?"

"Sure."

"Probably nothing," Kent shrugged. "I probably wouldn't want to be saved."

"Exactly. Lucky for us, you don't need to be saved."

"Right," Kent nodded.

"Wrong!" The handle of a shovel slammed hard into Kent's chest and he fell backward into the trench. Three looked up in shock, struggling to regain his breath, unable to see the sky for the man towering over him. "You have no idea what kind of war you are in." The biceps in the huge man's arms bulged as he gripped the shovel harder.

On his back in the trench, there was nowhere for Three to go. He was trapped, and the shovel-wielding tank of a human being loomed over him like a guillotine. The giant's mud-caked boots stepped forward and the shovel went high.

Then the man leaned in close and whispered, "Do you need to be saved now?"

Before he could squeak out a response, steel fingers caught hold of his arm and yanked him off the ground. The big man looked around to the rest of the crew and laughed. Then he looked back to Number Three and said in an overly loud voice. "Watch your step, son..."

The others laughed and went back to work.

When the big man spoke again, his shovel once more scraping along the sides of the trench, it was only for his guest to hear. "That right there is where you have to start. You want to steal from this guy you can't go in until you realize you are even worse off than he is."

"But I'm not..." Three was shaking, his heart blasting adrenaline through his veins, his mouth running off without him.

The shovel stopped moving and the man stood up. He glared at Three so hard that it made the thief's knees wobble. "You're not worse off than he is?"

Three gulped, profoundly intimidated. "No."

"How do you know that?" Anger flared in the big man's voice and his mouth went tight across his teeth.

Three stammered, but nothing came out.

"You don't know one thing about this man." The titan slapped his shovel hard against the side of the trench to make sure he had Kent's attention, but the gesture was unneeded. "Next to him you are a boy. You hear me? You couldn't carry his coffee cup. He's carried off more pain in one year than you will your entire life, and he's wrestled with questions you wouldn't understand even if someone explained them to you. So don't you dare stand in my trench and tell me that you are a better man than one who has actually walked the path."

An inch separated their noses, and the rest of the crew had stopped working to watch.

"What's going on over there, Malcolm?"

"Ah, nuthin boss." The man laughed out loud with a roar so forceful that the shingles shook on the next house over. "Just breakin in the new guy!" Malcolm went back to shoveling, and the rest of the crew turned away a moment later.

After a few minutes Malcolm spoke again, more gently this time. "The man you have been assigned is not a worse man than you. There are no worse men than you. Start there."

μ̄ μ̄

Three was done arguing out loud, but inside he was filled with protests and excuses, explanations and justifications. There were a million men worse than him, and at least a thousand ways he was better than the mailman. After all, who was the one being sent in after the other? Only one of them needed to be saved, and it obviously wasn't the one being sent in to do the saving. Besides, he hadn't done anything wrong; not really wrong anyway. Obviously, the mailman had.

Malcolm looked over and motioned up above the trench and suddenly Kent saw them. The guards. They were on him!

Their appearance was so shocking, so hideous, that Kent dropped his shovel.

Malcolm reached out and caught the handle of Kent's shovel before it hit the ground. "Pretty nasty, huh?" he whispered, handing the shovel back.

Three couldn't respond. He was too busy trying to process what he was seeing. Two guards loomed over him, one on each side of the trench. They were grotesque; the worst he'd ever seen. Their skin was so tight that it was nearly transparent, and though they were horribly emaciated they were also horrifyingly tall. If they were to stand up straight, they would easily be able to see over the few remaining pines still standing at the back of the lot.

The two guards were so tall that in order to reach him they had to squat down and contort their bodies so that their shoulders were between their knees. This was made easier by the fact that neither one of them had arms on their shoulders. Somewhere along the line someone had torn their arms from their sockets and crudely reattached them inside their mouths. These mouths were loose and gaping, coated in a watery slime that ran partially clear like the albumin of an egg and partially dark like crude oil. The clear slime and the black slime flowed together, sometimes mixing and sometimes remaining separate.

One of the guards moved to speak, and Kent watched in horror as its long skeletal arms unfolded from within its mouth to reveal a long and vigorous tongue. As the arms reached out and took hold of the cartilage around his ear, the guard pulled its mouth in close and its twisting tongue began to do its work.

103

Three thrashed to get away, but the grip of the guards was too strong. They held him tight, and he was helpless to stop the tongues from slapping against his ears, flopping and thrusting to get in. As he felt the slippery slime from their mouths pour into his ear canal, he longed to scream, to spew out what they were pouring in, but his body would not obey. Violated to the point of nausea, Three swayed and almost went over. Again, his trench mate held him up.

"The sickest thing," Malcolm whispered, "is when you realize they've been there the whole time."

It was true. Kent had never seen them before, but their presence was as familiar as his own skin.

He looked to Malcolm helplessly. "What do I do?"

"Don't believe what they are telling you. Test what they say."

Fighting down his panic and revulsion, Three looked straight ahead, trying not to see the sickening mouths of the guards. Instead, he paid attention to their words.

"You are better. You are special. You are what this life is all about. The rest are just extras in your story. You deserve more. You deserve the best. No one is as valuable as you. Everyone else is flawed. Everyone else is broken. You are better."

The words were repeated over and over in a voice that he recognized at once. It was terrible. They really had been there all along.

The guards never saw the change in Three's expression. They could not see him past their own enormous mouths. Their sight completely blocked by their gaping jaws as they spoke, they had no idea that he was finally aware of them.

"They are wrong, you know." Malcolm was watching him carefully as he worked the shovel along the edge of the trench.

"Yeah."

"No, I mean it. They are lying to you. You're not more important than anyone else."

Three considered Malcolm's words and felt one of the tongues loosening. He had believed the words for so long without even meaning to. He never consciously chose to elevate himself above anyone else, but now he saw that the words were dug in, deeply entrenched into his understanding of his place in the world. There was nothing he could do.

He believed what they were saying, not because he wanted to or because he chose to, but because he had heard it for so long. It is what he knew.

"I'm stuck." He looked again at Malcolm, pleading. "I don't know what to do."

One of the guards realized that something was amiss, and it jammed its tongue in harder. "This idiot knows nothing about how deep you are. He doesn't have your gifts. He isn't special like you. He's just a temporary shadow passing through, just an extra in your story. When your true size and value is revealed, he won't even be found. You don't need what he has to say."

"I don't want to believe them," Three groaned, "but they've been here so long."

Malcolm was beside him now. "You aren't alone in this. And this whole thing is not about you."

The fiendish hands tightened on his ears. They were on alert. Three felt them digging in.

"The one this is all about…" said Malcolm, "His is the one name they cannot stand."

The guards increased their volume, screaming and pounding against Three's head in an attempt to block out Malcolm's voice. Kent could feel the desperation in their grip.

"You are the strongest. You are the smartest. You are the best. You will go farther than them all," cried the guards. "You should be lifted up and put in places of power. You! You! Wonderful, beautiful you!"

"Manuel."

Three heard the name, even as the guards were rocked. They clung to his ears now just to remain upright. The ground beneath them had gone to jelly, and their sickly long legs wobbled with their knees splayed out to the sides.

The guards' screaming became like storm winds, so loud that Three could hear little else. He clawed at his ears, wanting them out.

"Manuel." Malcolm said the name again, and the trench went sideways.

Three did not need to ask whose name it was. In his heart, he knew. It was the one he had been unknowingly seeking for years. It was the name of the Sweet Thief.

"There is danger everywhere! You must run! No one will believe you. This is all in your head!" The guards screamed furiously.

Three grabbed his skull with both hands, squeezing back against the raging pressure of the sound. Waves of vertigo had him reeling from one side of the trench to the other. Still, there was hope. He knew the name that mattered. With all that he had left, he took the name on his own lips, and spoke it. "Manuel."

Everything went still.

When his vision cleared, Three was down on one knee in the trench, bracing himself against the wall with his left hand. In his right hand was the shovel. The guards were nowhere to be seen. For the first time in as long as he could remember, there was real silence in his head.

It was beyond wonderful.

Malcolm beamed at him, his protective presence even more enormous than his frame.

"Thank you. Thank you so much." The words gushed out.

"Sorry I had to push you a little bit," said Malcolm. "It isn't always easy helping people see those two."

"I'm so glad you did. This whole time…" Three shook his head in disbelief. How had he not seen them? Suddenly he looked up in alarm. "They'll be back, won't they?"

"Yeah," Malcolm nodded. "But they aren't hidden anymore. That's a big deal."

They were both silent as Number Three let that sink in. The immensity of future battles loomed huge in his mind. What had he gotten himself into?

Malcolm knew where Kent was. He could see it on his face. "One day at a time, rookie." His voice was gentle and his smile sincere. "You'll be OK. Just do one day at a time. That's all we are made for."

Three's shoulders rose and fell as he took one huge breath. Then he nodded to himself and returned Malcolm's smile. "You saved me." He felt silly saying it out loud, but he knew it was an important confession, a pivotal step. "I needed it."

"We all do." Malcolm patted both his shoulders at once, almost knocking him to his knees.

When Three regained his balance he looked back up at Malcolm one more time. "I think these are yours," he said. Then he held out a pair of enormous onyx coins, each with a shovel etched on one side and the mark etched on the other.

Malcolm accepted them with a smile. "You know, you just might be able to steal from the mailman after all."

17

Postage Due

The crew was on lunch break when the escort returned.

Three and Malcolm were sitting off on their own, laughing.

"So can he dig?" the escort asked with a smile.

"As a matter of fact, he can," Malcolm answered.

"How much did you tell him?"

"As much as I could remember."

"Thank you, Malcolm. Your time is a gift."

Three could not tell if Malcolm was blushing, but it sure looked like it. He had never seen such a big man look so much like a child, and he admired him more for it.

The escort indicated that it was time to go, and Three got up to follow. He turned to Malcolm and put out his hand. It was too tiny a gesture to convey the gratitude he felt for this man, and Malcolm laughed as he grabbed Kent's hand and pulled him in for a powerful hug. Three returned the embrace wholeheartedly, despite his suspicion that it would likely result in several broken ribs.

Just before he let go, Malcolm leaned in and whispered intensely, "Go get him, Kent. Please." There was no hiding the concern in his voice.

Number Three nodded as they stepped apart, offered what he hoped was a reassuring smile, then turned away and slopped through the thick mud of the construction site to catch up to the escort.

"Malcolm is good stuff, isn't he?" the escort commented as Three drew near, her tone warm and unusually casual.

"Yeah, he really is."

"He's been through quite a bit."

"Seems like it," Three agreed.

"How?" The escort whirled on Number Three and fixed him with a steady gaze. It was as if she stopped the entire world to make time for this one question.

Three did not have a clue how to answer. "What do you mean?"

"How? How does it seem like he's been through a lot?" The escort made it clear that they would not be moving forward until Three had taken time to answer, and answer carefully.

Three mulled over his answer before speaking. "He seems peaceful... wise... a bit like you, actually."

"What does that have to do with being through a lot?"

"Well," Three paused, then continued with confidence, "No one is born that way. No one starts out with those things. At least I don't think they do. Wisdom has to be gained. Or I suppose earned might be a better word. And if wisdom and peace are universally valued, and I think they are, then it stands to reason that the entire world should be filled with them, but it isn't. So they must be tough to earn, at least for real."

"For real?"

"Plenty of us put on masks, but they don't hold up. Eventually the truth comes out. People who have had those lessons carved into them by hardship, however, they seem to have them for real."

"Do you have any idea why that is?" the escort asked.

"None."

"Fair enough." The escort nodded and began to move on.

"Wait. Aren't you going to tell me?"

"No."

"What? Why not?"

"You just explained it yourself," replied the escort. "The heart holds dearest what costs it deepest."

"Yeah," Kent nodded. "But…"

"You own what you dig out, Number Three. Now I am more than happy to spoon-feed you the peripheral trimmings, but the deeper things are here for you to wrestle with until you own them or they own you."

"Or both and?" Kent asked teasingly.

The escort grinned. "Something like that. But bear in mind that not everyone earns the deepest rewards. The effort can seem too great, the cost too high. Many pass them by for closer, shinier things – things easier to win. Yet this truth remains: the best things are often hidden and placed up high."

"And it's meant to be that way I suppose."

"Yes."

"Can I ask why?"

The escort turned and put a hand on his shoulder. "Chase, Kent! Climb, run, live!"

As if a huge spigot had been thrown open just above his head, Kent was flooded by a fresh awareness of how wide open life really was. He was not trapped in a box. The world was full of chances, and he was invited to try! In his mind he was carried to a mountain range above the snowline, a layer of cotton clouds hiding the earth below. He watched birds soaring from the peaks, skimming over lakes blue enough to rival the clearest skies, and he was allowed, just for an instant, to know what it felt like to fly like that.

Still thrilling with the sensation of such wild freedom, he was treated to a taste of the moment of ecstasy known to the great champion who, after a lifetime of effort and struggle, finally raises the trophy above his head. It felt as if his heart was going to burst out through his chest, but Kent had no time to recover.

The incredible tour rushed on, sweeping him from the sweet rush of victory into the near-euphoric sense of accomplishment experienced by those who see their buildings rise at last; wonders greater than the pyramids standing in the world because of what their hands and minds had done. His heart swelled with pride and satisfaction.

Last of all he stood beside his wife and held his child for the first time. Kent could not take any more.

The greatest achievements he could imagine; Kent had been allowed to sample them all in one overwhelming revelation. Yet the next instant they were all placed next to an expanse that was so limitless that they seemed like nothing by comparison.

The expanse he glimpsed was not composed of rock and water and wind and fire. This greater expanse was altogether deeper, its elements carried around unseen by every living soul upon the earth. He saw it clearly. There was a greater thing going on!

Love was possible in this deeper place. Purpose as well. All of the deepest things could be found on these other peaks! The summits were not closed off. They could be searched. It could be chased. Wonder of wonders... it could actually be won!

Yet to set the value in place, to preserve the flavor's biting edge, the perils were allowed as well. He could plunge from cliff faces and be pummeled on the rocks. He could snap his legs at the ankles with a missed step during the pursuit. He could offer all he had and be outbid, or miss the last train by one sweep of the second hand. It was untamed, this proving ground, and his heart leapt and cowered at the sight of it.

Three could not speak as he glimpsed the gleaming fields. The wealth known to the thieves was stacked up like mountains all around, ripe for the taking. There was so much pain to steal! Every day was a fresh set of time to gather more, and the riches that were gained stretched beyond the mountains to eternity, never to be lost or spoiled.

The big picture was too large to comprehend, and Kent was suddenly exceedingly grateful for that. How awful would it be if it were not! To live forever in a realm that could be fully mastered and completed? Where the edges could be circumscribed and the story tied off like a final chapter, with nothing new to follow? How hopeless it would be to exist for all eternity in a world with an end...

Thankfully the expense had none.

Three had no idea how many steps they had taken since the trench and the digging and the thick wet stench of orange mud. It may have been ten. It may have been ten thousand. A change in the light brought him back.

They had stepped inside.

As Number Three paused to allow his eyes to recalibrate, the sweltering heat outside was quickly driven off by the breath of the air conditioner on his wet clothes.

But that is not why he shivered.

The portraits had changed again.

It was a subtle change, but confounding. How does a portrait change in size? Yet that is what he saw. The portraits here at the beginning of the hall were larger than they had been before, while those at the other end were smaller. Kent shook his head and laughed. He was almost not even surprised anymore.

He followed the escort toward the far door, surveying the portraits along the way. He could see it now! These were the ones who had chased! That is why they were here. Forsaking cheaper counterfeits, these people had poured out their lives pursuing deeper things, and now they stood on peaks with banners raised. Treasures that could not be bought, glory beyond that seen on earth, pleasures deeper than the world could begin to imitate... they owned them all! And every single one of them had the wounds to prove that they had paid the price to be here.

"Tell me what you see," the escort called over her shoulder.

"They are in a better place." It was the first impression that came to Three's mind. He wasn't just talking about a physical location. These people, after all was said and done, lived on a different level.

"Good," the escort turned to face him. "Now tell me what you see but don't see."

See but don't see? How was he supposed to know? Number Three stared at the portrait nearest him. What was he not seeing? He searched for a while, but eventually looked back and shrugged. "No idea."

The escort did not press him further. She simply gestured toward the walls. "Everyone you see here loses their lives."

The cryptic comment made no impact. Of course they had. These were ancient portraits.

Kent froze.

The very next portrait on the wall... it was familiar. With her sweet smile and kind eyes lighting up her face, Adelle stared out at him, more vibrant and alive than he had ever seen her before.

Number Three whipped toward the escort. "No! I just saw her. She was just in the den this morning!"

The escort ignored his protests. "What else do you see?"

"What else do I see? How can you ask me that?"

The hallway went still as a pine forest after a snowstorm. Three had never heard such a soft sound.

The escort asked again, patiently, "What else do you see?"

Shaken and upset, Three looked back at Adelle's face. He could not believe she was gone. His ragged breathing was the only noise in the hall as he fought to reclaim his focus. Searching the portrait for answers, he was struck by how peaceful she looked. She was completely surrendered. Three could see nothing else. His shock and sadness were too thick to fight through. "I don't see anything. I am tired."

"Try again. Don't give up."

Kent sighed. He was exhausted. His mind and heart ached. From the den to the trench and back again; it was too much all at once. He coveted the peace he saw in Adelle's eyes.

"I see peace," he murmured at last. "Incredible peace. Is that what I am looking for?"

"That is what everyone is looking for."

Kent regarded the escort from the corner of his eyes.

"If that peace is truly what you want," the escort added, "then I suggest you buy a watch."

"A watch?" Kent repeated, bewildered. What was she talking about? "You mean the kind that tells time?"

"Sort of," the escort replied, perturbingly unaffected by the death of one of the thieves. "The next time you stand before the mirror with a handful of coins, you will have the chance to buy a watch. If you decide to make that purchase it will remove your control of time."

Three scowled. "I thought the whole idea of wearing a watch was to give a person more control over time."

The escort stifled a laugh. "Do you really believe that?"

Kent did not have to think about it very long. "Never mind."

"The watch you will be offered by the mirror," the escort clarified, "is not a normal watch. It is a symbol – a reminder to pursue the decision you make when you put it on."

"Which decision?"

"That your time is not your own. That you will operate on the schedule determined for you."

"Determined?" Kent did not like the sound of that. "By whom?"

"I think you know," replied the escort.

"I'm going to be asked for more of my time, then?" Kent asked suspiciously.

"Maybe more. Maybe less. What you are agreeing to when you put on that watch is that you relinquish your ownership of time. Control is what is at stake, and time dominated by self-interest is what you will not find in any of these." The escort motioned fondly toward the portraits.

She was right. There was wisdom and peace and incredible strength on display in these portraits, but none of the people shown in them was operating on their own schedule. They had given that up.

He glanced again at Adelle's face. He was happy for her. He was sad for himself. He shuffled on, side by side with the escort.

The door to the den arrived swiftly, but before they could complete the journey there was one more obstacle to clear. He knew it was coming. In truth, it had not left his mind since the first time he had seen it.

His portrait beckoned to him, virtually glowing from the wall beside the door, and while it was slightly smaller than the last time he'd passed through, it still stretched from floor to ceiling.

To say that he tried not to look at it would be a gross overstatement. It would be far more honest to say that he tried to appear as though he wasn't going to look at it. That was the best he could do. It was, after all, the most beautiful thing he had ever seen.

Kent batted at his ears without effect. A familiar voice was whispering all kinds of delicious things.

The slime dribbled in and soon Number Three was hearing the cheering in his mind; the cheering of the crowds that waited just on the other side of the door. He pictured them shouting as they had last time, smiling with approval and raising their fists joyfully in his direction. Kent knew that he could have that again. All he had to do was exactly what he had done before.

Kent smiled at his portrait and patted the thick stack of coins in his pocket. That was his ticket. He'd slipped them right out from under the noses of Malcolm's guards – quite a feat considering how heavy they were. Anxiety is such a cumbersome thing.

Now everyone would watch him present his gift. Number Three could almost hear the trumpets sounding, announcing throughout the den what a great thing he had done, and with how valuable these new coins were the coming ovation was bound to be at least twice as big as the last one.

The escort said something as Three turned the doorknob. It sounded as if it might have been important, but hers was only one small voice in an approaching ocean of cheers. It bobbed between the waves of roaring applause, coming through only in pieces, but the waves were singing such lovely songs that he didn't stop. He didn't go back to discover what the lone buoy had said. He stuck his face into the sweet salt air and closed the door behind him. The ocean was all that remained.

Kent stepped up, tall and confident, ready to face the mirror. Yet as he glanced at his clothes and his hair in the glass to make sure everything was in place before his big moment, reality met him hard and fast. He was a mess! Brown-red trench mud clung to his shoes and speckled his pants. Sweat and dirt streaked his T-shirt with haphazard stripes. His knees were damp brown patches. He certainly could not go on like this. Kent looked around frantically. Where could he go to clean up?

"You look fine," said the voice from the mirror.

Three checked his reflection again. "I look fine alright. The mud goes well with my hair."

"It is well-earned."

"Thanks, but if it's all the same to you I'd rather get cleaned up before we do anything else."

"There is a washroom in the den," offered the one behind the mirror.

"Of course! That's perfect." Three clapped his hands in relief. "I'll be right back."

Kent stepped away from the mirror and made his way directly toward the washroom, moving as unobtrusively as possible through the den. Still shedding flakes of dried mud and smelling terrible, he kept his eyes down the whole way, hoping no one would notice him as he passed. Thankfully it was a short walk.

As he ducked into the washroom, Kent was delighted to discover that not only was it spacious and clean, but it even had a stone shower stall set into the back wall. He made a beeline for the shower, leaving a trail of faint orange footprints behind him on the white tile floor. Then he plucked up the bar of soap that was waiting in the stall and Number Three gave himself a good scrubbing.

Moments later the mud and sweat went slipping down the drain. Kent felt refreshed, completely clean. His clothes, however, were another story. He scrubbed and rinsed them several times, but the stubborn streaks of pale orange would not disappear. Sopping wet, they clung uncomfortably to his skin even after he wrung them out. There was no getting around it. He was going to look ridiculous out there in front of everyone when the trumpets announced his gift.

Three stood at the sink, staring at the disaster in the mirror. The wad of paper towels in the trash and the hand dryer on the wall had done little to change his appearance. Leaning forward on his hands, there was nowhere to run when the washroom door opened behind him.

In stepped a man in a tailored suit, his clothes so fine that Kent felt ashamed to be in the same room with him. A flawless jacket stood perfectly on the gentleman's shoulders, and he skated across the floor on shoes that shined like black glass. The man gave Three a smile and a nod, radiant with the confidence of one who always wins.

Three nodded sheepishly back and headed toward the door. His mind was made up; he would find a way to sneak out of the den without being seen. The cheering crowds would have to wait.

"Good day, friend?" the man asked as Three tried to slip by.

Three pulled up short. Had it been a good day? "Yes, I suppose it has been. And you?"

"Actually," shared the man in the suit, "I seem to have gotten myself into a bit of a situation."

"Oh?" Kent responded politely, still planning his escape.

"I'm afraid I was a bit clumsy with my planner," the well-dressed man confessed, "and one of my appointments completely slipped my mind."

"Too many red carpet events in one day?" Three joked lightheartedly. "I have that problem all the time."

"Interestingly enough," the man chuckled, "there was a red carpet at my engagement this morning." He shrugged off Kent's subsequent reaction as if the event had been no big deal. "However, I am scheduled to do a rather untidy job this afternoon and I did not bring a change of clothes." The man raised his arms out to his sides. "I can't go out like this."

"You're kidding," said Kent.

"Not at all." The man shook his head. "I'm in quite a pinch. I was due to be there ten minutes ago. I don't suppose... I feel like a dreadful buffoon for even asking... would you be willing to trade?"

Three laughed in disbelief. What were the odds?

"Well, I am not really in the habit of swapping my clothes for the dumpy sort of threads you are hauling around," Kent laid the sarcasm on thick, "but I suppose if it would make your day brighter I'd be willing to trade down."

The well-dressed man's eyes lit up. "Truly?"

"Sure. Why not?"

"Splendid!" exclaimed the man in the fine clothes. "We look to be near enough the same size. Let's have it then."

The whole situation was preposterous, and Three paused a moment at the absurdity of it all. Then he shrugged and got busy stripping off the mud. He realized immediately that he was going to need another bath just from getting changed, and he began to feel really guilty as his wet clothes slapped down on the bench against the wall. It would be disgusting to have to pull these things on. He thought of his counterpart who was carefully hanging his suit jacket on a stall door.

"Um... Are you sure about this?" Kent asked. "I can't help but feeling like this isn't very fair of me."

The well-dressed man looked up in surprise. "What? Oh, no! You are doing me a truly good turn, my friend. I can't believe I forgot about this. What a gaffe! Look, I'm already nearly thirty minutes late! If I am not out there soon I'll never hear the end of it, and these clothes are not made for manual labor. I don't want them ruined."

"But mine are pretty gross," Kent insisted.

"Nothing that can't be washed off later." The man smiled and went back to changing.

Five minutes later two men left the washroom; one decorated with mud and the other shined up like a new coin.

117

"I'll get your suit back to you the next time we meet," Three called in parting. "And I'll have it cleaned and pressed."

"Jolly good!" the muddy man cried as he waved and hurried for the exit.

Three couldn't believe it. He had gone from gutters to glory in the blink of an eye. He felt like a different man. Oozing confidence, he gazed across the room in delight. There would be no skulking around now, no need to look ashamed or apologize. He stepped up to the mirror like a peacock on full display. With long and graceful motions, he smoothed his jacket and tugged the cuffs of his sleeves. He looked good – almost portrait good. Ready for the crowds, Three held out his hand, the dark coins glinting in his palm.

Looking away from the mirror for a split second, Three stole one last sideways glance at the den. They had no idea what was coming. Lost in their own little worlds, their own little conversations, their own little concerns, the thieves were about to be rocked out of the seats. He wondered if a trumpet blast had ever been heard before like the one that was coming. Doubtful.

"I hope no one gets whiplash," he chuckled to himself.

Then, at the last second, Kent had a bout of indecision. How should he stand? What should he do with his hands? Should he put them in his pockets? Give everyone a wave? Maybe he should just keep them at his sides, as if the whole thing was no big deal. Cool and aloof would be pretty stellar if he pulled it off well.

He decided at last to unbutton his jacket and put his left hand halfway into his pants pocket, letting it hang there casually while he presented the coins with his right hand. Maybe then he would wave or give the den a thumbs-up. He would have to see how it felt, try to read the crowd. If they were on their feet, he might need to put both hands up in the air to recognize them.

Kent smiled at himself one more time in the mirror, then looked at the coins and opened his mouth. This was his moment.

The coins flaked into dust and gently wafted into the mirror.

"Thank you," the voice behind the mirror said quietly. "You are now Number Four."

The room remained as it was.

Confused, Number Four stood there waiting, one hand hanging ridiculously from his fancy pocket. But there was no fanfare, no applause, not even a nod in his direction.

After a few seconds he looked up, incredulous. "That's it?"

The mirror replied, "Yes. Thank you, Number Four."

This wasn't right. Surely there had been some kind of mistake. Something had gone wrong.

Kent looked down at his empty palm. What had happened? Why was there no cheering? Where was his reward? Clearly there had been a huge oversight. Number Four pulled his other hand out of his pocket, took a half step toward the mirror, and quietly pointed out the mistake, "I didn't say what they were for."

The voice behind the mirror was calm and steady. "Yes. You did. I heard you quite clearly."

Now Kent was really confused. "You heard me? But… I didn't say anything."

The mirror did not respond.

"I said I didn't say anything," Kent repeated, thinking that perhaps he had not been heard.

There was no sound from the mirror.

"You can't just guess what I was going to say!"

The mirror remained silent.

Now Number Four was angry. "Hey! Those coins were valuable. You said so yourself. You can't just take them!"

He didn't hear a word from the mirror. Instead, the surface of the glass trembled slightly, and Number Four watched in silent fascination as his image shifted back to exactly how he had been standing two minutes earlier. Kent lifted a hand in surprise, but for the first time in his life his reflection did not move with him. The one in the mirror remained locked in place. Then, slowly, the image began to shift. Trained in like a hawk, Kent watched himself pull the dark coins from his pocket and extend them out toward the mirror. He leaned forward eagerly. Here would be the proof! Here he would be justified!

Four pointed insistently at the image that would exonerate him, all set to witness the unauthorized disappearance of the coins. But he never said a word. A gasp escaped his lips as his entire body went rigid.

The rest of Kent's thoughts ceased to exist. Only one thing mattered. No one could ever see this mirror! Not ever. He stretched himself in front of it, but his body was not nearly big enough to cover the glass. Four spun around, frantic with shame, searching frantically for something he could use to hide the mirror. In desperation he scanned the walls for curtains that he could rip down and throw over the glass, but there were no windows in the den. His eyes bounced from the walls to the tables, searching for a tablecloth, but none of the tables were covered; and the napkins and bar towels were too small. When he saw that there was nothing he could use to hide the mirror, Number Four looked toward the exit. He would get out and never come back.

This was too much.

Nothing like this mirror should exist. Not anywhere!

Mercilessly honest, the mirror showed it all. It showed him primping and winking at himself, which would have been mortifying enough if that's all there was, but the rest was even more damning. In a seamless cloud around the reflection was a crystal clear display of every thought and heart whisper he had entertained since entering the den. No secret was hidden, no compromising thought held back. Kent tried to avert his eyes but found that he could not. Nor could he blink. Frozen in time and space, he saw what the mirror saw.

There were the adoring crowds in his mind, along with their standing, cheering accolades. There was the flawless portrait of his resplendence, the universe itself swirling around to pay him honor. There were the voices of the trumpets announcing his heroics. Not one thing in the glass even faintly resembled a man asking to purchase a watch, or anything else for that matter. The scene in the mirror revealed the ugly truth: that in his heart of hearts, at that moment, no one else had mattered at all.

Kent's reflection lifted the coins toward the glass. The decision had been made. His thoughts were like bubbles rising up through water, speeding toward the point of release, racing for the surface. No sound was uttered, but the words of his heart were absolutely clear. He saw what the mirror saw.

Only then did the mirror speak again. "I heard you quite clearly."

It was clear, his heart's contents on a stand of lenses and mirrors. No angle was off limits. No spot was too small.

Number Four crumpled to the floor in a heap. No one had touched him. Nor was he in pain. He was simply unable to stand. Kent's entire life had always included a comfortable layer of deception. Having that crutch pulled out from under him was like losing his legs. Only the ground could hold him up now – and tenuously at that.

"Number Four… know this!" The thundering voice from the mirror filled the room, the building, the surrounding countryside, and every tiny crevice of his shrinking soul. "We are not concerned only with what people say. People say a lot of things. We are not concerned only with what people say, especially when it does not agree with what they do. We are not concerned only with what people say. People say a lot of things."

With that, the speech from the mirror was ended, and Number Four lay with his cheek pressed down on cold tile, exhausted and trembling. How long did he lay like that? How many hours and days passed before he was able to move, able to cope with the terror of seeing himself with the deception stripped off? Kent had no idea. Was the mirror still watching him, still gazing right through his skin and his pretenses to the heart underneath? Kent covered his chest with his hands and closed his eyes. He was fully aware of the futility of such measures, but he had no clue what else to do.

There would be no hiding here. Not from mirrors that showed it all.

18

RSVP

"Number Four. Come and eat. Refresh yourself." The escort was holding out a hand, motioning toward the table where his friends were waiting.

How could he go before them now? Surely they had seen! The mirror was too enormous to miss. They must have glimpsed his vanity – his ridiculous appetite for fame. They must have seen that they held no larger place in his heart than the selfish uses he had for them. How could he join them now? And how much more had they seen in that cruel mirror?

"How can I?" he whispered, despairing.

"You are not alone," the escort assured him. "Not one person sitting at these tables failed to hit the floor when they were faced with the terrors of the truth. So do not fear them. All are laid bare by the mirror. Besides, your friends are waiting for you."

"My legs..."

"Take my hand."

As Four wrapped his fingers around the hand of the escort, his ankles became strong and the feeling returned to his knees. He wobbled gingerly over to the table and collapsed in a chair, hoping they were talking about anything other than him.

"You OK?" Jim leaned in. His demeanor made it clear that he would not be joking about this, at least not right now.

"No." Kent shook his head. His eyes did not leave the surface of the table.

"What did it show you?" Samuel tried to lay the question out gently, but he could not hide his fascination. He relished hearing about such revelations, and even his normally composed disposition was no match for his desire to hear about things uttered from behind the mirror.

"Me," Kent whispered. "It showed me."

They all got it. None of them spoke. None of them needed to. They had all been there. Samuel. Jim. Adelle.

Kent shuddered violently when he saw her.

Adelle was at the table. Alive!

Number Four stared at her, trying to understand. How many times in one day could a person be completely sideswiped before losing their mind? Four was dangerously close.

"How are you here?" he mumbled.

Adelle looked as confused as he was. "What do you mean?"

"She said you were dead." Four stared down at the table. Then his head snapped up and he glared over at the escort. He was so angry that he didn't know how to put it into words.

Samuel broke the silence. "Kent, what is going on?"

Four's eyes were smoldering as he jerked a thumb in the direction of the escort. "Not even an hour ago she walked me through the hall of portraits." Three glanced over to Adelle. "We saw yours."

Adelle started. "Mine?"

"Yes. It was you. As clear as you are sitting here now, but different."

"Different how?"

"Just different. Anyway, she said you were dead."

"Dead? Are you sure?"

"Yes. Ask her. She said every person whose portrait hangs in the hall had lost their lives. Didn't you?" Four turned a furious gaze on the escort.

"Loses," the escort corrected.

μ

μ

"But she isn't dead!" Four screamed. He pounded the table with his fist so hard that drinks spilled and food jumped. "It's not OK to go around telling people that their friends are dead when they aren't."

The escort went silent.

"And stop doing that!" Four stood to his feet. "Stop going silent when I am talking to you!"

The escort looked up with her weary, peaceful smile. "Number Four, it is not for you to give me orders." The gentle power of her voice swept the room up like a flood and squeezed it out like summer fruit. She had been here before any of them. She would be here after all of them.

Four slowly sat back down, realizing that he had been barking at someone utterly beyond him.

The soothing voice continued, "I have my orders, and I will follow them whether or not they line up with yours."

Number Four looked down and happened to notice his bare wrists. There was something about his wrists that was important. Then he remembered and closed his eyes in disgust.

The escort folded her hands and laid them softly on the table. "I'm sorry you misunderstood, Number Four, but I told you the truth. Adelle has already begun the process of laying down her life to gain something much better, as have you. That is why your portrait also hangs in the hall. You did not understand me because you assumed that journey was an instantaneous event. Many of the things you are sure of are not completely accurate."

"I didn't buy the watch," Four confessed.

"No," the escort replied. "That is why we are struggling to walk in step right now. We are on two different schedules. I advised you to buy the watch so that our schedules would be the same; so that we would be receiving our orders from the same place. Right now we are not."

"I failed," Kent mumbled. "Again." He shook his head, learning for the second time that day that there were guards he had never seen that had been playing with him his whole life.

Four's friends at the table nodded with him. They understood.

Adelle reached toward him from across the table, "Kent, just so you know, none of us saw what the mirror showed you."

Four eyed her carefully. "What?"

"The mirror shows us ourselves. It doesn't show us everyone else."

"So no one saw?" Kent asked, his tone betraying a hint of hope.

"No. Everyone else can only see the evidence of what you do," Adelle assured him. "The mirror doesn't reveal the rest to everyone yet."

"Yet?" Kent quaked.

Samuel stepped in gently. "It is rumored that eventually everything will be exposed."

There was a nearly audible gulp around the table. They were all in the same boat.

"For now, though," Adelle whispered, "only you can see your mirror."

Kent let out a huge sigh and his shoulders slumped as the weight lifted. Then his face clouded over again. "Now that's sad isn't it?"

"What's sad?" Jim asked.

"That it is an incredible relief to me to know that you all could not see the truth. That I am much more comfortable in our friendship knowing that I can continue to lie to you about who I really am."

Adelle and Jim nodded, but Samuel seemed more fascinated than troubled by what Kent had said. In fact his expression was almost appreciative, and Number Four pounced on him.

"That doesn't bother you at all?" Four demanded. "That I am sitting here being completely false with you?"

Samuel was calm. "Let's do one line of thinking at a time. First of all, you aren't being completely false with me. Part of what you are showing me is true. Secondly, yes. The fact that we hide our flaws and injuries is a sad thing. However, it is not a permanent condition, so I do not allow it to wrap my entire existence in despair." He winked at Four to let him know that he intended his words to be taken lightly. "And lastly, I think that is one of the beautiful parts of what friendship is. It is about a gradual revealing of the true self, as deception is trusted less and the friend is trusted more. The longer and deeper the friendship, the more lies are jettisoned. That strikes me as being a very good thing."

Four couldn't even stay upset. Samuel was right. It wasn't hopeless. On the contrary, it was as noble a challenge as friendship could face, and he saw even greater value as he looked around the table. He was being honest with these people. Maybe not all the walls were down yet, but some of them certainly were, and that had to count for something.

"You're right." Four surrendered gladly and relaxed back into his chair. Then he remembered something and stood up. He walked around the table to where Adelle was sitting and he wrapped his arms around her. He did not hang on long, but he meant it when he said, "I'm glad you're still with us." Then he returned to his seat, smiling gratefully as a tall glass of water was set in front of him.

Until he put the glass to his lips Kent hadn't realized how thirsty he was. He drained the whole thing before he set it back down on the table.

Jim tried to give Number Four time to breathe, but it was obvious that he had something on his mind and that he was getting kind of twitchy trying to hold it in. Finally Kent noticed the man's wide green eyes and clenched fingers. "What?"

"I'm not sure this is the best time to be asking you, but I can't wait."

"Obviously," muttered Adelle, rolling her eyes.

Jim turned toward her and, leaning in, put his fingertips on the table. "Well, we're kind of on a deadline with this one, aren't we?" Then he turned back to Kent. "Before you walked in, the three of us were considering a job, and we had decided to see if you wanted to come on as part of our crew."

"Your crew?"

"Yeah," Jim answered.

"You mean like doing a job as a group?"

The others nodded.

"Can you do that?"

"Of course," said Jim.

"How does it work?"

"Same as any other job... just with more people." Jim's answer was so deadpan that Samuel started to crack up, then leaned back and apologized wordlessly with a wave of his hands.

"So what is the job?" Four asked.

"Thanksgiving."

"What about it?"

"It's tomorrow," Jim replied.

"So... you want to steal Thanksgiving?"

"Not exactly." Jim paused to take a sip of his own drink. As he set the glass back down he asked, "What happens on Thanksgiving?"

126

"I don't know…" Four murmured. "A lot of people get together with their families, gorge on turkey and mashed potatoes, and then pass out in front of football games."

"I'd say that's pretty common. Who misses out?"

"The football players?" Four suggested.

"Who misses out because they have no choice?"

Four's mind swept over countless nameless, lonely faces. He did not know them, could not see them in detail, but he knew they existed somewhere. He said nothing.

Adelle stepped in. "We know a place that serves people who don't have very much. Tomorrow these people will face, yet again, the things that they don't have. There will be plenty to steal."

"What's the catch?" Four leaned forward. "A place like that must be pretty well guarded."

"Well, let's face it. You aren't going to be able to steal much in one short meal. There will be a lot of loot there that you will never even see. It's too deeply buried. But there is some on the surface, and you will be able to take bits of it without much resistance at all."

"What about guards?"

"You can expect regular patrols by the same guards that always try to keep us from making it out to this kind of job; apathy, distraction, selfishness… But once you get past them you aren't going to find too many fences, at least not around the kind of loot we are going after."

Jim nodded. "It's actually very easy to feed the hungry once you are actually handing them the food. It's getting yourself down to the kitchen that is the hard part."

Kent nodded in understanding.

"There is one more guard to be aware of," Samuel warned. "Keep your eyes out for the guard who looks like your portrait."

Number Four looked up guiltily, but the man with the scarred face was talking to all of them.

"This guard will lure you to despise your targets, and if you fall for it he will greatly limit how much loot you will be able to carry off. Men and women who are convinced that they exist on a higher plane than the rest of mankind do not carry bags or pull carts. They make other people do the pulling. Don't become one of them. Evade these last guards and we will most likely find a room full of people ready for the services of a sweet thief or two." He smiled.

Adelle looked at Kent enthusiastically. "So what do you think?"

Four smiled back at her, eager for an opportunity to try again before the mirror. "I'm in."

"Great!" Jim all but shouted. "Then we have some planning to do, which means I'm going to need some more snacks. Samuel?"

"I'm on it." Samuel slid back from the table and headed over toward the long bar.

As he walked away, Adelle turned toward Kent. "Sam has already heard the run down, so I'll catch you up until he gets back." She spread her hands flat on the table. "I've been out to this place quite a few times now, and it is blowing me away. Last time I met the most amazing family. They've been without a place to live for five months. The father developed some serious health issues about three years ago that keep him from working. They have no insurance, have exhausted their savings, and the mother makes so little at her job that they were unable to keep their home. Yet despite everything they are going through they have managed to stay together with their two precious babies." Adelle lit up with excitement, her face radiant as she spoke. "It is amazing to watch them love each other. It really is. They are there with nothing – and I mean nothing – and you can see the weariness and anxiety in their eyes, but when they look at each other... wow. You don't see love like that in too many couples these days. I don't know how they do it, but it sure is beautiful to watch."

So was she. The colors in her eyes almost swirled, and Kent could not look away. The way her lips moved, the sound of her voice, everything was getting to him...

"Kent?"

"I'm sorry, what?" Kent shook himself back to attention.

Adelle was looking at him as if she was waiting for an answer, but he had no clue what she had asked. Flustered, he glanced over and found Jim grinning at him in amusement. Kent tried to play it off, but it was no use. He had been busted, caught red-handed by those watchful green eyes. Jim raised his brow and glanced toward Adelle, his expression exposing it all.

Kent started to shake his head no, but found that his heart wasn't in it. He looked up helplessly and shrugged his shoulders.

Jim laughed out loud, and Adelle stopped her story.

"Are you guys OK?" she asked.

"I think Kent is feeling a little warm," Jim offered.

"A little?" Four murmured under his breath, gratefully staring down at the plate that Samuel placed in front of him. He grabbed a handful of fries to give him an excuse not to say anything more.

Samuel passed out the rest of the food, clearly confused by what was going on at the table. Adelle looked back and forth between Jim and Kent, obviously feeling left out. Happily, the awkward silence was broken a moment later as Jim stood up to leave.

"If you all will excuse me, I have some business to take care of."

"What, now? What about your food?" Samuel asked indignantly.

"Yeah, sorry about that. Things come up. I'll catch you all at the shelter tomorrow." Then he adopted a decidedly southern accent and added, "Y'all be good now, ya hear?" He nodded cryptically toward Kent and winked, then smiled to the rest of the table and turned to go.

"What was that all about?" Adelle demanded of Kent as Jim walked away, suddenly very self-conscious.

Kent wanted to say something reassuring, but a clueless shrug is all he could offer. Adelle clearly didn't buy it.

"Fine," she said. "I have to get going anyway."

"But…" Samuel began to protest.

It was now or never. Number Four stood up. "Excuse me Samuel, but I need to go, too."

"Wait! I got enough for all of us…" Samuel sat helplessly behind a mound of hot sandwiches as the others left the table.

Adelle headed for the exit. Kent was hot on her heels.

"Um, Adelle?"

She looked over a shoulder, half-turning as she walked, "Yeah?"

There were those eyes again!

"I was wondering… If you weren't busy. If maybe…"

"Kent, I really have to go."

"This will be quick. Just give me two seconds," Kent pleaded.

Adelle stopped and turned and Kent's momentum carried him right up to her. Standing face to face, with barely enough room for a breath between them, everything else in the den instantly became background.

"Ummm…" Kent balked awkwardly. "Where is this shelter?"

"Oh, right!" Adelle grabbed his hand and quickly scribbled a phone number on his palm. "Call me later and I'll tell you!" She laughed and disappeared outside.

19

Holiday Greetings

Only two of their foursome managed to slip out past their guards the next morning, but the pair was far from alone. Thieves from several other dens had showed up as well.

They all stood on the sidewalk outside of an old church, waiting for someone to arrive and unlock the doors. It was a frosty morning, and the sun was just beginning to peel the nighttime chill from the city streets when an elderly man in a bright orange knit cap shuffled over. Number Four thought the poor old fellow was the first of the homeless wanderers to arrive, but he walked right past the thieves and pulled a set of keys from his pants pocket. He fumbled with the keys and muttered, then made his choice and slid it into the lock. The deadbolt slid to the side, and he held the door open as they all went in.

"Thank you, Robert." Adelle paused in the doorway and gave the man a hug.

"Happy Thanksgiving," he returned briskly, then added. "I'll be in around one-thirty. Have Jared take the dining room. Thelma is scheduled to run the kitchen."

"Will do." Adelle leaned back, still holding onto Robert's arms. "Are you going to see family today?"

"Just did." Robert winked warmly at Adelle. Then he turned, shook Kent's hand, and slowly shuffled back to a white van parked on the corner across the street.

Adelle led Kent back to the kitchen where she handed him off to Jenna, a fiery Italian in her mid-thirties who quickly explained what she needed him to do. After asking about a few minor details, Number Four jumped in with both feet. It was a joyously stressful atmosphere in the kitchen as a dozen people hustled to prepare food for the day ahead, Christmas music playing in the background. It felt very much like the holidays, and the thieves sang and smiled as they assembled a feast of turkey and stuffing, potatoes and gravy, cranberry sauce and pumpkin pie. The smell alone was healing, and with every plate they armed themselves to break some prisoners out of solitary, if only for a few hours.

Number Four got busy cutting celery, Adelle's earlier words still ringing in his ears. "Physical pains are often the simplest to steal. Most people are glad to be rid of them, often far more willing to accept help with those than with some other burdens that they carry around. Still, be prepared to see people hurting in all kinds of ways."

Four glanced out a narrow window. The kitchen would not open for another half hour, but at least twenty people were already lined up outside, bundled in old coats and ragged mittens, the treasure piled high on the sidewalk. This was going to be the easiest haul ever.

When the doors opened at eight thirty, Four found himself smiling without having to try. Everyone was glad to be there, and as the hours and the hungry lines slipped by Four discovered that the people he had seen waiting outside were real. They had real smiles and they really meant it when they said "Happy Thanksgiving!"

Noon passed in a flash and one o'clock found Kent gently rattling the stacks of dark coins filling his pockets. He stepped out of the serving line for a quick break, and when no one was looking he pulled out one of the coins and examined it. It was a delicate coin; thin and not very dense. It almost felt like he could break it with his fingers, but a quick test proved that wasn't the case.

It was much harder than it looked.

Curious to see the stamps, Four ducked back into the farthest corner of the kitchen quickly held one of the coins up to the light. On one side was an empty plate. On the other was the mark. Satisfied, he slipped the coin back in his pocket with the others. All the coins he'd collected so far felt the same, and as he resumed his position on the line he wondered what other types of treasure there were to be had.

Trying to discern the burdens and sorrows carried by the morning's visitors was difficult, but not because the loads they carried were abnormal. In fact, the dark plagues he saw within the room were the same as those he saw on people all the time. What was different was the amount. Anxiety and suffering were like snow here, falling incessantly and piling up on those who sat still too long. Number Four noticed right away that one fat little man in the corner had a huge pile building up on his head. It was a target made to order.

Might as well hand it over now, little man.

Four walked toward the target and smiled; pity filling his eyes. The smell of alcohol and filth wafted from the man like a cloud, and Four wondered just how drunk the man was and how long it had been since he'd had a bath. Poor old dirty fat little man. Four searched the dull red eyes for any sign of a spark but found none. Covered in shadows, the man wore dark wounds like clothing. Creatures of varying descriptions clung to him, feeding. The man was a mess, a junkyard of damage. It would take a lifetime to clean this guy up.

"How had he let himself get like this?" Four wondered to himself.

"I see you, little thief."

Four almost jumped out of his skin. He hadn't even noticed the guard that now slunk past him and sat down next to his target, though it had clearly been tailing him all day. Cursing his clumsiness, Four looked around for a place to find cover.

"Awww, what's wrong?" the sleek figure purred. "You don't want to play anymore?"

The red eyes of the poor little fat man looked right at Kent, suddenly intensely focused and entirely clear of the haze. "You don't know me!" he roared, then reared back and launched a thick and rancid glob of spit and mucus from his mouth. It landed on Number Four's left cheek and nose and ran quickly down onto his lips.

Four shouted in disgust and jumped back, frantically wiping his face with his sleeve as the man cackled toothlessly.

The guard's slime tag went neon, glowing like a beacon as the sleek figure bent seductively and whispered something in the little man's ear. The man glared at Number Four with renewed fury and an instant later a plate still piled with stuffing and potatoes flew in the direction of Kent's head.

The plate missed its target, but it was clear that Four would no longer be stealing anything. The guard squealed and convulsed with mocking laughter, shrieking in victory as the treasure Kent had been seeking was swept away and locked down tight. Huge searchlights from the guard towers exploded and locked on the thief, the neon slime burning brightly on his skin.

Kent panicked, feeling hot and dizzy. How had he messed up so badly? It was as if the guard was waiting for him; as if it knew him.

From out of nowhere the mist swirled and Adelle was at his elbow.

"Are you OK?" she asked.

"I'm stuck here," he confessed, successfully taking out a huge guard that tried to grab him from behind. "And I'm not sure what I'm doing. Did you see what happened?"

"You were tailed," Adelle answered.

Four looked at her, determined. "Can you show me?"

She glowed in response. "I'll try. I'm sorry if this hurts."

Four nodded.

Adelle reached inside her jacket. When she pulled her hand back out, it glinted like a polished razor. She held the small mirror to his face, and Kent saw in the reflection that he was not alone. Over his shoulder a figure was stalking him, silently marking his trail and sending some sort of message to the sleek guard up ahead. The signal transmitted, the sleek one then whispered it to the little man.

Samuel's warning from the day before leapt to life, and Four growled inside when he recognized the creeping figure behind him. It was the flawless version of himself that still dominated his portrait in the hall.

Four spun on his portrait image and found the proud eyes glaring back at him from the edge of the mist. He seized on the first lesson he had learned from Malcolm in the trench and launched a reckless shot, "You are a lie."

The image flinched, then fired back. "No. I'm what you can be. Look at yourself. I am in there. With enough training, you could be good. Really good. The potential is there."

The image was right. He could feel it. Smarter than most, he had the gifts and talents to be a great thief. He just needed practice.

Four looked up again and the mist was empty. The image was gone, having apparently met its match. Satisfied, he turned back to the little man who was now screaming and pointing at him, crying and demanding a new plate of food.

"It was his fault!" the fat little man cried.

Dozens of eyes followed the little man's finger to where Four stood, off-balance and embarrassed. Questions and disapproval filtered through the crowd as the sleek guard danced gleefully from table to table.

Four fumbled, grasping at straws. He resorted to what he knew. "You are a lie!" he shouted at the sleek guard. The guard only laughed harder, whispering and further inciting its prisoner. The little man was now radiating pure hatred toward Number Four, and his example was gradually moving others to do the same. Treasure all around the room was disappearing from sight and more guard towers were flipping on their lights. This newcomer was clearly not to be trusted. The neon marker blazed condemningly.

Adelle put a gentle hand on his shoulder. "No, Kent. That one is not a lie. That one is true. That's what makes it such a powerful guard."

"What is it?" Four looked at it fearfully.

"Ignorance," she replied. "Your ignorance."

Four spun on Adelle. "Ignorance?" he cried, anger flaring.

"It is why they don't trust you," Adelle explained gently. "You don't know them."

"And you do?" he challenged.

"No, I don't."

"Then how do you know that I'm ignorant? Maybe I know things you don't."

"I'm sure you do, Kent. But you don't know these people."

"You have no clue what I know!" he protested.

"Have you known this?" she challenged. "Have you ever been this hungry?"

"Hunger is hunger." Four fixed his eyes on the mass of dirty faces scattered throughout the room. They wore expressions like ice. He was not welcome.

"The guard is building walls, Kent," Adelle warned. "Be careful."

The sleek one moved incredibly fast throughout the room, stacking dark bricks in rows between Four and his targets. The walls grew taller by the second. He could almost hear the concrete setting.

Four thought for a moment, his pulse quickening. He glared at the fat little man, then at Adelle. "So what, I need to go without food? Is that it? Make myself hurt so that I can relate to him a little better?"

"You can try that. You might learn some valuable things from the experience. But even if you starve yourself to the point of pain and beyond, you will never really be where he is, because your suffering will always have been by choice. You may allow yourself to hurt, but that is not the same thing as being hurt. Knowing the sensation of pain is not the same thing as being abused."

"So how can I know where he is?"

"You can't. Start there. And show the man some respect."

Something inside Kent sprang up. He hated his own words even as he said them, but they were in there and he could not stop them from coming out of his mouth. "Show him some respect?! How about being shown some respect? Or some gratitude! After all, we're here for them! It's not like they've come out to where we live with a bunch of food. It's not like they care about us!" The words gushed out, sweet and poisonous all at once.

Adelle whirled on him, pinning him to the wall with a stare stronger than he was ready for. The rest of the room faded into the background as she drew him into a place that was carved out for just the two of them.

"Have you asked yourself whether you really want to be a part of this?" she growled.

The world went still. Four could hear the swish of Adelle's hair against her jacket. He could feel the heat of her breath on his face.

"Of course I have!" he fired back. "A million times. You think I haven't counted the cost? I know how hard this is going to be!"

"So you know it is going to be hard?" she pressed.

"Yes!"

"Then you realize HE was just inviting you in?"

That stopped his mouth. She was right. It had been an invitation. A brutal, harsh, honest invitation to pick up his share of the load and get hauling. It was an invitation to steal pain, and he took offense at it. He had been wrong all along… he had no idea how hard this was going to be. He was hostile toward the burden before he'd even picked it up.

Adelle watched him soften and longed to ease up, but this operation needed to go all the way. Leaving this surgery halfway finished could damage him for a long time. This was not the time for pity. This was the time for truth. Once more, she whipped the mirror from its sheath and pressed it to his face. He could not avoid it, standing as close as they were, and the glinting silver suddenly occupied his entire field of vision. The eyes that met his were handsome, haughty, and cold. His eyes were the eyes from the portrait.

Four instantly realized what had happened. He had allowed the guard in. Like playing back a recording, he listened in his head to the arrogant words he had just been saying.

"You are being a jerk," he told himself.

"No," the image countered. "You gave up your time for these people, and they repaid you by spitting on you and throwing plates of food at your head. It is no wonder they are where they are. You are better than they are. Much better!" Four recognized the voice. He had heard that long, whipping tongue before.

"Actually," he observed, "I am looking down on a group of people I know nothing about."

The eyes in the mirror widened in fear.

"I have allowed you to convince me that I am more important than anyone at these tables," Kent continued, gutting himself, "but that's not true. And while I claimed to be here in order to help people, the one I have been most interested in helping was myself. I am the lowest one here."

This time the image said nothing. It had fled. His own softer eyes looked back at him.

Adelle lowered her blade.

"How did you know?" Four asked the question, completely disarmed.

Adelle smiled and laid a tiny finger on his chest. "Don't take this the wrong way, Number Four... but you reeked."

"Oh!" he remembered. "And now?"

Adelle closed her eyes and stepped in close, her lips bending happily. "Mmmm... Much better."

20

Stamp of Approval

There was a coin in Number Four's pocket unlike any he had ever stolen before. Marked with a broken bone, it was handed to him by the fat little man whose name, he found out, was Kermit. It was a large coin, and not easily won.

The battle with the sleek guard ranged throughout the room. Fast and well-trained, it would not allow Number Four to sneak past or hide from it, for the searchlights from all the neighboring towers moved wherever it looked. If any loot was going to be stolen, it was going to have to be done boldly and in plain sight.

Despite his initial failure, Four did not retreat. Instead he approached the battle with a new understanding. He left his long-sleeved hooded sweatshirt folded behind him on the ground. There would be no pretending anymore. Both combatants knew where they stood. Both knew what was at stake.

The guard raced forward, shuriken whispers shredding the room with mistrust as the wall went higher. From the tops of the surrounding towers spotlights sliced through the mist, focusing in on the glowing tag that was still smeared across the thief's face, reminding the homeless crowd that this outsider was not one of them.

The thief was not to be trusted.

Four accepted their hostility. These were real people with wounds and burdens that he did not fully understand. He did not shrink from their suspicion, nor did he pretend to be one of them. He was not their savior. He was simply a thief, willing and able to sit with them for a while.

Four approached the fat little man and apologized. Then he went to the serving window, got a fresh plate of food and delivered it.

The little man glared suspiciously for a moment, then shrugged and accepted the plate.

The whole interaction, from Four's perspective, was incredibly uncomfortable, with the sleek guard continuing to launch threats of rejection, but he committed to it and tore a huge brick from the base of the wall. He sat down next to the fat little man and poured himself a glass of milk from a plastic jug on the table. Together, they sat and ate. Fireworks did not go off. People did not suddenly grab hands and begin dancing in happy circles around the room. The lifelong troubles did not disappear. But now they were shoulder to shoulder instead of toe to toe.

Sitting beside each other, Four and the fat little man ate Thanksgiving dinner. It was a small thing, but it mattered.

Brick by brick, the wall came down. The sleek guard scrambled furiously throughout the room, trying to make repairs and keep the division in place, but it could find nothing to use for building. Other guards attempted to build in different places throughout the room, but the thieves had a weapon the guards could not answer. They cared. It was like sledgehammers on the walls. Warmth and conversation sent bricks flying away in powdery clouds.

"I'm sorry for being rude," said Kent. "I'm a little unsure of myself. This is my first time at a place like this."

"This is your first time in a cafeteria?" The fat little man glared at him with his far eye, crumbs spilling from his mouth. The eye closest to Kent was squinted shut in disbelief. He looked like a toad.

"No, not in a cafeteria. I meant…" Four thought about what he meant. It was exactly what Adelle was talking about. To this man, that is all this was – a cafeteria. It was not some special place to visit once a year to help poor people, feel good about yourself, and score loot. This was his life. His regular everyday survive however you can 365 days a year life. "You know, you're right. I've been in plenty of cafeterias. I am uncomfortable because I feel like an outsider."

"Well you are an outsider," the toad man said, grinning.

"And that's OK with you?"

"Sure," the man shrugged. "There's always room at this place. That's why I come back."

"Well thanks for having me." Four stuck out his hand. "My name's Kent."

"Kermit."

"Kermit?"

"Yup. Like the frog." Kermit smiled as if he'd just told the best joke in the world and was waiting for the laughs to pour in. Kent obliged.

"That is a great name. Nice to meet you, Kermit."

The body of the sleek guard sank and collapsed to the floor, mortally wounded from a knife wound in its back.

Still dirty and drunk, with breath that could knock you down at ten paces and wearing clothes that others had thrown away, Kermit dropped the blade and went back to his dinner.

Did he know what he'd done? It didn't matter. The guard was down. The rest of the room softened, conversation resumed, and the gravy was passed around the table...

That evening Number Four stood before the mirror, a mound of different coins piled in his hand. For the first time in years, he looked at his reflection and really examined what he saw. Kind eyes, but tending toward conceit when given their head. A healthy body, but with a little too much love for sleep and sugar. A heart for justice, but chained by selfish fear...

He spent several minutes gazing, no longer with the self-adoration that he had for the portrait in the hall, but with an honest eye. He was searching for an accurate assessment of himself and he found it.

There was growing to do. A lot of growing. And the more he grew the more room for growth he would be able to see! It was almost defeating.

Kent pushed those thoughts aside. One day at a time.

"Who are these coins for?" the mirror asked.

"I would like to make a purchase."

"Very well. What would you like to buy?"

"I have been instructed to buy a watch."

"Have you also been instructed as to what that will mean?"

"I have."

"And you still desire to make the purchase?"

"I do," Kent said.

As the words left his lips, the coins in his hand flaked apart into grains like sand, then re-formed and twisted around his wrist. The clasp snapped closed with a permanent sound, and he could not avoid the immediate associations his mind made with imprisonment and slavery.

He did not have forever.

The boundary raised by the watch was drawn terribly close to where he was already standing. Heavy and inflexible, it was not a new sensation, just a deeper awareness of the limitations that had always been there. All the growing he had to do and barely enough time to get started...

He raised his eyes again to the mirror.

"You must make a decision, Number Five. Who is your time for? Who gets your minutes, sets your schedule, and orders your seasons?"

"The Sweet Thief."

"Be alert, Number Five!" warned the voice behind the mirror. "This is not a secure decision. It is always under attack. The guards will constantly be suggesting alternate schedules and orders. The surrender of your time must be won daily."

"Daily?"

"Sometimes more often than that."

"How will I know?"

There was no reply. The mirror had gone quiet.

Already Number Five could feel the conflict between different objectives, the tension brought on by differing strategies, and the deeper power struggle at the root of it all.

As usual, he felt like he was in over his head.

Number Five stepped into the den, anxious to see his friends and feel like someone else was in this with him, but when he grabbed a chair and sat down he was disappointed to see that Adelle was not at the table.

Samuel glanced over and gestured toward Five's new accessory. He didn't say anything, but his expression was like that of a father watching his son catch a baseball for the first time.

Jim's reaction was more playful. He reached over with his own shackled wrist and clinked Five's as though making a toast, though his wide smile was also a grimace.

Now that he had his own, Five noticed many other thieves in the den wearing similar bands on their wrists.

"Does everyone have one?"

"No," Samuel said flatly. "And many of those who do struggle to keep them on." He indicated his own bare wrists. Five could almost make out a pale ring where one may have once been.

Jim was absently chewing at the tip of a fingernail, but Five looked over at him when he heard him chuckle.

"What?" Five asked.

The green eyes twinkled. Then Jim pulled his hand away from his mouth, examined his finger, and wiped it on the loosely rolled sleeve of his shirt. A mischievous grin was tugging at the corners of his mouth, and Samuel began laughing disgustedly before Jim even said a word.

"What is it?" Kent demanded.

"It seems," Jim teased, "that our illustrious sage, the venerable Sam..."

"Samuel," Sam corrected.

"Ah yes, Samuel..." Jim repeated, the thieves sparring laughingly with their eyes, "Samuel here, for all of his vast wisdom, seems to have a bit of a problem keeping his watch on. Apparently he prefers to steer his little ship around the pond on his own schedule."

Samuel's face was in his palm. "It's true! It's all true!" he wailed.

"While I..." Jim trumpeted the words and stood to his feet, his hand on his chest and his face blissfully pointed toward the sky, "have found that it goes much better when I surrender control to the one to whom we have pledged ourselves." Jim looked over quickly and winked at Five, then resumed his pose until Samuel groaned in agony.

His performance over, Jim walked around the table and took Samuel by the shoulders, roughing him up and patting him on the back.

"Like I said," Samuel continued, rolling his eyes at himself, "Some have a much more difficult time wearing them than others. You would do well to follow Jim's example on this one rather than my own."

"Timing is everything!" Jim crooned and stepped away from the table, disappearing into the den.

It was only Sam and Kent at the table when the barkeep brought their food a moment later. The two of them dove in, and the smells and tastes instantly transported Five's thoughts back to the heist at the shelter.

He finished chewing his first bite and looked over at Sam, "How is it that some guards are able to work together? I'd never seen that before. It was brutal. One was behind me, reporting to one up ahead, and they were launching attacks on multiple fronts at once. Just when I faced down one attack, another wave was coming right behind it. I thought they were going to swamp me."

Samuel looked up glumly. "The guards can do whatever they want." Then he shot Five a challenging, encouraging glance. "Just like you."

21

The Mailman and Malcolm

"At least you and I have something to do, love. At least you and I have something to do!" The prisoner was screaming, his hands curled like palsied claws. *"Pass it on, but never to this dread pale country. Throw it to the wind, the frost and the barn-side owls, but throw it not to them. Not to the ogre and not to the brood, for one clucks and the other throttles, and you'll have no rest at all. Oh, she carries her love in a tragedy box!"* Chains thumped in time against the wall as the huge man rocked back and forth, his arms wrapped around his legs.

"How long has he been like this?" asked the mailman.

"Ten years now," the attendant replied. "Though he's only been here at the facility for two."

"I assume he's received some kind of therapy?"

"We've tried everything. Shrinks. Meds. Electroshock. You name it, he's had it."

"Did anything have an effect?" the mailman probed.

"The pills can wind him up and slow him down, but that's mostly just metabolism. We never saw a significant change in cognition or awareness. None of the therapists who have seen him have reported anything to be hopeful about. And the electroshock just made him mad."

"Where was he before he came to the facility?"

"His family had him. Amazing people. The things they went through with him would blow your mind. They bawled like babies when they brought him in. They've been one of the most faithful groups of people I've ever seen. His mother hasn't missed a visit in two years."

"How often is that?"

"Three times a week," the attendant replied.

"Does he know when she's there?" asked the mailman.

"I think he does. There are slight differences in his activity levels for a while after her visits. I don't think she knows it since she doesn't see how he is when she's not around, but there's a difference. I wish she could tell. It breaks my heart watching her with him."

The mailman had heard enough. There was more than enough pain here. Even this guy – an observer three people removed – was filling up his mailbag just talking about it. Target acquired.

"When can I see him?"

"Well, you know that legally you can't just walk in there."

The mailman looked up intently. "I thought we had an arrangement."

"We do. But we have to be careful about how we do this."

"You can't just sneak me in under a cart?" the mailman grinned.

"Sure," the attendant shrugged, "as long as you don't mind both of us being permanently moved in here."

The mailman had already considered that as a last ditch option.

"So what's the plan?"

"We're going to sign you in as a visiting specialist from a clinic on the west coast. We've had to get a little tricky with the paperwork, but as long as no one digs into the referral too closely we should be fine. If you are willing to risk it we can slip you in right before the shift change this evening."

"Do it," the mailman confirmed without hesitation.

"And our arrangement?" the attendant prompted.

"Of course." The mailman handed him a small package.

The package rattled softly and the attendant nodded. "Be here at quarter to six."

The mailman walked back out to his truck and spent the rest of the route getting his mind ready. This one was going to hurt.

He returned five hours later; no longer in his normal uniform but in a short white coat. He wore glasses with no prescription and had his silver hair combed down neatly.

"Hello, can I help you?" asked the attendant.

"I think you can." The mailman waited a moment, saying nothing more.

Suddenly a flash of recognition swept the attendant's face and he lowered his voice. "Oh, it's you! I never would have known it."

"That's the idea, right?"

The attendant instantly brought his voice back up to normal volume. "Very good. Sign here then, Dr. Osbourne."

"Osbourne?" the mailman mouthed the question in silence as the attendant spun a clipboard neatly around and held out a pen.

A momentary panic hit the mailman. This was one part of the plan that he had overlooked. Times and locations and personnel he had completely figured out, but signing himself in was something he hadn't even considered. Conscious of every security camera in the lobby, the mailman took the pen. Trying to look natural, he ran a finger down the clipboard, hoping that there would be large blocks of text he could pretend to read in order to buy himself a moment to think. There was no such content on the form. It was just a list, and it was clear where his signature should go. He had to wing it, and fast. No one thinks long and hard when it's time to sign something. They just do it.

Luckily, the mailman had seen millions of signatures on the mail route. Some were intricate scrawling works of art, while others were little more than an X. The mailman went with something in between. Finding the space on the log where it read Thomas Osbourne, he looked to the right of the name and found an empty box. There he wrote a large T followed by a short, wavy squiggle. Then he added an O and a longer squiggle. It wasn't perfect, but it was done. He spun the clipboard back around and laid the pen on top.

"Very good, Doctor. Your patient is in room 118." The attendant handed him a laminated badge and pointed to the mailman's left, then looked back to a monitor below the counter.

The mailman turned away from the front desk and walked down the hallway on legs he could barely feel, nervous energy surging through his body like electricity. Not even halfway to the patient's room, the first shot rang out.

"You forgot to sign 'Dr.' you idiot!" cackled one of the guards.

"I wonder what the penalty is for what you are doing," a second guard chimed in. "Can felons work for the post office?"

"What other details have you forgotten?" screamed a third.

As expected, the place was infested.

A couple of the guards' barbs grazed the mailman, but he shook them off lightly as he fired back, pulling the pin as if from a grenade and rolling it down the hall ahead of him. "Can you all even begin to imagine how much pain I could steal in prison?" A moment later the hallway went silent and the mailman continued on, stepping over the motionless forms of the guards as he went.

Every door he passed was labelled with a number; odds on the left and evens on the right. About a quarter of the way down the hall the mailman arrived at a door with a placard reading 118.

This was it.

On the wall next to the door there was a small orange button. The mailman pressed it once and watched it light up. Then he inserted a keycard into a slot beneath the button and looked back to see the attendant wave in his direction and reach below the counter. There was a quiet buzz and the sound of a latch clicking.

As the door swung open to reveal the room beyond, it instantly became clear how insignificant a few layers of steel and brick were going to be when it came to really getting inside.

The prisoner rocked in the far corner...

"Sing to me, ancient traveler. Tell me of the palaces I've built. Cry for crumpled silver wings long hidden in the sand. Raise your darlings o'er your head and dash them on the rocks. Dance with me you scatterer! Ha ha. Hallow the ruts of wagon tongues that bore the floods away. Dredge the empty veins that bend vain bars of broken

gates. Aha! Now chant, rattling boneyards! Gleam, glinting portals!
Give no breath and take no breath from blooms of angry shores...
the wrathful tides are blossoming!"

The mailman could see beyond the padded room, well past the tiny cell made safe with shackles and restraints. He saw the immense maze that filled the space between the smoky walls. He heard the guards calling to one another from their nests and hiding places. He felt the agony of the one chained in torment on the other side.

It was thrilling. To stand here on the edge of battle and feel the strength surge. This was the one he had been hunting – a heist truly worthy of his skill – and the loot within the labyrinth was the haul of a lifetime.

Black gloves went tight as the mailman clenched his fists. The fear was gone. As excited as he'd been in years, he slipped silently into the maze.

It was time to play.

Darts came flying in from all sides as the first of the guards attacked, but their barbs were like snowflakes on desert dunes. The mailman repelled them before they even made contact, and the first line of defense quickly realized that whoever this was, he hadn't stumbled in here by accident. Twenty doglike guards lay broken in a heap as he moved past.

"What is your name?" The guttural question came from across the room and echoed through the maze. Though it rumbled from the huge man's throat, it was not a human voice.

The mailman did not answer, but raced silently through the shadows, dispatching lesser guards with such speed that they didn't even have time to gurgle a warning to the rest. A confident blur, the thief moved on.

"Tell me your name!" The demand was a powerful, ear-splitting screech.

Lesser thieves would have cowered at the awful sound. This thief, however, smiled hungrily. He heard the uncertainty behind the bellowing voice. *That's right. You should be afraid. The mailman is coming.*

The walls of the maze, though intimidatingly tall, were far from flawless, and the mailman found handholds everywhere. He exploited the broken surface to make his way past floor traps so clumsy and obvious that he wondered why they had been placed there at all.

Is this the best you've got?

The mailman padded forward quickly on his toes, eyes scanning and ears perked. On the floor ahead was yet another juvenile trap. It was not concealed at all; the tripwire placed too high. Only the least observant of thieves would set off such a snare.

The mailman leapt easily to the adjacent wall, then vaulted over the wire and moved on. It was as though a child had set this up just before going to bed, after the best of creativity had been drained by the day. The mailman was almost bored. Maybe this wasn't the test he had hoped for after all. He ducked below a rocky shelf and shot past a spring-loaded blade that he set off on purpose.

Another trip wire up ahead made him shake his head. What a waste. His legs tensed and he sprang to the wall, rebounded and came down on the other side of the wire. This time, however, he heard the sound of cracking ice as he landed.

Now that's more like it.

Had it been the thief's first assignment he would have been impaled on the spikes beneath the crumbling floor, but the mailman was more than ready. With balance honed by trial after trial, he absorbed the fall with his legs, slowing his body and coming to rest on top of the spikes. They punctured only the soft rubber soles of his shoes. Precisely poised atop the spikes, the mailman slowed his breathing and closed his eyes, sensing everything around him. The movement of the air. The change in temperature. It was all perfectly clear. So when the blast came from behind, the mailman was ready.

He ducked, lunging forward to lay flat upon the spikes as a raging ball of fire shot past and exploded on the edge of the pit. A shower of red and orange flew in all directions as drops of molten rock splattered on the floor among the spikes. The mailman heard the rock sizzling as he shuffled his hands from spike to spike.

There was no time to recover. Another missile was inbound, this one headed straight down. Concentrating all his energy on his hands and feet, the mailman tensed and pushed off of the spikes, launching himself to the edge and scrambling up out of the pit. He rolled to a stop on the floor of the maze, inadvertently tripping the wire he had hurdled an instant earlier.

As the meteor slammed into the pit, shattering the spikes and melting the surrounding rock, the mailman lay on his back and tried to catch his breath. The tripwire he had just set off triggered nothing more. It had already done its job.

The last of the sizzling bits of rock fell to the ground and the mailman leapt to his feet. He quickly brushed himself off, dislodging a few glowing embers, and when he surveyed the burns on his clothes and examined the skin underneath he found several shallow blisters.

It was a good wake up call. This was no game.

Again the inhuman voice called out, *"What is your name?"*

The mailman was tempted to respond, but still he remained silent. If and when he spoke to this guard, it would be on his own terms. Then again, he might not speak to it at all.

He continued steadily up the canyons, careful to mark his way at each intersection. While the attacks kept coming, he would not allow the guards to rush him. This was not a one day job – he knew that going in.

Time and again the mailman returned to the clinic to take on the maze. He returned so often that the entire staff knew his face and waved him through without examining his badge or signature. He returned so often that the dark one bellowing from the large man's throat ceased asking his name and merely screamed at him in fury. He returned so often that the attempts of the guards to erase his marks on the walls no longer mattered. He knew the maze by heart. He knew where false paths led to snares. He knew where the powerful guards lurked – those that could not be damaged but only avoided. He also knew where the weaker guards were posted, and he trampled them for sport.

Finally, after many days, the mailman walked into the maze for the last time. He was utterly weary of the burden. He had paid the price and then some, every scar well-earned. Deeply, profoundly... he hurt.

It was just as it should be, and it would end today.

"Happen. Happen. Happen. Happen."

The mailman heard the voice muttering as he opened the door. It knew he was coming. The vast maze stretched out at his feet, and he looked across the tops of the jagged crooks and crags. Smoke hung thick and low over the peaks like a living shroud, rolling and flashing, and a dim red glow came from within the maze itself. To some, it would be a vision of hell. To the mailman, it was nothing more than the smoldering embers of a backyard campfire. That is what he told himself. That is what he needed to believe. This job had cost him much more than he wanted to feel. It had wounded him more deeply than he dared let on.

"Nothing has changed!" the guards screamed from their perches.

"You have spent yourself for nothing!" they taunted.

"So much pain. All your suffering. Meaningless." A thousand voices shouted, sounding like the whole world. "You are older, slower, weaker! You have nothing left to give and nothing to show for all you've given. This will end as nothing, and you will have poured yourself out for no reason at all."

The ache and the weight of the load pressed in on the mailman's forehead. The memory of every sting and freezing touch sliced into his skin. For a moment he faltered. Of course they were right. He had nothing left. The battle had worn on far longer than he expected. Besides, there was no victory to be gained here. The moment that it ended they would simply move on and rebuild. The attack would never really be over.

The mailman longed for the thousandth time to simply lie down and be done. But he would not. The odds against him, his strength gone, the guards were on high alert... there was no way he could win. It was exactly what he had come for, and he smiled and took them all by the throat.

"Though I fall, I win." For the first time the mailman spoke out loud to the gloom and the fire and the twisted figure on the other side of the maze. *"I do not fear you or the death you hold in store. This will end today, and the captive will go free. I will take it all, and you will watch. Prepare yourself."*

With that, the mailman stepped down into the smoke.

On the other end of the room the helpless man contorted and writhed, skin nearly bursting from the pressure inside. Bound with belts and buckles, he strained with such force that the shackles could not hold.

The mailman was halfway through the maze when he heard the first of the straps give way. The tearing sound echoed through the room.

The mailman quickened his pace. He was a powerful thief and a death sentence to guards, but he had little in the way of physical strength. If his massive target broke free of his restraints in this tiny padded cell, he would be torn to pieces before help could arrive.

Leaping over traps he would have preferred to inch around, the mailman took on guards three and four at a time.

A guard with three heads and owl wings screeched as it flew above the canyon, "It's dangerous to change your strategy now! What if you make a mistake?" Another of its heads called out, "Better hurry, he's almost loose!" The third head cooed warmly, "Safety resides in the hall outside. You can still make it out if you turn back now."

The mailman skidded to a halt and looked up at the guard. For more nights than he could count he had labored under a constant barrage of discouragement from the ugly bird, and he would endure it no longer. The guard's wings flared too late as the mailman raised his hand.

"*Manuel!*" The name erupted from the mailman's mouth, thundering through the body of the guard and spraying bits of feathers and carcass across the room. The rest of the guards covered their ears and screamed in pain. Enraged at the mention of the name, they filled the air above the maze with a deafening roar. The room rocked and the floor buckled as showers of dust rained down from overhead. A second strap tore loose.

"Blood and bile and venom!" the voice of the oppressor bellowed. **"The beast is freed and heaven quakes! Westward blow the scales of all your favorite ghosts! You are nothing to me, slave of thieves! So kick the skies and fill the air with shards of hope and fruitless prayer. You will not leave this place unfettered. Your life for his!"**

"*So be it,*" came the unyielding response.

The mailman raced on, hurdling obstacles and cutting down foes. Nothing could stop him. Nothing could slow him down. Nothing could keep him from conquering the maze. It was only a matter of time.

"Time. Time. Time."

The maze was breached at last just as the last strap tore loose, and the mailman leapt up onto the dais only to find himself face to face with a foe he could not match. The huge man rose to his feet, restraints dangling uselessly from his massive arms. Upon the captive's back rode a perversion too revolting to look upon directly. The mailman could only squint at it from the corner of his eye.

153

It was the nearness of the thing on his back that had driven the large man mad, and now the victim wailed through spit and snot as the guard spoke through his mouth. *"What is this? A milk bug creeps up from the cracks, intent on theft and mischief. Come then, bug! Skitter close. Hear the cracking shell. The juice squirts far as you go flat, wiped up with smoke-stained curtains. A fistful of candles held tight by fools, snuffed out with careless giggling, the children will play in a sandbox of your ashes as I smudge their faces with what's left of you."*

The mailman moved to speak the name that he knew would send the darkness scurrying, but no words came out. A huge hand had gripped his throat, crushing his larynx with a single twist.

The pain was blinding. The mailman fell to his knees as consciousness began to slip away. The power of the guards he could fight, but not this. There was no air to breathe, to speak, to scream.

Rising exultantly from the huge man's back, its tentacles quivering in the air, the guard stood in the saddle and shrieked. The awful sound filled the room. Even the padded walls were unable to dampen the wicked voice of the guard. The roar bounced from floor to ceiling and back again, first in victory, then in surprise, and finally in terror.

"Manuel..." Impossibly, the thief had somehow found the strength to reach the saddle's straps, and with one swift and desperate whisper he sliced the harness free.

The guard tumbled to the ground like a spider flicked from its web.

Liberated all at once from years of cruel subjugation, the huge captive looked around in shock. There was no darkness pressing down, no wicked words inside his head. He was free! As he glanced down at the one who had made it through the maze, he relaxed his grip and let go of the mailman's neck.

The mailman immediately began crawling toward the guard, determined to finish it off. Delirious with pain and suffocation, he dragged himself along with one hand clinging to his throat. Tears streamed down his cheeks. There was still no air!

The guard scrambled up on kinked and crooked legs and tried to run away, but there was nowhere to go. Trapped in the corner of the tiny room, it turned to face the approaching thief. It hissed loudly, as it no longer had a human mouth to use, but its words were clear in the mailman's mind. *"I told you... Your life for his!"*

The mailman's silent response was just as clear. *"So be it. I win."*

It was true. Robbed of its captive, the sick creature began to shiver and shudder in pain, the chill of the ground working up its legs and freezing them so quickly that they started to splinter and break off. The mailman would not be the only one to die here today.

"We could both live," the guard hissed.

The mailman's lungs were on fire, the pain beyond description as his body convulsed, demanding breath. He lurched forward on his knees, desperately seeking pockets of air that he could not take in. Where was his help? Where was the den? He tried to cry out but could not.

Again the disgusting darkness called, *"We could both live."*

The mailman said nothing. He lay heaving in agony, waiting to die. But when the guard crawled over, so broken and fractured that it was no longer much more than a speck, the mailman did not close his mouth. Meeting no resistance, the guard crept inside. It pushed his throat open and cleared the shattered path to his lungs.

The air went in and the fire went out.

22

Transfer of Funds

"Simmer there, my wounded one. Stolen breath a shackle sore. Raw and weeping, last year's figs. Burn and let the crooked play. The hot lash cracks snaps fast bent backs, Unbearable! Yet bear you will, just barely. So much rage and fight remains. Aha! Doubt digs in like trenches deep. Fire the guns and file your teeth. Suck the air between long fangs and fan these lower flames. The throat hole such a sweet nest here, though cramped; too cramped to stay. Enjoy the air while I am small. I'll ride you before long."

The words were sour on the mailman's tongue as he muttered them over and over. He was careful not to speak so loud that anyone else would hear. He had enough problems to deal with as it was...

"That you are lying is clear. Why you are lying is not." Two men in suits glared at him.

The mailman scribbled his answer on a notepad that lay open on his hospital bed. *"Why would I lie?"*

"That's what we'd like to know," answered one of the suits. "You are clearly not a doctor, so you can drop the act. We know your name and how long you've been visiting the treatment center. We also know that you have no license to practice any kind of medicine anywhere. What we don't know is who helped you, or why you had such a keen interest in this particular patient."

The pen flicked fast and aggressively. *"Is there something wrong with helping people?"*

"When you pretend to be a doctor? Yes."

Again, the pen scratched. *"What is a doctor?"*

"A doctor…"

The mailman waved him off with an angry gesture. Then he wrote again. *"No one was helping that man. I did. End of story."*

"I'm afraid that isn't the end of the story. Impersonating a member of the medical profession is illegal."

The mailman's next statement did not involve pen or paper.

"I see," replied one of the suits. "Well it is clear that – "

The mailman pushed the call button on his bed and made himself look as frantic and in pain as he knew how, pleading for help with his eyes as the nurse rushed in. She came to his rescue immediately.

"I'm sorry," said the nurse as she shooed the suits from the room. "The patient needs his rest."

Greatly relieved to see them go, the mailman smiled gratefully and laid back in the bed. But right before the door closed one of the suits leaned back inside.

"We'll be in touch," he smiled, and a cloud of dark darts came flying.

The mailman flinched in pain as the darts hit home.

Now he was confused. Those darts were child's play. He had been dodging those since day one. So why had they suddenly found their mark?

Anxiety and fear leaked from the darts, pouring into the mailman's veins. At the same time a tiny burp bellowed up from deep inside his throat and filled his mouth with a rotten stench.

"Hello."

The mailman trembled at the sick feeling of having the guard inside him. Where was the den? Where was the support? He had needed them. He still needed them!

The silence was chilling.

"They aren't here," the voice whispered from his throat.

The mailman longed to reach in, rip the poison out, and smash it against the wall. But he couldn't. The guard was right.

"They left you. They left you. They left you."

The guard taunted him for hours and the mailman could do nothing to stop it. He just lay there, broken and alone. No rescue arrived. The den never showed.

There was one person who did end up dropping by that night.

It was late. The oxycodone was working its magic, the pillow under his head growing softer and softer until it felt like he was floating. As he lay there, teetering on the brink of consciousness, the mailman suddenly caught a glimpse of something moving near the foot of his bed. The curtain near the window swayed out from the wall as if it had been blown by a breeze. But there was no breeze. The window was closed.

"Why'd you do it?" a voice asked.

The mailman was too drowsy to turn his head to see the face of the one who had finally come. Not that it mattered. It was obviously one of the thieves – here to find out what went wrong. Desperate to explain why there was a guard living in his throat, he groped in the dark for his notepad, unaware that it had fallen to the floor. After a minute of feeling around on the bed and finding nothing he abandoned the search in frustration and simply tried to force the words upward – shocked when they actually came out.

"I was dying," he croaked. His voice was weak and raspy, but it held.

"That's why you did it?"

"Yeah, that's why I did it!" he heaved. Each word was a fight to push out. "I had no choice."

"That don't make no sense."

Suddenly the mailman's eyes snapped open and he strained to turn his head. The one standing above his bed was not who he thought it was.

Towering over him, almost too tall to be human, was an enormous figure. Loose clothes hung like wings from his shoulders, and his head, though bowed toward the bed, seemed to be no more than a few inches from the ceiling.

The mailman was too afraid to move. His arms were rigid, his legs unresponsive. He couldn't even cry out as doom descended upon him.

"Why'd you do it?" the figure asked again. The voice was pleading, almost desperate. "I gotta know. Why?"

The mailman looked harder and all at once he saw that it was neither a thief nor a guard standing there in the dark. It was the madman from the padded cell! The one who had crept into his hospital room was the same man he had been creeping in to see in his cell – the one who had been bound for years in restraints and straps and buckles.

The huge man looked so different that the mailman couldn't believe it was the same person. There was intelligence and warmth in those eyes that for so long had stared back at him like hollow pits. Surely this could not be the same man, but it was. It was patient 118, the one they called Malcolm.

"You can't be here," the mailman choked out the words. "There's no way they let you out that fast."

"No," Malcolm stared at him without blinking. "I left up out of there on my own. I had to know before one more minute went by. And now you gonna tell me. Why?"

"Why what?" the mailman cringed.

"Why you came and got me." Malcolm stood there trembling. He wasn't going to leave. He wasn't going to do one more thing until he knew the truth.

The fear on the mailman's face melted away and was slowly replaced by a scowl. As he dropped his eyes to the sheets that were draped lightly across his stomach, his visage went cold. He sat in silence, not saying another word. The answer Malcolm was looking for was not one he was willing to give.

The giant man glared down at him, but the mailman was unmoved. The den had betrayed him, and as imposing as Malcolm was, the mailman's rage was larger still.

When he saw that no answer was coming, Malcolm sat down on the edge of the bed and looked up toward the dripping IV bag. His gaze was unfocused, swimming in a peculiar concoction of remembered pain and very present relief.

"So long…" he spoke again, much gentler this time. "So long I sat there in the dark. All alone… Nobody to be wit' me." Malcolm's cheeks sagged and his bottom lip hung loose as he stared through the hospital walls back to his padded cell. "People would come – even my momma – but nobody could get to where I was." Malcolm took in a long, shuddering breath, a wave of pain streaking across his face. "Then one day you came. I thought you was just passin by. Steppin in and then back out like you was just lookin; the way people do when they out window shoppin. I heard the door swing open and shut. I was sure you left, that first time. But you was still there…"

Malcolm tore his eyes away from the IV bag and looked straight at the mailman.

"Again and again you came back, and every time you got a little bit closer." Malcolm grabbed the mailman's arm like it was made of pure gold. "They wouldn't let me look, but I knew it was you cause they would get real quiet like they was scared. When they finally did scream at you it was always louder than they screamed at anyone else. And boy, would they cuss and fight after you left!"

Malcolm paused as a tear like a wrecking ball suddenly rolled off his nose and crashed down onto the hospital sheets.

"It was the only good time for me – knowing you were there; knowing someone was coming. I couldn't see you, but I could feel you. And it made me feel… not alone." He wiped his face with a huge hand. "Feeling not alone ain't all that important when you got people. But it's all kinds of important when you don't – when you by yourself in the pit."

The mailman swallowed hard, ignoring the searing pain in his throat. "What about now? Are you OK now?"

There was a tremendous intake of air, followed by a powerful sound of release. The words that followed came straight from the core of the big man's soul. "I can breathe. After so long, I can breathe! I don't know how to say it so that you'll understand, but every breath of air is like sugar on my tongue." Malcolm's eyes flashed. "And they can't reach me no more! Not like they was. They can't tie me down or chain me up. You saw how they had me… Now look." Malcom spread his arms out wide. "It's like flying with my own wings all the time. Yeah, I would say so. I'm a whole lot more than OK."

"Good." The mailman relaxed and sunk back into his pillow. At least that part was right.

Malcolm wasn't satisfied. "You gotta tell me why," he insisted, gently shaking the mailman's arm. "Please. I gotta know."

"Tell you why?" the mailman echoed hollowly.

"Yeah. Why? You don't know me. Now look at you… all laid up. What did you do this for? I was there in the dark… I know what you went through – what they did to you. Why'd you do it? Why'd you get me loose? The best gift anyone could give a person, and you gave it to me. Why?"

All his life the mailman had waited for this question. He knew the answer better than he knew his own name, but now that the moment arrived he couldn't bring himself to say it. Put this man in the hands of the ones who abandoned him when it mattered most? No! He wouldn't do it. He refused to lift up the cause of those who had betrayed him.

A mighty, unseen conflict erupted in the mailman's heart as years of ready conviction warred with the disillusionment of a shattered man. In the end it ended as a stalemate. He would not give credit to the one great thief. Nor could he bring himself to denounce him. His heart was completely divided.

The man from the cell stood resolute. He was not leaving. After the siege he had endured throughout the last ten years, this was nothing.

Finally, seeing that he would not outlast him, the mailman pointed weakly to a plastic bag that sat on a chair in the corner of the room. In it were his clothes and personal belongings.

"In there…" he said.

Malcolm wasted no time. He rushed to the corner like a man possessed and ripped the bag wide open.

"Heaviest thing…" the mailman whispered.

It wasn't hard to find. Everything else in the bag was feather light by comparison. It was only a matter of untangling it from the folds of cloth in which it had been hidden.

A moment later Malcolm turned toward the bed, mouth halfway open, the disheveled contents of the bag left forgotten on the chair. With both hands he held a bar so dark that it stood out against even the deepest shadows in the room. The sheer weight of the bar threatened to bring the powerful man to the floor. Malcolm's arms swelled with the effort of lifting it, and the mailman could see the strain showing in his neck.

"Know what that is?" the mailman groaned.

Malcolm nodded in awe. "Not sure I should be holding this," he murmured. "It ain't mine." It seemed an odd thing to say, seeing as it was his own face that was stamped on the top of the onyx brick.

"No, it's mine." The mailman sat halfway up, ignoring the pain for rage. "But I'm giving it to you. And you better take it, cause it's the last good thing I'm ever giving away for free. To anyone." He collapsed back into the bed, sweat beading.

Malcolm paused, unsure. It felt like something vital was at stake.

A minute passed in silence. Then the mailman gathered what remained of his strength. He needed this to be over. "You want to know why?"

"Yeah," Malcolm whispered, still staring at the lightless ingot in his hands. "I got to."

"Good. Then you take it. Take it to the place I write down and you ask them to tell you why. Then, once you find yourself hip deep in why, you find the one in charge and you ask him why for me."

The mailman motioned toward the pad of paper on the floor, and when Malcolm handed it to him he scribbled something quickly on the top sheet before tearing off the paper and handing it back.

Malcolm looked down at the paper in his hand, wrestling to hold the dark bar in the crook of his arms.

2212 Bismuth Vale

"Find that place," the mailman spat. "Or don't. I'm done with the whole thing." His throat burning from the effort, he lay back, closed his eyes, and fell asleep. He never saw Malcolm leave the room. He never felt the huge hand squeeze his own. He never heard the thank you that came all the way from the middle of the big man's heart.

When the mailman left the hospital a week later, he began to practice a different kind of discipline. He was going to get some answers. The thieves may have chosen to abandon him, but they would have no choice about this.

Like farmers do with foxes, he would smoke them from their den.

23

Signed, Sealed, Delivered

Number Ten dialed the number that Adelle had written on his palm a week earlier, hoping that maybe this time the call would go through.

"We're sorry. The number you have dialed has been disconnected. Goodbye."

"That's so weird," Kent said to himself. The number had worked fine the day she had given it to him. He tossed the phone onto the couch and sat down beside it in front of the coffee table. The puzzle pieces stared back at him. Running a hand through his hair, he went through them one by one.

The old photo of the people from three generations back. He still had no idea what that was about.

A broken silver chain. His note scrawled below it read "freedom?" and "precious…"

The hospital wristband. "Wounds?" "Healing?"

The empty space. He thought it might have something to do with the emptiness in the world. Or his unfinished assignment. He wasn't sure.

The tiny vial of water, etched with the mark. His note read "cleansing" and "refreshing?" The same slip of paper showed his own sketch of the mark. He traced it with his fingers, feeling oddly reverent. Why was this symbol so significant? Why this mark?

The yellow note... this was the one clue that felt like it had been solved. The old, faded note began and ended at the den.

A small silk sachet filled with dark lead pellets. "Burden carried?" and "ammunition?" were the only two ideas he had come up with.

The blank wedding invitation. Lists of names and images of his married friends scrolled through his mind, but none of them stood out individually as being the specific subject of the clue. Instead, he had written "unity," "bond," "permanent," and "celebration."

A spent bullet casing. "Death?"

He looked at the collection as a whole, trying for the thousandth time to tie it all to the Sweet Thief. It didn't take him long to give up and lay back on the couch. It wasn't happening tonight. He had other things on his mind.

Two things, to be specific.

Two people, to be more specific.

Both of them raised his blood pressure in very different ways. He hadn't seen Adelle since the Thanksgiving heist, and was hoping to change that as soon as possible. The mailman, on the other hand, he had never seen at all. Both intrigued him. Both were drawing him further down this path. Both were proving difficult to find.

Several missions had slipped by over the weekend. Ten was becoming aware of how very many opportunities there were to steal pain. The world was swollen with it. Money and time and other resources might be in short supply, but the one thing there was always plenty of was pain, and there was relatively little competition for it. It was untapped wealth. Millions walked past it every day without recognizing others' suffering as the prize it was. Ten knew better now. He had tasted the reward and found it infinitely more satisfying than the countless other things he had gone after before. Something in his life really mattered. Finally.

Thoughts of Adelle and pain-theft swam in and out of his thoughts, as did the greater mystery of the Sweet Thief himself. And of course there was the constant awareness, the unrelenting tug that never left his mind… he had to find the mailman.

The phone jumped to life beside him on the couch, shattering the quiet and catching him off guard. He was overcome with the hope that Adelle was calling him back. He snatched up the phone, but didn't recognize the number.

"Hello?"

The other end of the line was quiet. He tried again.

"Hello?"

Finally a voice answered, so casual and relaxed that Ten wondered if the person was on something.

"Do you know who this is?" the voice mumbled.

Kent paused, ticking off possibilities. "No. I don't think I do."

"That's too bad. You've been trying to find me for a while now."

Kent was fully alert at once. He sat up and gripped the phone tighter, staring straight ahead as if talking to someone seated just on the other side of the coffee table. What should he say? Should he ask for a name? You can't just call someone 'the mailman'.

The process of deciding took too long.

"Lost for words, eh? The strong silent type? Well, good for you." Confidence resonated in the voice despite its lack of volume. "I'm the mailman. You have a letter."

Ten instinctively grabbed a pen and a slip of paper from the table in case the mailman said anything helpful. He was sweating. His throat went dry. It didn't matter. The line had gone dead.

Kent looked around the room in confusion. He tried to get his bearings, but how? The man he had been trailing and asking about and looking for non-stop for weeks had just called him in the middle of his apartment, and he had sat there! Mentally, he punched himself in the face. He might not get another chance like that.

No, wait… There was something about a letter.

Ten raced around the apartment, thinking that somehow he may have overlooked a piece of mail over the last several days. There was nothing on the counter, nothing in the kitchen. Irrational, he swept his clues around the coffee table before realizing that a letter would not be small enough to be hiding under any of them. Besides, who would have hidden it there?

What was he doing?!

As if he caught a glimpse of himself from the outside, Ten stood up and put his hands on his head. "Alright, you have *got* to calm down." It was unusual for him to talk to himself out loud, but the situation seemed to merit it. "He called you, remember? The clues are all from him. He wants you to find the letter. So just calm down… chill out… relax."

Kent took a deep breath. Then he walked to the front door, opened it, and picked up a letter from the threshold as if he knew it was there the whole time. To prove to himself that he was completely back in control of his emotions, he walked all the way back to the couch before he tore it open.

"It seems your attention is becoming somewhat divided. I assume you can understand how this might be a problem for me. Hopefully I did not make a mistake in selecting you. I would hate for this to turn into one of those messy things."

Below the typed message were two addresses, numbered one and two. Below the addresses was a postscript.

"Just to make sure you and I are on the same page, you should come to the address labeled 'one' first. You should come now."

Kent felt like the boy who takes the dare to pick the snake up by the tail, but now that he has it up in the air he has no idea what to do with it. Could he just walk into a face to face meeting with the mailman? Malcolm said he was not ready. Still, it was his assignment. It hadn't been given to anyone else. What would happen if he blew off the summons and didn't show up? What did the mailman mean by messy?

Questions rattling in his brain, Ten found himself walking toward the door with his car keys already in hand. He almost stopped to think about what he was doing, but he had a feeling that if he reconsidered at this point it might land him back on the couch for the rest of the night. That would be real torture. Ten quickly decided that he would rather take his chances with the mailman.

The car door handle squeaked, the floor mat caught on his heels, and the ridiculous plastic blue feet swung backward as he punched the accelerator and raced down the street toward the first address on the letter.

Fifteen minutes later Kent was sitting outside of an impound lot.

The tall chain-link fence was locked and a large dog was pacing inside. There didn't seem to be anyone else around. Kent stepped out of his car and approached the guard shack, but it was dark. Even the large pole lamps inside the fence were out. It felt wrong. Something was very wrong.

Kent got back in his car and locked the doors, then looked around one more time. Across the street was an open garage; a single light bulb burning inside. It caught his eye, largely because everything else was so dark, but upon further inspection the garage was off, too. Not only was it standing wide open at night with the light on, but it was completely empty. There wasn't a car parked inside. There wasn't even any stuff. No racks. No shelves. No tools. No trash. Nothing. It was also not attached to a house. In fact, there didn't appear to be a house on the lot at all. It was a yard with an empty garage left open at night with a light on.

The alarm on Kent's watch suddenly went off, nearly giving him a heart attack. Pulse racing, he reached down and silenced the alarm, then looked at the tiny display. "Meeting with Mailman" flashed over and over again in iridescent indigo. Kent forced himself out of the car and across the street before he could change his mind.

"You are wanted at the den," Number Ten announced as he arrived at the garage.

He stepped to the battle like one landing troops on a beach. There would be no element of surprise. The defenders were dug in and they knew he was coming. Even as he approached, the ground beneath him surged and buckled. Snake heads on towers rose up through the floor and flares began to litter the sky with flashes of red. The swift pounding of boots could be heard rushing into place.

"I've been waiting for you..."

The light bulb went out.

Number Ten did not shrink back. "It seems that way," he observed calmly. The garage was now so dark that he could barely see the figure standing in the shadows.

"You took longer than I expected," the mailman drawled. He sounded unimpressed.

"Yeah, well part of that is on you." Kent matched the mailman's bored tone. "Your clues weren't that great."

"They were good enough to get you here," the mailman pointed out. Something about his voice sounded familiar. "Besides, in order to make them any simpler I would have had to drive to your apartment and pick you up myself."

They stood for a few moments, sizing each other up, listening to the unspoken words swirling in the room. Neither was hasty to make the first move.

Finally Kent spoke. "I do have one question that you may be the only person who can answer."

"You want to know why," suggested the mailman.

"Yes," Kent smiled. "Why?"

"Isn't that always the question?" The mailman mused. "Everyone wants to know why."

"Well?" Ten pressed.

"Oh, I don't think so," the mailman laughed from the darkness. "I've been waiting far longer than you have. You'll have to get in line."

"Fair enough."

The mailman went quiet.

Silence threatened to take a firm hold on the battlefield, and again Kent fought it off. "So you brought me here, knowing full well that I would try to steal from you. Is that what you want?"

"That's just a tricky way of asking why," the mailman countered, revealing nothing.

Kent was at a loss. "Fine. Then how do you suggest we begin?"

The mailman did not reply.

"You know," Kent observed, his eyes beginning to adjust to the darkness, "for someone who is so concerned with how long it took me to get here, you certainly don't seem to be in much of a hurry to get things started."

168

The mailman smiled cruelly. "We started months ago."

So far it was a draw. Kent attempted to move in, trying to connect with his target. The mailman approached in his own way while still keeping the thief at a distance. They circled the ring; testing, evaluating.

"You can't steal from a thief." Icy shrapnel flew at last.

You're not a thief anymore. The words sprang to mind, loaded and ready. However, Kent did not turn them loose. Instead he shared, "Of course you can. I have been stolen from many times since joining the den, and I have stolen from other thieves as well." The ice fell short and the shrapnel was deflected away.

The mailman smiled knowingly, "Very nicely done, Number Two. Trying to focus on loving me yet?"

Ten bristled at the condescension, but again he chose not to rise to the bait. "Yes. Many people at the den have begged me to do just that. You have touched a lot of lives there."

"Oh! Self-control! Very impressive. Though the flattery could have been disguised better. You rushed that a little bit. Next time try to tone it down a few notches. Then people will think you actually mean it," the mailman sneered, spitting every word. "You know, Number... wait, what number are you now? ... It doesn't matter... You know, Kent, the problem with the formula they drill into your head – the one that they use when they brainwash you? It's all so predictable. I know all your moves before you do."

Ten longed to lash out, to thrust and parry with the mailman over the code and the truth and the Sweet Thief. The desire to prove that he was in the right was dizzying, tugging him toward harsh words and hard proofs. Point and counterpoint, logic and reason, a great debate, raging and hinging, twisting and twirling on the nimble toes of agile minds as foils whipped the air in an artistic display of wit and control. His heart swayed toward it even as something inside him warned against it.

Ten pushed away the desire to attack and calmly held his ground. "We can play this game all night or you could just tell my why you brought me here. It's your call."

"No need to empower me," the mailman blocked. "Thanks anyway."

"Then tell me what you want," Kent suggested honestly. "Maybe I would agree with you. Maybe you are right."

"The problem with the identification strategy," the mailman whirled, "is that it smells so much like patronization."

"So the goal is just to go round and round in this little dance you've designed?" Number Ten asked.

"Yes," the mailman nodded. "For a while."

"This doesn't feel like wasting time to you?"

"Wasting? No. Not at all. We have time."

"OK." Kent surrendered to the watch on his arm, accepting its authority, laying back into peace.

"Well, well…" the mailman said with a smile. "Good things do come to those who wait. I am glad to see that you have arrived so well trained."

Kent weighed the words and crouched low, barely dipping under the net of vanity that spun overhead. "I thought you didn't like flattery."

"It's not flattery if it's true," the mailman offered.

The words sounded genuine. Perhaps the mailman meant it. Coming from such an accomplished thief, that was pretty high praise.

Kent sprang backward. He almost fell for it the second time. This guy was dangerous.

The mailman sneered as Kent dodged the second net.

Kent looked up with a challenging gleam in his eye, "I would have thought you'd be a little faster, given your reputation." The words were no sooner out of his mouth than he felt a cord slip around his ankles.

"Ah, and you were doing so well…" The mailman yanked the cord tight and Kent went down, landing hard on his back.

"You're right. That was arrogant. Sorry." Kent was instantly back on his feet.

"You're not forgiven, Number Two." A spray of shells went loose, speeding through the air toward Kent. "We both know it's what you wanted to say. You are just fighting it."

"That's true," Kent agreed. "So why aren't you?" He asked the question carefully, without malice or condemnation, and gracefully sent the mailman's bullets screaming back the way they had come. Three of shadowy guards that were running across the beach to take him out were instantly ripped off their feet. The rest turned back and ran for shelter at the base of the cliffs.

"That word again," the mailman growled, holding his throat. "I already told you... I get my answers first."

The light suddenly flipped on, blinding Kent and forcing him to shut his eyes. When he opened them again, Number Ten found himself alone in the empty garage.

The mailman was gone.

24

Mail Tampering

"So how did it go?" Two thieves peered at him from across the table.

"He was just toying with me."

"What did he do?" Jim asked.

"Well, he definitely hasn't drawn me in to steal from him. I walked away without a single coin. He doesn't want company or friendship or help. I don't even think he wants anybody to care. He's after something else, and he wants to use me to get it."

"Did you get any sense of what he's after?" Samuel asked.

"No. At least not anything specific. But he's angry. He's angry and smart, and he knows the thieves' code better than I do."

"He's just not following it…" Jim said.

"No. He's not." Kent frowned. "But it's not because he's ignorant."

"Did you get his name?" Samuel asked.

"No," Kent grumbled. "He wasn't giving up anything."

"But you saw him at least," Jim suggested helpfully.

Kent shook his head. "Not really. I mean, I did, but it was dark."

For a moment the table went quiet.

"So what's your plan now?" Samuel looked up at Kent.

"I'm not sure. I have to admit, he is faster than I am. When he wanted the conversation to be over, he simply vanished." Number Ten raised a hand to rub his eyes. "This thing might have to happen on his terms."

"I'm sorry," Samuel responded. "Sounds pretty bad." When Kent remained silent, he continued, "These paths we choose… they can lead in all kinds of different directions. Some wind around and crisscross each other. Some run straight away and never come back. Ride those diverging roads long enough and we can end up too far away to touch."

"You might not be able to steal from him at all," Jim agreed.

Kent could see guards creeping through the den, eying their table hungrily. The topic needed to change. "So what about you guys?" Kent forced a light-hearted tone into his voice. "How are your assignments going? And where has Adelle been lately?"

Jim and Samuel exchanged a dark glance and Samuel's face went stony. Reluctantly, the scarred thief reached up and laid an envelope on the table. The flap was loose, leaning freely in the air, tiny shreds of paper and glue hanging where it had been torn open.

"What is it?" Ten asked plainly.

"I'm afraid it's for you," Samuel answered.

"I didn't know until I read it," Jim explained. "There was no name on the outside."

Ten grabbed up the letter and unfolded it, expecting to see the mailman's familiar handwriting or one of his standard old typewriter style messages. But the letter was not from the mailman.

Jim and Samuel watched expectantly as Kent did a double take.

The words were handwritten, flowing across the paper like artwork. Scanning quickly to the bottom, Kent found what he was looking for.

The letter was signed "*Adelle.*"

"I'm not going to pretend not to be surprised. You're good. I never saw it coming. Especially after Thanksgiving. You had me convinced that you were the real thing.

So much of me wants to be cold right now, to keep you at arms' length and say nothing about how badly you've hurt me. But I've never been very good at being that heartless. Guess you either have it or you don't.

You don't have to worry about me talking to anyone. That's obviously not going to happen, though you could have done this without involving my family. I'm trying to forgive you for that, but it's proving a lot harder than forgiving you for simply hurting me. I mean, my family? You don't even know them! It's an ugly thing you are doing, Kent. You must know that the path you are choosing is not a good one. Of course, you probably don't care. Not if you are able to do all this. You're basically one of them. I should have smelled it coming, huh?

The instructions you gave me to follow are almost finished. I expect everything to disappear as soon as this is over, and I mean all of it. I won't be back at the den, and this is the last contact I ever want to have with you. I hope you take a minute to look over at Samuel and Jim and remember the friendship I had with them before you showed up. You killed that. At least admit that much to them. I'm sure you can figure out a lie that will make that work. I don't want them thinking I just left for no reason. You tell them I had no choice, that I love them, and you figure out a story that will make it all fit. You have a gift for that."

Kent dropped the letter to his lap and looked up, dumbfounded. He glanced across the table. "Did you guys read this?"

"Yeah," said Jim.

"Just before you came in," Samuel added sadly.

"I don't get it," Ten said, scowling angrily at the table.

"The way I see it," Samuel stated, "you are either one of the vilest and most deceitful creatures on the planet... or you are being set up."

Kent considered that for a moment, wondering how he must look to the thieves sitting across from him.

"Which way are you guys leaning?" he asked.

"Doesn't much matter," Jim replied. "We obviously can't tell if you are lying, and if you're not lying then it doesn't matter that we can't tell. In either case, our duty to you is the same."

"Which is?"

"We're here." Samuel grabbed his arm. "What can we do to help?"

"I have no idea," Ten shook his head. "If you could get in touch with Adelle and let her know what is going on, that would be great."

"We don't know where she is either," said Jim. "Even if we did, she would probably just think you have us fooled."

"So what do I do?" Kent asked.

"Seems like you've got to continue what you've been working on the whole time," posited Samuel.

"The mailman?"

"The mailman," Samuel confirmed. "If you are being set up, it's pretty clear who's behind it."

Number Ten frowned. "That plan would be a lot more doable if I knew where to find him. Like I said, it's all on his terms right now."

"How did you find him yesterday?" Jim asked.

"He's a mailman," Kent replied facetiously. "He sent me a letter."

"A letter?"

"Yeah, he sent a letter with ..." Kent leapt to his feet.

"Where are you going?" Jim called out after him.

"I have an address left!" Ten called back.

"An address?" cried Jim.

Kent didn't answer. He was scanning the crumpled letter for the second address as he ran out of the den.

25

Ambushed

The second address on the mailman's letter led Kent to a quaint little shopping area downtown.

Whipping his car into the first open space that he found, Number Ten stuffed a handful of quarters into the meter and sprinted up the sidewalk. Three blocks away. Now two. Now one. Guards leapt out from behind every post and sign to pelt him with darts, but he ran right through them, anger boiling so hot that he could barely think.

Whatever Kent was rushing into, he was going there full speed. No turning back. No halfway. His claws were out. And while the young thief admitted that he was no match for the mailman, he was more than ready to go down swinging!

Kent stopped as he came to a corner store, checking the address again just to make sure. This was it.

It was a neat looking little place. The words "Olde Town Apothecary" were painted in an arc across the large storefront window, the platinum lettering – skillfully accented with a ribbon of burgundy – leaping from the glass. Overhead, a black and tan striped awning stretched three feet out from the wall, providing shade for the better part of the sidewalk.

The building itself was in excellent shape. Composed of pale gray brick and black steel, it was one of the newer places downtown.

All in all, it was a charming little shop… a strange place for a battle. The mailman was as crafty as ever.

Ten stepped closer and leaned toward the glass, his hand above his eyes. Peering inside, he scanned the shop for signs of the mailman, ready to start swinging.

But there was no mailman.

There was only her.

Kent's breath caught in his chest. Inside the store, on the other side of a long polished counter, was the woman who could make him forget all about assignments and mailmen. She was up on a step ladder, stocking the shelves built into the back wall.

"Adelle."

Kent pried himself from the window and flew to the door, suddenly as nervous as a teenager. What would he say? How would he explain? He grabbed the brass colored handle before he could second guess himself.

As he stepped into the store his senses reeled with delight. The air felt cool and clean, yet it was filled with a potent array of different fragrances. Pine, cedar, lilac, rosemary, sandalwood, sage … What else? He closed his eyes for a split second in appreciation, then opened them again to drink in the most delightful thing in the shop.

Adelle did not turn around. Busy behind the counter, she continued arranging bottles and jars on a shelf above her head.

Thinking that she hadn't heard him come in, Kent stood for a moment and watched her, his heart racing.

He stood staring too long.

"Can I help you with something?" she asked without looking back at him.

Kent blinked and tried to cover. "I'm looking for someone. Maybe you can help me."

Her ears perked involuntarily at the sound of his voice and she turned to look at him for the first time.

Kent's mouth dropped open in confusion.

The woman on the stepladder behind the counter was not Adelle. He had been so sure it was her that he had already begun the conversation in his head. He would explain that he'd received her letter but had no clue what it was about. He would tell her about his meeting with the mailman. He would straighten all this out.

But it wasn't her.

The woman staring at him from her low perch on the tiny ladder could have been Adelle's sister. They looked so much alike that Kent felt drawn to her just by association. With the same hair, same shape, and almost the same smile, this woman was practically her twin. And her eyes… It was uncanny. She had the same eyes! A light blue-grey in color, the woman's eyes would have been too large for most faces, but they suited hers perfectly. It was like staring at Adelle. But it wasn't.

"I guess that depends on who you are looking for," the woman intoned. There was a challenging edge to her voice that was unmistakably playful.

Kent was completely sideswiped. "I'm sorry. I thought you were someone else." He stood frozen in the middle of the shop.

"Hmmm. Too bad." She turned easily back to the shelves. "Of course," she murmured, glancing toward him one more time, "maybe I could be."

Kent smiled uneasily, not knowing what to do. He had come here as a man on a mission, focused and ready to face the mailman. Then he had been sent reeling at the sight of Adelle. Now everything had changed yet again. He was completely off balance. With the mailman's second address leading to this dead end, and him once again completely out of clues, he had no pressing reason to leave. Of course, he hadn't come here to buy incense, either. With no Adelle and no mailman in sight, there was no reason to stay – nothing but this beauty behind the counter.

Still bewildered, Kent stood there gawking, his feet doing nothing to change his situation. Too much was going on in his head and in his life. His clueless smile, however, only satisfied the woman behind the counter for so long. She raised her eyebrows in expectation.

"I'm Kent," he stammered at last.

"Well hello there, Kent," she teased. "You're one of those overly chatty guys, am I right?"

"Yeah, sorry." Number Ten shook his head slightly as if clearing his thoughts, his brain stumbling over itself and pouring out whatever words it could find. "You kind of stunned me a little."

She lit up at that, unable to hide a smile. "Oh. So it's my fault?"

"I think so," he batted back, unaware of the guards closing in. "You really should know better."

The watch on his wrist began to beep, but Kent silenced it immediately. This was nothing to be alarmed about. This was just fun.

"I should know better?" she challenged.

"Of course. You've obviously been beautiful long enough to know how dangerous that smile is."

"Oh really?" She was not used to being out-teased.

"One of these days you are going to hurt someone, and you won't be able to claim you didn't know. Gross negligence. Plain and simple."

"I see," she laughed. "So I suppose I should walk around with a big frown on all the time?" She pouted prettily as a demonstration

"No, that is definitely dangerous too." Ten silenced the watch a second time, still failing to see the guards.

"Well what should I do?" She left the door wide open.

"You should climb down and tell me your name so that I'll be able to identify you when they call me in to testify."

"You're ridiculous." She laughed at him and shook her head. Then she stepped gracefully down to the floor and moved toward the counter. She smirked at his outstretched hand, batted it playfully away, and tucked her hair behind her ear.

"Trina."

Kent smiled, again unsure of what he was still doing here or where to step next. This woman was exquisite. There were no dark birds around her. No shadows. No suffocating chill. Everything felt fine. Everything except the name that was now inexcusably shifted to the back of his mind...

"So I know you probably didn't come in here looking for me," Trina somehow pouted and smiled at the same time, "but you found me just the same." Her fingers landed lightly on his hands. "And I think you really want to take me out tonight."

Number Ten agreed before he realized the words were coming out of his mouth. Standing this close to her, with only a counter between them, it felt like he was being carried downstream. And he really didn't care at that moment about swimming for shore. He'd never been so intoxicated by anyone so fast – not even by Adelle.

"You're lucky, Mr. Kent. I'm never like this. You caught me at just the right time." Trina spoke lightly, not looking at him. Her hands had moved from his to glide along the counter as she pretended to walk away. "I guess I'm in the mood for a little excitement. Something other than the same old routine. So here is my idea." She stopped walking away. "We meet tonight at the most elegant restaurant in town, we pull out all the stops, and we open a chapter that would, under all normal circumstances, never be read. What do you think?"

"I think it's completely irresponsible," Kent said admonishingly. "You don't even know me. I could be crazy."

"Right on!" Trina smiled at him excitedly, her tongue curled playfully behind her teeth.

"And I don't know you," Kent continued, looking down to the counter in mock terror. "You could be some creep!"

Trina threw her hands up in the air, pretending exasperation. "You boys are all the same! You dream about wild crazy nights, but when a girl finally shows up ready to play, you chicken out!" She fixed him with a teasing glare and made out as if she was flapping tiny wings.

Kent laughed out loud. Then he nodded and leaned in challengingly. "So where do you have in mind?"

26

Stepping Out

Kent met Trina that night at an elegant little bistro downtown that boasted "the most distinguished wine list in four counties." They shared a smirk at the grand scope of that achievement, but both agreed that the atmosphere was flawless. Candle flame danced atop bottles in woven wine baskets and the soft voices of a string quartet swept gently between ivory-shrouded tables. The glorious smells, the delicate sounds, the tantalizing flavors that fell upon their readied tongues… every moment was excellence itself.

And none of it compared to Trina.

Kent had considered cancelling a dozen times after leaving the little shop and coming back to his senses, especially with his watch flashing all afternoon a message that read 'stay home'. But he decided at last that standing Trina up wasn't necessary. He would simply go out, be kind, enjoy a nice meal, and leave. There was no reason to be rude. He might even find a little pain to steal along the way. In any event, he would not stay long. He would be back on the trail of the mailman the instant the next clue arrived. And he had his phone on in case there was any response from Adelle – who he had called ten more times throughout the afternoon. He had done all he could. If there was nothing left to do but wait, there was no reason he had to do it sitting on the couch.

All of Kent's justifications and good intentions were forgotten the moment Trina arrived. The unexpected compliments she had received from the stranger in her store had unwittingly turned a week of rejection into a day of delight, and she decided to reward him for it. With a dark green dress that slipped over her shoulder and plunged to her waist in the back, Trina had everyone staring as she walked into the restaurant.

None of them stared more than Kent.

He could not take his eyes off of her, and she loved it. The attention was like candy. She had come out tonight to be adored, and Kent was as indulgent as a man could be.

Just like in the store, he never even saw the guards.

Blinded by his eyes, Ten did not see the empty space passing right through the middle of Trina's chest. He saw only her beauty, and heard only the roaring of his own appetites. Even thoughts of Adelle and the mailman and the Sweet Thief, thoughts that had been his constant companions for months, were forced to wait in line behind the force of his desire. He was drawn to Trina in ways he was not prepared to resist. She was not just gorgeous. She was also broken. It would not take much... just the right words. A few kind gestures and she would hand herself over.

Her emptiness pulled like gravity, betraying her own defenses and beckoning him closer. She would give anything to fill that void for a little while. Though the wound was sure to follow, she would embrace each injurious touch if it meant she would be wanted.

Kent could feel it. She would let him enjoy her for almost nothing at all. Excitement flared to life, racing across his own empty places and leaping from spark to prairie fire in an instant. Her beauty the fuel, his desire the spark, they burned.

That is when he finally saw them. Not until he was falling, careening toward her like a shot down plane, did he notice the hard, shallow plates laid all across her shimmering surface. Held locked in place by wickedly barbed anchors buried deep within her, the plates were gorgeous and cold. They covered her body in a flawless exterior as the barbs injected emptiness underneath, erasing her from the inside out.

Number Ten watched Trina's heart disappear like an eclipse. The loss could not be hidden, not even by her radiant smile or her captivating eyes. He hurt for her and wanted her all at once.

Trina despised his compassion. What she wanted was his desire, and she fed it as one stokes a fire. Reaching over to him throughout the meal, she made her intentions clear. She would play with him. But she would in no way allow him access to the vaporous chasm just behind her shell. This was just for fun, she told herself. Nothing more. It was a harmless quenching of a temporary thirst, she lied.

Kent craved what she offered, but he also longed to reach through and satisfy that empty space she guarded. She would love him for that. She would adore him with those eyes, even as she gave him her sighing surrender.

"Don't."

The alarm on his watch went off and the screen flashed indigo.

Ten heard it clearly but it seemed like a very small sound next to the roaring of his hunger, and the blinking blue light was lost in the flashing images of Trina relinquishing that green dress, willingly letting down her armored plates.

"Don't!"

The alarm grew louder and the watch glowed insistently, ushering in a moment of decision. Kent could not simply be a spectator here. He had a choice to make, and for one split second he knew how important it was for him to make the right one.

But it was too late. He had walked too close. Kent smiled and reached for Trina's hand as he dropped the watch into his pocket.

The alarm echoed on, unheeded.

The blue light flashed unseen.

Kent was free to feed his appetites, and feed them he did.

27

Sealed With A Kiss

"Cravings sated, hungrier. Press the auger deeper. Dry hearts drilled like failed wells, anthem of the empty. Embrace the cheap wind, primp your feathers, wear the tempest like a hat. Now tear each other, tots! Is my voice yours, or is yours mine? Too hard now to tell, we've danced so long... and the show never gets old."

Tormented by the guard's twisted words, the mailman sat at his desk, his fingers on the keys of an ancient typewriter. To either side were stacks of blank paper and empty envelopes. They were both his fortress and his weapons now. He could hide here in safety while striking from a distance, dealing out wounds to anyone he desired. He had but to point and fire. The addresses of a dozen current targets were pinned to a bulletin board above the desk. One in particular was working out extremely well. Of all the prospects he had tested over the past several years, this one might just prove to be the tipping point. This one might force the issue far enough.

Fingers tapped rabidly on the keys, his strokes sending waves of hammers to slam poison into paper. The room sounded like a firing range. It looked like a cell. It smelled like a morgue. The mailman cared about none of that anymore. The battle was the only thing he concerned himself with, and the battle was going well.

He finished typing, his words sounding more and more like those of the guard in his throat, and he tore the sheet from the carriage just as the phone began chirping. Growling in disgust, he put down the letter and envelope and pushed himself back from the desk.

"Hello."

"He took the bait."

"Wow…" the mailman nodded slowly. "To be honest, I'm kind of surprised. I guess he wasn't as taken with Adelle as you thought he was."

"Maybe not. Or maybe we've just found his Achilles' heel."

The mailman laughed. "Achilles and all the rest of us. Well good. That should do it. He'll be useless to them now, and we'll have another man inside."

"You think so?"

"He's no hero. He won't pull out of this."

"What about Adelle?"

"She still won't bend," murmured the mailman. "She's too devoted."

"I thought you said you had her."

"I do, but only because she is protecting her family. When I threatened her directly she stood her ground."

"Spunky little thing. I always liked that about her. In any case, it doesn't matter how you get them, so long as you get them."

"Yeah, let's hope we don't lose our leverage. Once we can't hit her family anymore she'll resist us to our face."

"We can always hit her family."

The mailman was not convinced, but instead of pressing the issue he changed course. "So you said he took the bait?"

"He did. It was as if his mission meant absolutely nothing."

The mailman chuckled. "Never underestimate the power of a beautiful woman."

"I don't." The voice on the other end of the line was not laughing.

"I need to get going," the mailman said indifferently. "Keep tabs on the other two, and let me know when our boy is ready. I just finished his next invitation."

The line went dead.

The mailman sat there, not moving for several minutes, his hands and his phone forgotten in his lap. The skin of his face felt heavy and tired. He didn't roll back up to the desk. He didn't get up and leave the room. The mailman didn't do anything. His head fell against the back of the chair and he let his mouth hang open.

"I'm not leaving," the darkness said from his throat.

"I know…"

The mailman let his head roll to the side, too weary to fight the pull of the planet, and his eyes fell upon the mountain of bags that took up the rest of the room. Soon there would be no more room for him.

"That load is eventually going to kill you."

"Yeah," the mailman agreed, hoping the darkness would get bored and shut up. It never did.

The bags were full now. Far too heavy to carry, they sat and oozed, overflowing with pain. The fumes that rose from the top of the heap were toxic. They burned his eyes and his throat, and looked like smoke from the stack of an oncoming train.

Somewhere in the midst of that steaming mound was the mailman's tiny checkers bag. He couldn't imagine anymore how that one little bag was once big enough for all the burdens that he carried. That seemed like a different life.

He still remembered the day it got too heavy. He'd been carrying it for a while without turning anything in. He could handle it. Besides, the coins looked pretty impressive stacked up in the corner of his room. It was like a monument – or some sort of ancient altar. But he could never get them all out of the bag the way they dissolved in front of the mirror. So the bag got heavier and heavier until one day he dragged it home and dropped it on the floor. It hit like a bag of cement. He could almost hear the floorboards shudder.

The next morning it was too heavy to pick up. He tried to unload the pain into garbage bags, to spread it around enough to at least be able to carry it, but all that did was leave mounds of darkness scattered around the house. The piles grew a little more each day so that soon he had no room to eat in peace. And when they grew so large that he was forced to sleep on them he found the darkness creeping into his dreams. It was taking over and he knew it, but he couldn't bring himself to go back.

There was only one place where the darkness was ever truly and completely removed. But the mirror saw it all. It would see everything he had hoarded. It would see all he had done. No, he would not go back. Not until he had himself cleaned up.

That was when he'd gone in after Malcolm. If it was possible to purge away darkness without the mirror, surely that would do it. A job that big should let him earn his way out of the piles he had stacked up. All it would take was a big enough sacrifice. Or so he thought. But it hadn't worked, and now he had another reason not to go back to the den.

The darkness was in him.

Desperate for relief, he had begun carrying some of the pain out and dumping it on others. But while the release felt wonderful, he always returned home to find that it was all still there and then some. There was only one place where the darkness was removed, and he wasn't about to go groveling there.

They owed him answers, and he would wage war until he got them.

28

The Hunter's Mask

Guilt gored Kent all week, eventually driving him out of his apartment in search of refuge. The guards hounded him relentlessly, their screaming accusations so loud that he could barely hear anything else. He couldn't sit still – the guards were louder when he sat still – which made his delivery route a nightmare. Strapped in behind the wheel, locked in the cab like a cell, there was nothing he could do but sit there and take it. They swarmed around his fresh wound, their attacks growing more and more distracting until he almost ran his truck off the road.

He needed an escape.

Kent locked the door behind him and walked away from the apartment without any idea where he was going. All he knew was that he had to get out. But there was no out. Like a drowning man flailing at the water looking for the air, all he found was more water. The guards were waiting for him in every bush and behind every tree. The alleys were packed with their angry voices. He even saw them riding in the cars that sped by.

Number Ten wandered the sidewalks for hours, trailed by guards the whole time, until he finally found himself at the base of a knoll that crowned a sprawling park nearby. The breeze was just picking up as he arrived, making it feel like something was about to happen. He clambered up the hill in full retreat. Upon reaching the peak he turned a slow circle, surveying the slopes all around. It was the high ground. It would allow him to see them coming. He would make his last stand right here.

The tall grasses on the hillside waved like water, fleeing from the ridge in a dozen different directions. The way they moved made them look softer than they really were, as the different shades of green shimmered and flowed down the hill. It looked like fur, so soft that he wanted to pet it, or roll in it, or walk on it with bare feet. But he knew it wasn't that soft. It would scratch. It would itch. It would leave him with red lines all over his skin.

Still, it was lovely to watch. It made him do the one thing he had been trying not to do. It made him feel. The wound reopened and he saw things in himself that made him squirm. There were worms in his flesh, the same things he had always hated in other men. He was one of them now. He had taken a broken woman and added to her injuries.

Oh, he could tell himself that she wanted it. She was no child, after all. But the excuses were paper thin. It wasn't her motives he was responsible for… it was his. And while he could embrace what society said about consenting adults just having fun, it wasn't society to whom he was accountable. There was a higher standard and a greater judge, and he felt them both like a crushing weight. He had used her. The green velvet breezes rolling down the hillside cut like knives. Instead of stealing away a measure of her pain he had dropped in a little bit more, carving away another chunk of her heart and adding another layer of tile and shield. The worms wriggled, and the feel of them in his belly made him nauseous.

Not even the dragonflies' dancing could distract him from the truth. The knoll was much like the mirror that way. Unlike the rest of the world, with its smoke and speed and noisy cover, there was nowhere to hide up here. There was no one to lie to. There was no one around to tell you what you wanted to hear. Here the truth was laid out plainly, and the truth was hard today.

The worms bit hard, and Ten's belly stung with their teeth.

His army of excuses immediately leapt to his defense.

"She knew what she was doing."

"She was already broken."

"It's not like you did anything that other men hadn't done before. On the contrary, you were nice to her! At least you cared a little – that was probably more love than she'd seen in years."

The lies were thick and comforting, and the guards began to rebury the wound, hiding it away.

"No!" Ten shouted. It was perfume on a corpse and he knew it. There was no justification for using her.

Kent stopped brushing away the mosquitoes, forcing himself to endure their stings as some weak form of penance.

Another breeze grew and bathed the hilltop in honey, soothing his skin. He closed his eyes and let it blow through him, hoping it would carry away the cruel conviction in his heart, but it was not strong enough. It was only wind, and the relief that it brought did not last.

The guards were just getting started.

Kent felt them approaching before he saw them. There were four of them. Called by the screeching of the worms in his wounds, they came skulking through the park, stopping at the base of the hill. They looked up at him, their faces hidden behind white masks. The masks were tall and slender, oval-shaped, and looked as though they had been carved from ivory. Graceful curves and intricate lines spiraled out and down at the cheeks. Alone, they would have been exceptionally beautiful works of art, but the beauty of the masks was spoiled by the gruesome faces behind them. Wickedness strained at the seams and edges so hard that the masks were cracking, barely holding back the tide.

The masked guards started up the hill, one on each side, one coming straight on and one approaching from behind. It had the distinct feel of a hunt. The voices of the guards went terribly silent as they drew closer, and Ten watched in horror as their masks came stalking through the grass like lions.

Then all at once they charged. Leaping out from cover, the guards bounded forward up the hill. Each of them carried a small round shield and a thin spear, and the distance between the hunters and their prey dissolved in an instant.

Ten closed his eyes, hoping to escape the awful vision, but found that he only saw them clearer. With his eyes closed the masks disappeared, and his soul shuddered involuntarily at the sight of the guards' shriveled faces, red lines of fresh infection streaking their rotting skin.

Ten opened his eyes and the masks reappeared, causing him to dread his need to blink. Out of habit and instinct he turned to flee, but there was nowhere to go. They were on him.

The first spear bit in, hitting hard into the meaty part of his left thigh. A second came almost immediately afterward, plunging between the ribs on his right side.

Kent clenched his teeth, expecting to feel the terrible burn of the barbs. To his great surprise, however, the initial sensation that he felt was not one of pain, but of intense pleasure. Caught off guard, Ten inhaled sharply and closed his eyes in bliss, but as soon as his eyelids fell the masks disappeared. He saw the hunters ogling him. Sick with terror, he opened his eyes just in time to watch the third and fourth spears punch into his body, and he gasped in pleasure.

Waves of euphoria screamed through Ten's veins and soon he was flying. High and light, he felt gravity lose its grip. It was amazing. He had never felt such unrestricted freedom. Clouds were within reach, the burdens of life no more than a mist. The very essence of divinity was between his teeth. Luscious, tantalizing, irresistible, he had no choice but to bite down, and as he did a thin liquid poured out over his teeth and gums, sliding down his throat to the worms in his gut. The ravenous worms slurped up the liquid and instantly exploded in size and number. The weight of them swelled until the worms were so massive that they dragged him down.

Faster and faster he plunged, screaming from the sky until he slammed back down onto the hill. He crashed through and past the place where he had started. Pleasure fled away, leaving a gaping hole, and the four with masks stared down at him as he looked up from the pit. The wicked barbs of their spears went sour inside him, the initial sweetness forgotten as the poison began to burn.

Ten gagged on the squalid air in the pit. Gravity pressed down hard. Every burden seemed unbearable. There was no way out.

It was in utter hopelessness that Kent looked up to see the four hunters raise the ends of their spear shafts to their mouths. Then he screamed in pain as the hunters began to feed. They were drinking him alive! He swatted furiously at the spears, but his hands went right through. Not predators after all, but parasites, the voracious guards were latched on tight.

The hideous worms joined in, squirming alive through his flesh. As their tails wriggled in deeper and as their waste went fetid in his blood, the worms began to fashion something from his bones. Like something out of a nightmare, Kent could do nothing but watch as their bug-like mouthparts chewed his bones into a paste. Then they pulled the paste out in tiny chunks and glued it back together on the surface in a shape that was all too familiar. Tall and slender and beautiful, the mask was perfect – covering all the ugliness that was spreading underneath.

29

Hazardous Contents

"So now you know." The mailman's words were casual and cold, a hard edge of resentment slicing underneath. "You've been set up. You can blame me for that, of course. I admit it. But I was set up, too. They fooled me first. I just passed it along. It's all been nothing more than a big, sick game. The victory they talk about in the den? It doesn't exist. Everything about the thieves is a lie."

Kent had been hesitant to open the door when the mailman showed up at his apartment unannounced, but when he saw who it was he let him in. What was the point in fighting anymore? After dragging himself home from the hunters' pit he had hoped to be hit by a car. Getting finished off by the mailman wouldn't be much different. Kent felt like he had nothing left to lose, especially once he saw who it was.

"Not everything you told me was a lie," Ten replied darkly. "The pain is real enough."

The mailman grinned cynically at the sight of Kent's mask. "Yes, the pain is real, isn't it? Better you learn that now."

"I already knew that," Ten growled back. "So did you. That's why we went to the den in the first place. To stop it."

"Stop it?" The mailman almost fell off the couch he was laughing so hard. "You can't stop it! It's faster than you are. Even now it's spilling forward. You could spend every second of your life stealing and still never get back even the pain that you yourself have started in motion, much less all the pain caused by the rest of the world."

"The pain I've started…" Kent said the words to himself, feeling the worms squirm sickeningly in his gut. Yet even as their poison burned he saw that it was only one mistake. "No," he said defiantly. "I've stolen more pain than I've caused."

"I see!" the mailman grunted in surprise and nodded admiringly. "So you think you have stolen more pain than you've caused, huh?" he mocked, pretending to be impressed. Then he paused and held up one finger as if he had just remembered something. "Tell me, Kent. Do you know a man named Francis Lanoire? He's just a few years younger than you."

"No," Number Ten answered confidently. Whatever game the mailman was playing was not going to stick this time. "I've never heard that name before in my life."

"That's because you've never met him," the mailman answered, "and you never will. Yet – and here is the funny thing – you have just ensured his destruction, and the suffering that he is going to unleash on countless others down the road is a direct result of what you've done."

"What are you talking about?" Kent scowled.

"Right now," the mailman said, his voice both pleasant and bitter, "Francis is struggling to walk a very high and narrow path." The mailman's eyes flashed with anger as he imagined the burden the young man was carrying. "You see, he has been drawn to the thieves' path since he was very young, but he's never had anyone to teach him. He's never heard of the den. He's just been drawn in that direction. Now, without a second of training, Francis has begun stealing pain – all on his own mind you." The mailman paused, clearly delighted by what he was going to say next. "Now, even if that were all there was to the story it would be a great tragedy for him to fall. But it gets better, Kent! For unlike you and me, Francis can't see the guards. He can't smell them. He can't hear them. He

194

can't feel a difference in temperature at their approach. He has none of the senses we have. He hasn't even heard the Sweet Thief's name. But he is following."

Number Ten leaned in, fascinated.

"Exciting, huh? But here's the neat part…" The mailman's eager expression was horribly disconcerting. "If Francis manages to follow the path just a bit farther, he has the makings of a purist. Can you imagine? An actual purist!" The mailman's grin twisted. "But he won't get there. Want to know why?"

"No," Kent whispered, dreading the answer.

"Trina!" the mailman cried manically. "Down the road Francis will meet Trina, and she will no longer be the empty girl you took advantage of. Unfortunately for Francis, she will also not be the wife that would have helped him on his path. You tipped the scales, Kent."

"She wasn't…" Kent began to argue, but the mailman cut him off.

"Don't bother, Number Ten. Trina may have seemed like she wanted to be used. She may have dressed herself up like candy. But the truth is that she was a woman that needed, like all of us, to be honored and protected from the guards. She needed to be defended so that she would remain trusting and loving. But that is not what culture demands, is it? And it is certainly not what you did. So now, where there should have been a loving partner waiting to meet our young thief, he will fall hopelessly in love with a hunter instead – the hunter you helped her become."

Kent felt ill. "How do you know all that?" he challenged weakly.

"Let's just say I have a little inside information." The darkness shifted and tumbled in the mailman's throat, swelling grotesquely as he spoke.

"No!" Kent recoiled.

"Yes," snarled the mailman. "It's in there. It's the only thing that kept me alive when the den left me to die."

"There is no life in that," Kent blurted. "Can't you see it?"

"See it? Can't I see it?!!" The mailman's face contorted in rage and he grabbed Kent's shoulders so hard that his nails dug through his shirt. "Take a look boy! It is your turn to see…"

Kent could not move. The grip of the mailman was so strong – much stronger than it should have been for a man of his size. He had no choice but to stand still and watch as the mailman opened his mouth.

There in the dark Kent saw it. The wicked creature was in there, throbbing in the mailman's throat, and it showed Number Ten exactly what the mailman had said.

"You helped this happen," the guard said. **"Watch carefully."**

Staring in horrified silence, Kent shuddered as the images from the mailman's throat raced up to envelop him. There was no escaping the scene as it played out.

Trina stood in the darkness – colder, emptier, and more attractive than ever. Even now he wanted her, and he hated himself for it. There was no time to battle with that, however. Trina was moving. She was aggressive now, and the starving hunger that had drawn at him before was multiplied a hundredfold. Dazzling blue and red fabric clung to her like water, and the man with her was clearly struggling to control himself.

"You want me, Francis. You're a man. I'm a woman. That's how it's supposed to work." Trina was whispering, but Kent heard it all as if he had a front row seat. Every word she said echoed with emptiness. The void behind her flawless shell was even greater now.

"You are beautiful," Francis returned, "and valuable. But that isn't the path I'm on."

"The path you are on?"

"I have devoted my life to something very specific," he answered, "and it doesn't involve one night stands. This isn't love, Trina. This is just hunger."

"But aren't you hungry, Francis?" She laid one hand lightly on his chest then slowly, deliberately, ran her fingers up around his neck. The pull of her emptiness grew stronger.

Kent watched helplessly as he saw waves of dark heat spreading across the young man's skin. He'd seen this before. Number Ten tried to shout and warn both of them, but no sound came out.

"They can't hear you," the guard laughed. **"This hasn't happened yet. And you won't be there when it does. You just get to watch."**

Trina's smile grew more alluring. It was all she had. Her guards had convinced her of that. She'd never even caught a glimpse of her own higher calling. She'd never learned how to fill the void instead of feeding it. Seduction however… this she knew how to do.

Francis was weakening.

"This isn't right," he said again. "Not like this." He tried to make one last stand, but desire betrayed his words. They crumbled apart even as he said them. "We can't. You can't… have me."

"Awww…" Trina let the sound purr, then gave him a look that would make most men stop breathing. "Don't you want me?"

"No," Francis lied halfheartedly.

"Then why did you come over?" Trina called his bluff.

"I came to help," he gulped.

"To help?!" Trina stepped back, indignant. She pulled her hands off of him and fire flashed in her eyes. "I'm not yours to fix, Francis!" she spat. He could keep his attention… She didn't need this!

Walls went up and Trina's guards changed tactics. If this guy wasn't going to fall they would need to get her out of there fast; before he could start to peel away any of her plates.

"No. That's not what I meant." Francis extended his hands in supplication, not wanting to hurt her. "That came out wrong."

"Oh really?" Trina shouted. "How was it supposed to come out? That you feel sorry for me?"

"No. I don't. You are a wonderful person. All I meant was that people need each other," he tried to explain. "There's nothing wrong with that."

"But not you," Trina glared, tension crackling. "You don't need anyone. You're too strong for that."

"Of course I'm not. I need people, too."

"Just not me…" she reeled him back in.

"No, you're great!" he insisted. "Just not like this."

Trina wasn't buying it. "What's wrong with this?" She moved closer, pushed her body into his, and forced the issue. When he didn't pull away, she knew she had him. Her eyes closed and she sighed with pleasure as his hands made their way to her waist.

Just like that, the battle was over.

"So much for me not being able to have you." Trina said an hour later. Her cold smile was victorious. He had wanted her after all.

"Yeah," Francis said. "You win."

The next things they said to each other were deep and unsearchable and did not involve clumsy words. They did not need them. Something in their souls had been bonded, and now when their eyes met they saw new things.

As she looked over at Francis, tangled helplessly in the net of sheets, Trina caught a glimpse of the innocent person she had once been – the one who had been used to satisfy the appetites of selfish men. She saw the victim in his eyes and recognized herself. Yet she also recognized that she was not the victim this time. She was the spoiler now. Hers was the crime. However, it was not some child she had robbed. It was one who had waited and saved for many, many years. A lifetime's treasure, given away in an instant…

While for Trina it had been little more than sport – a simple conquest to prove she was still desirable, still valuable – for Francis it had clearly been much more.

"That's his problem," Trina's guards assured her.

"Plenty of men do it all the time. You are just evening the score."

"You don't owe anyone anything. Besides, he wanted it."

Trina tried really hard to believe them. But as she ripped her soul away from his and spilled the contents of Francis' heart out on the ground, she saw the lie for what it was.

He merely looked at her and she cracked.

Inexperienced, yes, but Francis was not ignorant. He knew what she had done. He lay there for a long time working through the layers of it, his features hardening into the stony scowl of those robbed of their innocence. The spark in his eyes was gone, carried off like battle spoils, and he was left with his heart clinging to one who would not stay.

Trina was already miles away, ready for the next fool who would prove her worth with his desire.

Left alone with his failure, Francis saw her clearly now. The perfect plates no longer hid the void, and he watched her losing a much greater battle than the little skirmish she had won. But it did not matter. He had lost, too.

"The cycle goes around again, huh?" His words carried both acceptance and disgust.

Trina flinched. It was true. She had taken the darkness that had been dumped on her and had passed along a copy, heaping onto someone else the same damage she had endured.

Delirious guards celebrated as they raised new towers and added more chains to her heart. "You are the monster now," they whispered.

Trina's guilt immediately flared into anger, but since she didn't know about her guards she fired back at Francis instead. "Are you going to cry?" she asked, trying to shame him into silence.

"Probably," Francis admitted. "But not yet. I can still feel the tearing working its way through." He wasn't really even talking to her. It was more like he was narrating his observations, giving an objective account of the destruction of his heart.

The detached, passionless tone sounded utterly foreign coming from him. It was like a doomsday prophet looking on as the first of the fire begins to fall. Resigned to the damage that had been done, there was nothing to do but endure it, and Francis' simple honesty left his heartache out there for her to see.

Trina loved and hated him for it, but neither emotion was powerful enough to make her change course. She would leave – but there was something she had to see first.

Trina watched him lying there, unable to ignore the effects of the collision she had caused. In slow motion she saw the blue minivan swerve across the median, glass exploding and metal shrieking as the body bent and crumpled. She felt the power of the wreck, gasping as she caught sight of the child in the backseat. This was no place for something so fragile. She never had a chance.

Trina and Francis both felt the death, though they didn't understand what it was, and the daughter they would never have bled out invisibly among the soft grave of sheets and pillows.

Trina grieved without showing a thing. She felt it all through him. The disbelief, the shock and disillusionment, the cold empty hole that was left behind… she experienced the first breaking all over as she watched her victim tasting it brand new. For an instant she touched that place once more. It brushed by fast, that innocence, and her heart leapt just to glimpse it. It had been so long. She'd almost forgotten.

Francis sat there much longer. He was old enough to expect the searing emptiness. Still, it was deeper and colder than he had feared.

This wound went all the way to the gates.

μ

μ

30

Mass Distribution

Number Ten stood there, tortured as he watched. He felt their pain with them and saw his part in it. The negated marriage, the unborn child, the brutal heartache and cruel coldness… He saw the cost and realized that the mailman was right. Tearing each other apart was the way people worked, and there was no reason to believe that it would change.

He had done as much himself.

For all his good intentions Kent had merely added to the problem, increasing the wretched inheritance and passing the curse around again. He was no thief. He was just like the guards.

Trina's future victims? The rage Francis would unleash on the world? It was all ugly. And it was all because of him!

The images playing in the mailman's throat faded away at last, but the show did not end for Kent. His heart was now full of them.

Ten was nearly catatonic when the mailman spoke again. "All our time and energy and heartache. All our effort and sacrifice poured out. And for what? So we can end up weaker and worse off than when we started? It's all a lie, Kent. One big setup…"

Kent said nothing. He was so sad. All his pretty ideals were falling like icicles from warm gutters. Where had it all gone wrong?

"Maybe we chose the wrong side," mused the mailman. "Have you ever thought that?"

Ten had, but he didn't say so.

The mailman shrugged at his silence. "Anyway, that's why I switched. Remember when you asked me why? Well, there's your answer. I left because the den is a lie. Their promises are just bait to get you in the door, and once they have you on board all they do is tear you down. I see it now. There is only one person you can trust, Kent. Only one who has your best interest in mind."

"Yourself?"

The mailman nodded. "I may let myself down from time to time, but at least I know who I'm dealing with. And I know I'm not going to cheat or lie to myself. I can always trust myself to give me what is mine."

Kent said nothing. The mailman's words were much like the hunter's poison – sweet and bitter at once. But the more he spoke the clearer it became… The mailman was full of it.

The funny thing was that he obviously knew it. That is why he talked so loud; why he kept going on and on. He was still trying to convince himself.

"What about the den?" Kent asked. "Will you ever go back?"

The mailman scorned the idea. "The den can burn."

"Even though you are a rich man there?" Kent pressed.

"Rich?!" the mailman exploded. "Are you still falling for that? What is wrong with you? I swear you people are the dumbest, most ignorant bunch of backwoods…" The mailman threw his hands in the air. "How much more do you need to see before you get it? No one is rich at the den! The thieves are without a doubt the poorest, most miserable people on the face of the planet. They pour out their very best, give all they have, and they end up with what…? Worn out bodies and unfulfilled dreams! No, in all the time I was with them I never saw those promised riches."

"Then you weren't paying attention," Ten replied, picturing the faces of all those who had begged him to bring the mailman back. "I have personally seen the wealth you have stored up there."

The mailman shook his head. "You're a fool. I don't have a dime to my name. The courts bled me dry when the den didn't show. I lost it all betting on the lies you're still clinging to. Take it from me, Kent. Get out while you can. There are no riches in the den."

"But I've seen…"

"You've seen what you wanted to see," the mailman cut him off. "But the numbers don't lie. The harder and longer I gave, the farther I got left behind until finally I was lying there gasping for air… alone. That's what I got paid for all my trouble." The mailman's scowl somehow grew even darker. "That is my story. I lived it. Lured in. Used up. Left there to die. The den abandoned me, and now my debts are larger than I can ever bring in. They will do the same thing to you."

"If you say so." Kent would not reveal how swayed he was by the mailman's words. He felt them all sharply, his guards twisting the knives of guilt in deep, reminding him of his own current debt.

"It's not too late for you," the mailman said after a long silence. "You can still change sides." When Kent did not answer the mailman grinned icily. "It actually feels really good to give, you know. To deliver…"

The words caught Kent by surprise. It was then that he realized he had still been trying to engage his assignment. Despite his failure and self-doubt, he was still trying to bring the mailman in. Now the mailman had taken things in a different direction.

"What?" Ten asked, apprehensive.

"To deliver… To give instead of take." The mailman spoke as if to a visitor in a new country.

It was an entirely different set of rules.

"What do you mean?"

"Think about it," the mailman motioned with his hand, "you work hard to steal, but those efforts leave you tired, emptied out, and frustrated, right?"

"Sometimes."

"So what do you think happens when you do the opposite?"

Kent was stunned. He had never looked at it full in the face before. Causing pain accidentally was one thing. But delivering it on purpose? Planning it out? That was an entirely different way to see everything. Part of him was afraid to even get close enough to that cliff to peek over, as if merely imagining what it would look like might taint him somehow. What if it pulled him over the edge?

As he considered the idea of handing out pain, Ten felt one of the hunter's spears surge with pleasure. He instantly recalled the sensation of conquest he'd felt over Trina, and to his horror it lit in him a craving powerful enough to widen his eyes. He wanted to feel it again. Now!

"You know what I mean, don't you?" the mailman smiled. It was as if he'd seen the frightful images flashing in Kent's mind. "They train us to run from that hunger, so we turn away, unwilling to experiment, never really knowing both sides. But doesn't it make more sense to have all the information, to be educated before you make a decision?"

"But you can't really know both sides," Kent argued. "You can't truly embrace both innocence and depravity. One will eventually obliterate the other."

"That's what they train us to think. But it's not true. I tried it."

Kent looked up sharply. The mailman had his undivided attention.

"I went on an assignment – it was quite a while ago now. At first it was just like all the others. I crept around and stole some pain. But this time I changed the game, and on my way out I left some of my own."

Kent's face scrunched in reflexive disgust and the mailman regarded him as if he were a trained poodle.

"Oh please. Don't look so appalled. We both know that you very recently did exactly the same thing."

Kent's eyes blinked as if he'd been slapped.

The mailman wielded his weapon flawlessly, driving the tip of the blade into the chink in the thief's armor. He waited until Kent winced and then stopped. His point made, he withdrew the dagger and slid it into its sheath behind his back. It was painfully clear that he would ever have it close at hand.

"I know…" the mailman continued. "It hurts at first. I felt terribly guilty as I started, too. But once I really dove in it was intoxicating. There was no more holding back. I gave all I wanted, completely in control, and the effects on my target were instant. No more waiting around for slow healing. The pain is there as soon as you strike. It was so satisfying. It was the first assignment I had gone to in a long time that I left laughing."

"So you left more pain there than you found when you arrived?"

The mailman nodded significantly.

"Whose did you leave?"

"Ah, now we're getting somewhere!" The mailman looked pleased. "I left some of my own. Then some from others that I was still carrying from earlier assignments."

Kent considered this for a moment. "That sounds a bit like you were simply sharing your burdens." Maybe what the mailman was suggesting wasn't as bad as he feared.

"No," the mailman sneered. "The real pleasure is found beyond that. You don't feel it, and I mean really feel it, until you give someone more than they can bear. That is where the pleasure is. Not just in the relief of laying the burden down, but in watching them being crushed beneath it. Don't misunderstand, Kent... this is not burden-sharing between capable comrades. This is pouring dirt on the grave of one buried alive, drowning one who cannot swim, chaining one who will never get out of their cell. This is irreversible. This is power."

Kent did not know how to respond. It was completely outside his way of thinking. Thieves didn't talk this way. Not ever.

"And get this," the mailman leaned in. "I've learned how to create it."

Kent felt numb.

"There's not a finite amount. The suffering monks missed that. They beat themselves, trying to steal from the world's pile of pain in order to create a vacuum that would offer others relief. But there is no vacuum, because the pile is not finite. We can create it."

Ten glared angrily. Create pain? Make more work for the rest of them? Add to the pile? Why?

The thief didn't ask the questions aloud, but the mailman answered as if he had. "Because it feels amazing! Don't you see? That is where the freedom is. It's not in doing assignments and hauling loads. Freedom is doing what you want when you want how you want to do it. Anything less is slavery, regardless of who your master is. Well now my master is me. I am done scraping by." The mailman clenched his fists. "Instead I will take what I want."

"But the Sweet Thief!" Kent pled. "You really want to fight against him? You really want to tear things down?"

"Hostility is in my blood," the mailman said. "It's in all our blood. We crave the base and carnal even as it turns sour in our stomachs. We chase things we know are destructive. That's not by accident, Kent. We do it on purpose, and deep down you know why. It's because, though we never say it out loud, part of us longs for our own undoing. Like all injured animals, part of us cannot wait to die."

"You must hate yourself," Kent observed.

"Yes." The mailman didn't try to deny it. "I've embraced that as well."

The apartment went quiet. Kent was so stunned that he didn't notice when his target got up and left.

"There!" the mailman thought to himself as he pulled the door closed behind him and stepped out into the street. If that didn't force the issue, nothing would. The den wouldn't be able to ignore him now. He would have his answers, one way or another.

31

Retreat

It was four days before Kent could work up the motivation to head back to the den. He was hurting, tired, and ashamed. What is more, he was now seriously questioning the path he was on. Maybe the mailman was right. Maybe he had bought into a lie.

Part of him just wanted to ignore it all, but there was no peace in his apartment. The guards had overrun the place. Ever since the mailman's visit they had occupied the living room, slowly but surely wearing him down. Most of the time they kept him tied to the couch, but while they were willing to let him gorge on hours of guard-approved propaganda on TV and online, often goading him on into the wee hours of the morning, they never let him get any real rest. And whenever his thoughts drifted anyway near the den they were right there waiting.

"It's nonsense!" they screamed. "I can't believe you ever fell for that."

Kent sank back into the couch, but the conflict was far from resolved. Every time he glanced at the counter he saw the metal band that he had bought from the mirror. It was a constant reminder, and it flashed with daily messages from the escort calling him back.

"Are you seriously still thinking about the den?" the guards resumed their heckling each time he touched one of the clues on the coffee table. "You realize that stealing people's pain really does nothing but provide them with room to create more… Think about it! Have you ever, even once, seen a person benefit permanently from your sacrifice? Or do they eventually just find other needs and hurts to cry about? You don't free people for good. You bear away burdens that are replaced the next day. And do you know why? Because people are stupid. They aren't worth it."

Ten's thoughts were ugly. The hunters' barbs were working him over. He had to get out of the apartment.

It was late Friday night when he finally forced himself outside. He walked straight to his car, wrapping the watch around his wrist as he went. Then Number Ten pulled the creaking door open and slipped behind the wheel.

He knew immediately that he was not alone. As expected, the guards had him under constant surveillance, and they called in a strike the instant he stepped out the door.

Ten turned the key anyway, and his headlights sliced through the dark as he pulled onto the street.

For a while everything seemed fine. He was just driving across town. But halfway to the den his car suddenly made an awful sound and began to shudder. Kent pulled quickly onto the shoulder, but before he could get himself stopped the car bucked violently and seized up with a jolt. All his dashboard lights came on and smoke billowed up from underneath the hood.

Kent didn't call a tow truck. He didn't raise the hood. He just tore the keys from the ignition, climbed out of the car, and slammed the door. Then he started walking. He walked until he could no longer smell the smoke. He walked until he could no longer see the beams of the headlights that he hadn't turned off. He walked until he began to see a familiar skyline rising up in the distance.

Sadly, he did not walk fast enough. A group of guards appeared in the street behind him. There were a lot of them. Ten watched the twisted figures lurching after him and he quickened his pace, but the guards had no problem keeping up. In fact, the more he looked back the faster they closed the gap.

Kent fixed his eyes forward and kept going.

The street up ahead was eerily quiet. He'd expected to find plenty of people out and about – at least a car or two driving by – but the only living thing he saw was a half-starved cat that bolted across the road and disappeared into the shadows. Many of the tall arcing lamps stretching from the sidewalk out over the street were either flickering or had gone out completely, making it difficult for Number Ten to tell which dark shapes were harmless objects beside the road and which were lurking guards. It was with a creepy sense of panic that he watched in disbelief as some of the shadows began to move, staggering out from both sides of the street to join the mob behind him.

Ten endured the awful feeling of dread spreading up the back of his neck as long as he could, but he finally gave up and broke into a run.

As he hurried past the decrepit remains of a dead gas station, he glanced at the old sign. A buck twenty-seven a gallon? Clearly no business had happened here in a long time. Ten wished there were someone there. Someone filling their tank, an attendant in the booth, anyone with a heartbeat... but there was no one. The lights were out. The street was empty. It was just him and the guards, and he could hear hundreds of feet scraping along behind him.

Kent raced further into town.

There had once been a school up ahead on the corner; and a bank after that. Both were now boarded up. Kent had assumed, when he first saw the empty parking lots and dark windows, that the closures were the result of shifts in the economy. His eyes were different now. Around the base of both buildings Ten saw large, irregular holes, many of which were still occupied by the bulbous pale bodies of the huge concrete-devouring termites that had made them.

It was not simple lack of funds that had done these places in. It was corruption. The guards were destroying the city from the bottom up and from the inside out, their jaws making the communities weak and turning its roots to powder. As he ran on Ten saw signs of them just beginning to gnaw on the foundation of the local hospital, and he recognized their bite marks in the sidewalks that led back and forth to the courthouse.

Sad for the city and its people Kent pressed on, dangerously unaware that his gloom was a beacon for every dark creature within smelling distance. They were circling him now. There were dark birds, like those that had plagued the old woman at the diner. His solitary shadow called to them. He could also feel the insatiable barbs of the hunters burning beneath his skin. There was the new sting of doubt planted by the mailman as well. And if all that wasn't enough to drive him back home and into hiding, something far larger was watching him, waiting just out of sight. He could not see it, but he could feel it breathing.

"You can't go back," it called. "Just imagine what the mirror will show."

Kent dropped his head. He hadn't even thought of having to see his latest darkness exposed by the mirror. What an awful thing to consider. "Who are you?" Kent called out angrily to the empty streets, unable to completely hide his fear.

"Why do you ask our name?" The words seemed to come from everywhere.

Kent spun in a slow circle and slowed to a jog, staring hard and powerlessly into the alleys. All around him, they were watching. All around, they were closing in. There was no doubt what they were after. Kent took off again. With all of his strength he bolted down the street like a man running for his life. He did not spend another second looking to the right or to the left. His mind was locked on one place, and he drove himself toward it.

Pebbles sprayed behind him. Buildings blurred on either side. A thousand details dissolved around him as he ran.

Meanwhile the pursuers hounded him.

"You are one of us now."

He ran on.

"Our hooks are in you. There is no getting loose."

He sprang over the traps laid out in the road, looking toward nothing but the door still miles in the distance. He had to reach it.

"They will not want you there. Not anymore."

Kent began to tire and his pursuers gained ground, hauling themselves closer with the cords of the harpoons in his back.

"You are unfit to walk the hall," cackled the guards.

The thief stumbled, barely staying up.

"Even in your best attempts you create pain."

Kent tried not to listen, but the truth of the words could not be avoided. They slammed into his shoulders and wrapped around his knees, sending him sprawling to the pavement. He landed hard, his hands burning as the skin on his palms tore open, but as he hit the ground the alarm on his watch went off.

"Keep running," the display flashed.

'Keep running' was all it said, but that was enough. It was enough to know someone was there. Kent pushed his face up from the gravel and strained against the darkness. The hunters clinging to the cords in his back were pulled off their feet as he lunged forward, but more guards immediately piled on, bringing to bear their full weight. The load was crushing.

Ten had to get out of the street. Tearing across the pavement, he dodged several parked cars and vaulted up onto the curb. He needed a place to hide, if only long enough to catch his breath. Thankfully he had finally reached an inhabited part of town.

Kent sprinted several more blocks, speeding past insurance offices, pharmacies, and restaurants before pushing his way in through the glass doors of a movie theater. The howling of the guards outside went quiet as the doors swung closed behind him. Gasping, his hands on his knees, Kent stole a quick glance around the brightly lit lobby and flashed a small smile at the crowds of people staring at him. It was comforting to see lights and people, though he wished at the same time that they could not see him. Kent inhaled, and found his sense of smell dominated by the aroma of salt, fake butter, and the slightest hint of popcorn. Behind him the dark ones pounded the doors in frustration but they did not enter, apparently afraid of the bright lights inside.

Kent did not waste time standing around. He quickly made his way to the bathroom and turned on the water. It stung the places on his palms that had been scraped raw when he went down, but it felt good on his face and neck. He wiped his eyes, splashed his cheeks one more time, and then mopped himself dry with a handful of paper towels.

"Everything OK in here?" A man in a cheap vest had entered from the lobby. He now stood behind Kent with his arms folded across his chest, obviously trying to look larger than he really was.

"Yeah, sorry. I thought I was late for my movie." Kent almost scoffed at himself as he said it, but the excuse seemed to work. The man's expression suddenly cleared.

"Oh. Sure! What are you going to see?"

Kent's mind raced. What was playing? He had no idea! Again he put his hands on his knees, trying to buy time by exaggerating how out of breath he was. "Theater Four," he gasped at last.

Cheap Vest started to laugh. "Seriously? Where's your kid?"

Kent rolled his eyes at himself. "I guess I just never grew up." He gave the man what he hoped was a reassuring grin and stood up.

"Well, you should get yourself something from the concession stand and relax." Cheap Vest turned to leave the bathroom, then pulled up short to check one more time. "You sure you're OK?"

Kent waved him on. "Oh yeah. No problem."

The door swung closed and Kent glanced at the mirror. Even after rinsing his face, he was still a mess. No wonder he had gotten so many strange stares in the lobby. It must have been alarming for those who watched him crash in through the doors, sweating and gasping for air like a maniac. They probably thought he was crazy.

"And why not?" he thought to himself. "I'm seeing all kinds of things that aren't real. Might as well look the part..."

"But we are real."

The tiny, high-pitched voices came from the mirror above the sink, and Ten cried out at the sight of miniature faces staring back at him from the gaping wounds in his reflection. Terrified, Kent jumped backward and looked down, patting his chest and stomach to find the wounds.

There was nothing there. He was fine. But when he looked back up at the mirror he was met again by pale faces peeking from all the places the where hunters had sunk their spears.

"Did you really think you could outrun us?" the awful worms smiled.

Kent fled the bathroom in a panic, unaware of the fact that Cheap Vest was watching his every move.

He raced out into the lobby, right into the teeth of flashing lights and glowing posters. A fresh batch of kernels rattled and snapped inside a stainless steel kettle. The soda machine hummed and hissed at the people standing in line. Kent cringed, alarmed at the sight of so many mirrored surfaces scattered throughout the room. From the shining metal trim on the glass counters to the reflective covers of the light fixtures, everywhere he looked he found himself being ogled by tiny pale worms glared.

The line waiting for popcorn looked up in unison as Kent rushed out of the bathroom, on guard and curious to see what the madman would do next. Several arms pointed in his direction. One woman in particular stared directly at him while she whispered to three others.

Ten felt like the main attraction for all the wrong reasons. Desperate to get away from the crowds and himself, he ducked under a velvet rope and hurried down the hall, oblivious to the cries of the teenager calling out after him for his ticket.

He wasn't interested in seeing a movie. He didn't care what was showing. Looking only for a place hide, Kent slipped into the nearest theater without bothering to check the title or the time.

"No! Oh, no no no…"

Kent stopped and clenched his fists, horrified by what he saw.

Inside the theater, rows of men and women sat silent and still, shackled to their chairs. Even with the lights out Kent could see the steel bands that pulled their foreheads back and the ugly sutures that held open their eyes. They all wore blank expressions, complacently open to the streams of guards marching in.

Kent's shoulders slumped in defeat.

How could anyone fight this? The havoc that this many guards would hatch out in the world… no one would be able to steal it all. Not in a hundred lifetimes! Ten burned with the desire to shake the people awake, to scream out a warning, to tear down the screen and silence the guards.

"Sir. I need to see your ticket," Cheap Vest whispered intensely.

Kent could not pull his eyes from the crowd.

"Sir!"

Kent whipped toward Cheap Vest and took hold of one of his sleeves as he pointed frantically toward the audience. "Are you seeing this? Do you see what's happening here?"

"Yes. I see that you are trying to sneak into a movie without paying for it. Now this is your last warning. You can either leave with me now or I am going to call the police. Which is it going to be?"

213

Kent was trembling, his eyes so huge with horror that Cheap Vest took a moment to glance up at the screen. But there was absolutely nothing scary about the movie. Then he realized that Kent was not facing the screen at all, but was pointing at the crowd.

This guy was not right!

Ten stiffened with panic as another wave of guards began marching into their new hosts. Every passing second the darkness gained more ground. This had to stop! Nearly hysterical, Ten mouthed mute warnings until one word finally exploded from his mouth.

"Manuel!"

A hundred guards froze in midstream before being obliterated against the far wall of the theater. Hundreds of heads snapped toward the thief. Enraged, the guards that were already safely entrenched in their bunkers spun to glare at the intruder.

"Shut up down there!" one guard screeched.

"We're trying to watch the movie!" cried another.

The fury of the crowd came at him like darts.

Ten had no problem dodging the darts. He knew they could do nothing to hurt him. The man beside him, however, was no dart.

Cheap Vest grabbed Kent's wrist, twisting his arm and pinning it behind his back. "That's it, buddy. Let's go call the cops." He used Kent's face to open the door as he forced him from the theater.

Kent realized he had made a mistake. He would find no shelter here tonight. He stomped down hard on Cheap Vest's foot, then yanked his arm loose and spun away. Ignoring the angry man's shouted threats, he sprinted through the lobby, breaking through popcorn line and looking ahead to the main doors. The army of guards he had left behind when he fled into the theater was nowhere to be seen, and he suddenly understood that the glass doors and movie lights had not kept them out. The whole thing had been a trap.

Cheap Vest was already on the phone, glaring at him from across the room, while the crowds and the teens working the concession stand stood gaping. They were anxious. They were afraid. They were angry.

Number Ten realized that he was spreading darkness again!

He couldn't do this on his own. He was a mess. Confused and exposed, Ten latched onto the last message from his watch.

"Run."

Ten bolted from the lobby, away from Cheap Vest and the popcorn stand and toward the glowing red exit sign at the end of the opposite hallway. Kent was to it and through it before another rational thought went through his mind.

The night sky welcomed him with its gorgeous black beauty, a color somehow altogether different from the suffocating darkness rushing up from behind. Cool air swept his lungs clean as he began sprinting once more. For almost an hour he pressed on, willing himself not to stop; ignoring the burning in his lungs and the voices telling him that the journey was too long.

Up ahead at last he saw the door. He did not worry about being followed. He did not consider whether he might be giving the thieves away. Kent raced forward, scrambled up three concrete steps, wrapped his fingers around the handle, and prayed that it would be open.

32

Face to Face

"You are to meet the Thief. Wait here."

Had it been day one Kent would have been thrilled.

This was not day one.

He was too tired to argue, but as the escort walked away Number Ten seriously considered fleeing back into the street. Meet the Thief? The darkness outside seemed like nothing by comparison. How could he meet the Thief now?

The thought was mortifying. If he had been able to complete his assignment, then maybe. If he had been able to steal enough to get himself cleaned up, perhaps he could face him. But not like this... He recalled his reflection in the mirror from the theater bathroom. This was more than wearing muddy clothes in a nice place. This was about him being a habitation for evil, an active participant in the spreading of darkness. He had things living in him that did not belong in this place.

The Thief would see all that.

Kent shuffled over to the nearest wall and slumped to the floor. He felt cold.

The room where the escort left him was not one he'd ever seen before. It was tiny, with rough rock walls. Fresh mud and clay ran in streaks from floor to ceiling, leaving diagonal ribbons of dull orange and blue on top of the gray. It felt nothing like the rest of the den.

Miniature rivulets of icy water trickled here and there through cracks in the ragged walls, quickly soaking the seat of his pants, but Kent didn't move. Such things were of little consequence now. He'd been beaten by the mailman. He'd failed his assignment. He'd caused pain instead of stealing it. Now, infested with the hunters' worm-like barbs, he would stand before the Thief and account for everything.

"Take off your shoes." The escort's summons was like that heard by those about to be led out to the gallows.

Kent obeyed, even as his stomach knotted with fear.

Then the escort held out a used hospital gown. "Put this on."

Covered in stains and dried blood, the gown smelled awful, even at a distance. Kent gagged as he took it, holding it as far from his body as he could. The thought of wearing the putrid thing against his skin, especially with his open wounds, was revolting.

"Won't this make me sick?" Kent asked doubtfully.

"That's no longer something you need to worry about," the escort said flatly.

The gown felt even worse than it smelled. The fabric was so encrusted with filth that it was stiff. Scratchy and unbending, it was not something a person puts on and forgets. Ten felt like he was contracting a new disease every time he moved.

The escort did not say another word, but led him from the dripping room into a corridor that was lined with cloudy green tiles. The lights in the ceiling were bright but cold. The floor was frigid on his feet. Kent shivered as he trudged after the escort. Fatigue and shame hung on him like the stains of the gown, and he couldn't wait to leave this whole place behind.

As he shuffled along the chalky green tiles, Kent tried not to see the door in the distance. He had no doubt where it led. This was the lair of the Sweet Thief; the one that the den whispered about in awe; the one whose name could obliterate armies of the most powerful guards and splatter them against the walls.

Too fast to be seen.

Victories beyond counting.

So powerful that guards would simply hand over their treasures and flee rather than face him in battle.

The stories went on and on.

Kent had his doubts. Much of what he had heard seemed impossible. Yet there was proof in the den. The trophies Ten had seen did not get there by themselves. There were pictures of entire cities that were built and populated by those the Thief had freed. Number Ten had even seen the darkness flee with his own eyes, sent running at the mere mention of his name!

No, the Sweet Thief had no equal. Not even Kent's doubts.

Number Ten shuffled forward, barely able to keep his feet moving in the direction of the door.

The Almighty, the Invisible, the spoiler of darkness waited up ahead. And he himself was dark…

The realization stopped Kent in his tracks. He would not take one more step forward! He too would flee. He would run for his life like the rest of the guards.

"Kent." The voice was no longer that of the escort. "Turn around." The power was no longer behind the door.

Trembling, Kent did as he was told. He would not shake his fist like the mailman. He would face the end just as he was… broken.

The Sweet Thief was smaller than Kent expected. He wore all black, his tunic tightly wrapped around a lithe, graceful frame. And when he moved – Kent could only assume he was moving – it was indeed too fast to see. His speed made it hard to pin down any other details regarding his physical appearance. It wasn't that he was blurry at all. Then again, there wasn't really a better way to describe it.

The Sweet Thief looked Kent over, and as soon as he saw Ten's wounds the kindness in his eyes flooded over with sorrow and anger.

Without another word, the Sweet Thief sprang forward.

There was no following his movements. Wherever he stepped, gravity and time and the air itself rushed to meet him. Even the turning of the earth stayed in sync with the Sweet Thief's steps, and his feet balanced nimbly on every speck of dust.

Kent never felt the strike. It was over so fast that he didn't have time to raise his hands in defense or try to step to the side. He didn't even have time to gasp. And in that instant he came to understand the plight of the guards.

Many things can be said when a person isn't around. Many threats can be muttered behind a warrior's back. But it all fades to nothing when you are alone with them face to face. Mocking turns quickly to groveling. Proud claims dissolve into shudders. Threats turn into fleeing feet.

There was no case, no argument. Kent, like the guards, was helpless. Even if he had wanted to fight he would have never gotten his weapon drawn. The only reason he even knew something had happened was that he heard the motion of the air racing to catch up.

Number Ten looked down slowly, hesitantly; expecting to see his insides spilling out. What he found instead was the shaft of a spear.

The spear was familiar. He'd seen one before – far too closely. It was the spear used by the hunters, only this time the glinting point was facing away from him.

"Take it." It was not a suggestion.

Kent wrapped his fingers around the weapon and immediately the urge to destroy surged through him like it never had before.

"Now use it."

"What?" Kent sputtered.

"Use it!" the Sweet Thief ordered.

Involuntarily shaking, Kent cried out, "You'll kill me!"

"No." The Sweet Thief's jaw was set.

Kent was baffled. Surely the Sweet Thief did not intend to allow Kent to murder him. He was far too powerful, far too important to let that happen.

"I won't…" Kent whimpered.

"Yes. You will. Do it." Again, it was not a suggestion.

"I don't want to hurt you!" Kent tried to escape.

"You already have." The Sweet Thief pulled his tunic to the side, revealing the damage Kent had done over the years. Deadly scars littered his skin, and Kent recognized each one. "Before, you struck me without having to see it. That is over now. From now on, you will wound me to my face. Now do it."

219

Grief-stricken, Kent lunged forward and the body of the Sweet Thief jerked. The spear slid through his flesh with a slick punch and the butt of the spear rattled on the floor. Kent stared in shock at his empty hands, unable to grasp what he had done.

The Sweet Thief staggered away and fell to the ground, gasping and clutching his stomach. Then he looked directly at Kent.

"This is what it costs. Remember this. Stop taking it lightly. It costs this." Holding out his hands, he showed Kent the price.

"What have I done?" Kent was shaking uncontrollably.

"What you have always done," answered the Sweet Thief. "This time you just get to see it."

The Sweet Thief lay back on the floor, blood spreading out across the green tiles.

Kent knelt beside him. "Why you? Why not me?"

"Because," the Sweet Thief gasped, "you can't afford this." He took Kent by the arm and pulled in one last breath. Then the Sweet Thief gave up his spirit, and Kent saw at last what it was all about. For the briefest of moments he glimpsed the beauty and riches and glory and love that were approaching. Then he saw nothing at all. The drape fell back upon the world.

The Sweet Thief was dead.

Kent took his hands slowly from under the Sweet Thief's head and stood up. He moved to wipe away the tears flooding his eyes, but as he raised an arm up to his face, he was shocked to find that he was no longer wearing the filthy hospital gown. The putrid, stained-covered rags had been replaced by a flawless jet black tunic, so light and strong that he felt immune to the world.

The wretched gown was now upon the Sweet Thief, finally revealed for what it was – a burial shroud.

Had Kent switched them? No. He was barely able to hold himself upright. The escort? No. She had already left the hallway. Then who? Who could have stolen his clothes that quickly?

There was only one answer.

Kent frowned as he looked down at the body on the floor.

The Sweet Thief's last theft… a disgusting old rag? What a sad ending. Of all the amazing things he had stolen, of all the multitudes he had set free, of all of the dark guards he had disarmed and defeated, he ended his life stealing a piece of ruined cloth not fit for a person to wear. It seemed too small.

Then Kent felt it.

Tentatively, he opened his tunic and examined his belly, relief pouring in like a flood. The gaping wounds from the guards were gone! The worms slithering through his flesh had been removed…

Kent screamed out joyfully and threw his hands in the air. The weight was gone. The wound was healed. He was free! And there wasn't a thing the guards could do about it.

One more beautiful piece of the puzzle was filled in as the meaning of the empty bullet casing became clear.

The Sweet Thief had not just stolen his rags.

He had stolen his death.

33

Return to Sender

Kent looked around, unsure of what to do with the Sweet Thief's body. It didn't feel right to leave him lying on the floor. He glanced toward the tiny room at the other end of the hall, but the thought of leaving the body there made him sad.

Only one option remained.

Number Ten slowly turned and inched cautiously toward the door of the Sweet Thief's lair. There was no telling what he would find behind that door. Would it be locked? Was it an irreverent act to find out? Kent paused for a moment, but then he looked down and saw that he was wearing the Sweet Thief's clothes. If he had given him his clothes, surely he would be welcome in his house.

Kent opened the door and was surprised to find a room that was roughly the same size as the tiny cell on the other end of the hall. Unlike the cell, however, the walls of this room were clean and dry, and the air was warm. A stone shelf, about knee high, extended from the far wall.

There was no doubt about it... this was a tomb.

Kent went out and retrieved the body, then brought it in and laid it gently on the stone. He paused a moment and bowed his head, but in his heart he knew that no vigil was needed – the Sweet Thief was no longer there.

Kent did not stay long. The watch on his wrist began beeping and he looked down to find a number blinking on the display.

Three hours and thirty minutes.

It flipped to three twenty-nine and he watched as the seconds began to tick off.

Fifty-nine... Fifty-eight... Fifty-seven...

Having no clue what the countdown was about, Ten backed out of the tomb and quietly closed the door. Then he turned and stepped, intending to return the way he had come. He thought of the cell at the other end of the corridor, took a second step, and was there.

Ten gave a small cry of alarm and put his hands out to protect himself. Just inches from his face was a gray rock wall. It was streaked with mud and clay, tiny streams of water slipping gently toward the floor. The entire corridor was behind him.

"You're moving pretty fast."

Number Ten spun around, turning back toward the green hallway, only to find the escort standing there smiling.

Kent's mouth moved but no sound came out. He'd never seen it before. He'd never been able to...

The escort was beautiful!

She wasn't pretty. She wasn't hot. It was something else; something far more profound. It was the kind of beauty that Kent felt when he stood staring at the sky, the beauty of the green waves flowing down the knoll when the wind bent the grasses, the beauty of his niece's hugs and of his dad always being there. The escort was all of these and more, for beauty was not just something she put on. Beauty is what she was.

Unable to fully bear the sight of her, Kent dropped his eyes to the floor and could not raise them.

"Your time here is over," said the escort.

"But I – " Kent tried to protest.

The escort held up a hand and the thief went silent. "This is not a common place, Number Ten, nor is it a place for what is common." She did not wait for him to reply. "You have heard it said that there is a time for every purpose. Well the purpose for your visit has been accomplished, and it is time for you to go. You may not return this way again until you are invited."

Invited… Kent shifted uneasily. Should he tell her what he had done? Should he confess to the escort that he had just killed the Sweet Thief?

Oh no! No one could know that.

But she would! She would eventually walk down the corridor to the tomb and see his body on the stone.

Suddenly terrified, Kent considered running back to the tomb himself.

But then what? Could he hide the body? No. There was nowhere to hide it. Perhaps he could lock the door! But did the door even have a lock? It didn't matter; he had no key!

His thoughts were a jumble. He was trapped. There would be no hiding this. The escort would discover his crime and alert the den.

Ten couldn't imagine what they would do to him.

"Be on your way," the escort ordered. It was clear that there was no option this time. Kent was not allowed to stay.

"How?" he trembled.

"You don't remember?" the escort asked.

Number Ten shook his head.

"In the corner," she said.

Kent looked to the corner of the cell and found a hinged panel in the floor. It pulled up easily and a lamp made of emerald glass flipped into view, revealing an opening to the floor below.

"Down there?"

"Yes."

"Where does it lead?"

"Go find out." The way she said it left no room for argument.

Kent took a breath, trying to steady himself. Then, with the shoes of the Sweet Thief on his feet, he dropped through the hole in the floor and landed silently before the mirror.

He recognized it all immediately – the mirror, the tables, the emerald lamp that swung back down into place… everything about the den was the same. Everything except himself.

"Welcome back!" said the voice behind the glass. "Have you completed your assignment?"

"I have not," Ten confessed.

"Do you have anything to turn in?" the voice asked.

"I don't."

"Very well. Make yourself at home."

"I do have a question," said Kent.

"You may ask your question," the voice invited warmly.

"My assignment..." Kent began, "it is the mailman."

"Correct," confirmed the voice.

"He's lost."

"Yes."

"So how do I get a new assignment?" Kent inquired.

"What do you mean?" asked the one behind the glass.

"A new assignment," Ten explained. "To replace the mailman."

"The mailman is your assignment."

"Yes," Ten allowed, wondering why the one behind the mirror was having such a hard time grasping the situation. "But he is lost."

"Yes," the voice agreed again.

"So?" Ten prompted.

"So... what?" The even tone behind the mirror was unchanged.

"So he is against us!" blurted Ten, unable to hold it in anymore. "He is no longer a victim. He is an enemy!" Kent glared into the mirror, trying to make them understand. "The mailman is not going to let me steal from him. Even if he did, there is no way I would be able to carry all of the pain he is stockpiling. He is actually creating it on purpose!"

There was a slight pause.

"Did you expect this to be easy?" The voice behind the mirror was completely calm.

"No," Kent grumbled, "but I didn't think it was going to be impossible, either."

"No new assignment will be given," came the firm response. "The mailman was, and still is, your assignment."

Kent threw up his hands in exasperation, "He's gone over to the other side! You must know that. He's knowingly delivering pain!"

"Thus the urgency of the assignment." The voice was unfazed.

Kent's demeanor grew cold. "You don't understand," he said slowly. "It's too late. The things he was saying… there will be no turning him."

"Turning him…" the mirror echoed. "Who said anything about turning him? That is not your job."

"I thought we are supposed to make things better."

"You do."

"But I can't fix him," Kent argued.

"Fixing him is not your assignment. You are only a thief."

"I don't understand."

The voice continued patiently, "What do thieves do?"

"We steal."

"That's right."

"So why bother stealing if it won't fix him?" Kent pressed.

"Why bother stealing if it does?"

Kent went silent, baffled by the question.

"Kent, there is something you need to hear."

The thief looked up in surprise. The one behind the mirror had called him by his name!

"A thief's assignment…" the voice explained, "is certainly about the target. But it's more about the thief."

Kent stopped arguing. The mirror had never been clearer, and as he looked into the glass Number Ten saw something there that the mailman had failed to mention in his diatribe against the den…

He saw depth.

He saw value.

This road was a tough one. There was no doubt about that. It was costly and often exhausting. At times it even seemed hopeless. But it was worth it!

Kent's shoulders eased, and he took in and let out a huge breath as he let the burden fall away. His assignment had never been to fix anyone. It was to steadfastly and willingly bear away a measure of pain on behalf of someone else, and he was supposed to spend himself doing it. Even in the midst of obvious defeat, even if it didn't change a thing, it was a worthwhile battle – perhaps the only worthwhile battle there was.

The few remaining barbs in his flesh flared in protest, and Kent was filled with doubts so strong that for a moment his reflection in the glass was occulted by a cloud.

"You can't do this!" screamed the guards within the cloud.

But the voice behind the mirror called through the cloud, ignoring the guards and addressing Kent directly, "You can't do this alone. That is very true. But you aren't alone. You never have been."

The guards' howling died down and the cloud was swept from the glass.

"I have one more question," Kent said. It was a question he'd been wrestling with since his meeting with the mailman.

"You may ask your question," the voice allowed, no less warmly than it had before.

"If a target proves impossible to steal from, and if that target is doing harm to others, should a thief ever simply take him out?"

There was a great sigh from behind the mirror. "Thieves are not assassins."

"Are there assassins?"

The mirror was quiet for a long time. When it finally spoke again, it was no more than a whisper. "Be very careful, Kent. Eliminating targets often looks good on paper. It seems like it will solve the problem. But it's usually more complicated than it looks. There is collateral damage in killing and violence that ripples out in all directions and causes more pain that must then be stolen and hauled away. It also taints the thief that does the killing, sometimes making him every bit as dark as the one he thought was bad enough to destroy. What is more, the moment you take a target out, you end their story. We are almost always poorer for that. It is much more effective to steal pain. That is where transformation happens. That's where thieves are made. Only in the worst cases is eliminating a target a better option than trying to steal from their guards."

Kent stood thinking, wondering if this might be one of those cases.

"Go in after him." The voice behind the mirror cracked unexpectedly. "Kent." The passion in the voice could not be hidden. "Go in after him. Don't think any more about taking him out. That is not your assignment. Disarm his guards. Steal what you can. Don't leave him there alone."

The command was not issued with a drill sergeant's barking or with a royal ultimatum, or even with the irrational fury of a boss screaming about an order for tile adhesive. What Kent heard was the unmistakable pleading of a desperate father. "Go in after my son."

Number Ten felt the request in his bones. It soaked through his skin, climbed his limbs, and hardened like steel in his spine. This is what the training was all about. This is what he was for.

Kent Hentrick stepped away from the mirror fully resolved. Come what may, this was his war. He turned and walked toward his table in the den with a singular focus. There was but one target left, and he was the spearhead on the end of an airborne lance.

One thief was sitting at the table as he approached.

Samuel stared at Kent through the mish-mash of scars on his face like an inmate looking out through the fence in the yard. Nothing escaped his attention — not the new clothes, not the speed of movement and sublime peace, not the gleaming weapon at his side.

"You saw him." It was part statement, part question.

"You are right about him," Kent replied. "Everything..."

"Everything?" Samuel asked.

Kent nodded. "I have to be honest. I had my doubts. Even after all I've seen I still had trouble believing it all."

"But you saw him," Sam squinted.

"Yes. Now I understand. Now I've seen what you have seen."

"No." Samuel went strangely quiet.

Ten waited for him to continue, but the scarred one said nothing. Something immense hung upon the air. Ten didn't move. He would sooner gouge out his right eye than interrupt the silence. He would wait until the earth buckled if that's what it took.

Minutes passed in stillness before Samuel finally looked up through thin tears, joy and jealousy vying for the field. "You are the only one."

Kent didn't understand.

"You are the only one of us that has seen him," Samuel clarified.

Kent should have answered more gently, but his surprise left his tongue unguarded. "You've never seen him? But... you know so much. I thought surely..."

"No." Samuel stopped. "No." Another pause. The tearing of his heart was almost audible. "I haven't. Most thieves don't."

"I don't get it," Kent whispered.

Samuel sighed and pulled up his chin. "Neither do I."

Suddenly the lights in the room dimmed, returning to their usual level, and Kent realized how abnormally bright it had been the whole time he was standing before the mirror.

"What was that?" he asked, motioning toward the dimming lights.

"The Sweet Thief has left the den," answered Samuel.

Kent's entire demeanor instantly plummeted.

"What's wrong?" Sam asked.

There was no way that Kent could carry the hidden burden the rest of his life. It was already eating him alive. He decided right then that it would be better to get it out and deal with the consequences than to have it rot inside. Still, actually forming the words was a struggle. He tried three times before he finally spit them out. "The Sweet Thief didn't leave the den. I killed him."

"You killed him?" Sam asked, trying not to laugh.

"He told me to," Kent explained quickly.

"And did you steal his weapon and his clothes?" Samuel asked.

"No." Kent slowly shook his head.

"Of course not," Samuel observed. "He is the Sweet Thief. You did not steal from him. He stole from you."

"But I held the spear," Kent muttered.

"Don't take this the wrong way, my friend," Samuel said. "I think you're great, but you're not that big a deal." Before Kent could protest, Samuel pointed to the lights. "And the Sweet Thief has just left the den."

34

C.O.D

Kent smiled gratefully to Samuel as he got up from the table. The scarred thief begged him to stay a while longer and tell him what he'd seen upstairs, but Kent heard the escort call and that was that.

His watch read three hours.

Eager to get back on the mailman's trail, Ten followed the escort swiftly through the hall of portraits to the door that led outside.

"You know what you are doing now?" the escort asked.

"I think so," Kent smiled.

"Good. We'll see you when you get back." The escort's expression was radiant.

Kent almost jumped at the visceral feeling of joy that washed over him, and he glanced up to read the maxim scrawled above the door.

"A few will spend their days etching eternity.
The rest are merely scribbling on the wind."

He clapped his hands in excitement. It was time to do some etching.

Ten practically danced down the three steps to the sidewalk. He didn't know exactly where the mailman was, but he knew how to find him.

The streets flashed by and Kent stood in a brand new trench.

"Well, well... Look what we got here. I almost didn't recognize you!" Malcolm laughed and patted Kent on the back, nearly sending him into the wall of the trench.

"I need to find him, Malcolm." Kent peered up at the giant man who had helped him learn to see his guards. "You said you know where he is."

"Sure do. I'll take you there myself." Malcolm stepped out of the trench.

"You don't have to do that," Kent tried to wave him off.

"You're right," Malcolm declared. "I don't." Malcolm signaled to the foreman and walked over to stash his shovel in a truck. Then he came back. "Let's go."

Kent broke into a smile, thrilled for the company.

A moment later the two men were scuffing down the sidewalk, both all too aware of the cracks in the music.

"I'm scared for you, Kent."

"It's alright..." Kent nodded reassuringly. "I'm ready now."

"You think so?" Malcolm glanced over doubtfully. "Have you met him yet?"

"That depends on which him you're talking about," Kent answered.

"The mailman," Malcolm replied.

"Yeah," Kent said calmly. "He's whipped me twice now."

"And what... you think the third time is the charm?" Malcolm looked at Kent like he was crazy.

"No..." admitted Kent. "I think I met someone stronger."

Malcolm looked up in surprise. "Stronger than the mailman?"

"And faster."

"Who's that?" Malcolm asked suspiciously.

"I think you know..."

Malcolm's eyes went round as dinner plates. "Wait. You saw *him*?"

"Mmm-hmm."

They both stopped walking.

"You met the Sweet Thief?" Malcolm exploded.

Kent nodded, smiling significantly.

"What's he like?" Malcolm's face lit up with the excitement of a child.

"Like everything you've heard," Kent replied. "And then some."

Malcolm's mouth fell open.

"It's funny," said Kent. "I heard so many incredible stories. There was no way it was true. People were just exaggerating. But no… All the things they say about him; climbing walls faster than other men run, being able to disappear, disarming guards with a thought? I believe it all now."

"Oh man!" Malcolm rubbed his head. "You actually saw him though. That don't usually happen. That's big, you know that?"

"Yeah," Kent nodded. "There's a reason for it."

"What's that?"

"I don't know yet, but I'm as sure of it as I am that you are standing here. It's like, for the first time in my life, I am right smack dab in the middle of where I'm supposed to be."

"Wow." Malcolm clapped his hands together eagerly. "Wish I could feel that."

"You will," Kent said with a wink.

"Think so?"

"Oh yeah. I think so. But even if you don't, you keep on going. You're on the way Malcolm, no doubt about that." Then he added, "You've got a piece of the puzzle that I'm still trying to learn."

Malcolm motioned Kent in closer. "Tell me what you got."

"The journey toward the Sweet Thief…" said Kent. "Contrary to what I thought for most of my life, is not really about me. All of this… up, down, left, right… all of it is about him. You already knew that, I can tell. I'm still getting there, but I know it's true. The Sweet Thief is not some little part of my story. I am a little part of his."

Malcolm slapped his legs with his hands and stood straight up. "Now I know *that's* right! Come on Kent. Let's go find our mailman." He began walking again, this time with a spring in his step that Kent had never seen before. It made the coming battle seem a little bit more hopeful.

As he matched Malcolm's stride, Kent reached up and put a hand on the big man's back. He was deeply grateful for his company.

Malcolm was right – feeling not alone was all kinds of important as they headed into the pit.

The mailman was clearly not expecting visitors as he finished his route and pulled into the fenced-in parking lot behind the post office.

Malcolm and Kent were sitting on a curb waiting for him.

Kent's watch ticked down to zero.

"You guys aren't allowed to be back here. This area is for post office employees only. You'll have to find somewhere else to sit around." The mailman walked toward them with his empty mailbag hanging heavy on his slumped shoulders.

"We're actually waiting for someone," Kent said as he stood up.

The mailman froze mid-step.

"Alright, little thief," said the mailman, trying to hide the fact that the ambush had caught him completely off guard. "Nice move. You got me. Now what?" He motioned toward the figure beside Kent without really looking. "Did you bring a friend to watch you get destroyed again?"

"No," Kent replied easily. "He's actually not here for me."

Malcolm rose to his feet and for the first time the mailman recognized who it was.

"Hello, my friend."

The mailman's legs wobbled, but he didn't say a word.

"I did what you told me," Malcolm said. "I went to that place you wrote down."

The mailman looked so stunned that Kent couldn't tell if he was hearing anything that Malcolm was saying.

"I turned in that brick you gave me, too." The big man nodded in corroboration with his own story. "I even asked them why."

Finally the mailman came to life. "It's too late for all that," he said dismissively, dropping his mailbag to the ground. The bag hit the pavement like a boulder. "You shouldn't have brought him here."

"Don't pin this on him," Kent forward. "I would have found you one way or another."

"You would have done nothing," spat the mailman. "Every step you have taken has been one that I laid out. You are a pawn in this game. I point, you move."

"Are you sure?" Kent smiled. "Are you sure it was you who laid out my steps?"

"I don't know, Kent, you tell me…" the mailman's voice oozed with contempt. "What led you to the den? Did you find it on your own, or did you show up there after I handed you the address? And where did the clues come from? Have you even figured out what they mean? Let me give you a hint… They don't mean anything! I found everything I sent you in the dead letter bin. That's right… It's all just a made up jumble of nothing, Kent, just like the den. You're living out a man-made myth, and do you know how I know that? Because I made it up for you."

"You made it all up? That's interesting. I guess that means you built the den, too. Impressive… Where do you find the time?"

The mailman snorted derisively. "I'm talking about your path, Kent. Yours. The den is its own lie. But I wrote yours. And you swallowed it; hook, line, and sinker. The lead pellets? The vial of water? Ooo… It's all so mysterious. It must mean something! And the mark… Well that just ties it all together nicely, doesn't it? Except I made up that stupid mark! You think those letters delivered themselves? You think Adelle hates you for nothing? Who is behind it all? Tell me, Kent, since you obviously know! What is this all about?"

"The Sweet Thief." The words were calm, peaceful, and gentle as they came out of Kent's mouth, but the entire parking lot rocked at the sound. Only the mailman remained still.

"There is no such person," the mailman said coldly. "It's all just a story people tell each other to keep ignorant saps busy cleaning up their messes and carrying their burdens. There is no Sweet Thief."

"Are you sure?" Kent asked again.

"Yes I'm sure!" the mailman roared. "I went to the end to find him! But he wasn't there. The only thing waiting there at the end was darkness. That's what I came back with. No den. No rescue. No One Great Thief! Just the evil riding in my throat." The mailman glared at Kent, an inferno of pleading and rage. "Tell me, Kent. Have you actually seen him? Have you ever truly seen the Sweet Thief with your own eyes?"

The mailman went silent, demanding an answer.

"Yes," Kent said softly. "I have." He used no more words, but suddenly exploded in such a display of speed that he seemed to appear and disappear throughout the parking lot at will. Both the mailman and

Malcolm looked on in stunned silence as Kent flashed through the arena, cutting down the multitude of guards that trailed the mailman.

The guards cranked their sirens and scurried for cover, but there was no escape from the weapon that the Sweet Thief had given to Kent. Over and under and around the mail trucks they fell, crushed against the walls and the curbs. None of them had an answer. None of them could stand. They soon covered the pavement so that there was nowhere to step.

A lone group of guards made a final stand in the southwest corner of the lot. There were twelve that looked like giant crabs, three that moved like people, seven that shed their skin like snakes, and five with owls' wings. Every one of them was armed.

Screaming hatred and defiance they all attacked at once, wielding every weapon known to man plus a few dark designs that the world had not yet stumbled upon. Their heads lunged out in snapping strikes. Blades and bullets filled the air. There seemed to be no place to move in the midst of the sharp and brutal cloud.

Kent stepped into the heart of their attack, moving in rhythm with each thudding heartbeat of the earth. The shrapnel and the poison, all launched in violence, were turned aside as he spun and whirled lightly between them all, the world slowing down to match whatever pace he set.

To the mailman and Malcolm he was a blur. To the ranks of falling guards he was disaster. To the world through which he moved he was nothing short of life.

A moment later Kent turned to face the mailman. Behind him was an enormous mound of darkness. Wings and tongues and legs and eyes were piled up like spent coal in the parking lot, every misused limb removed.

"I am not against you," Kent said to the mailman. "You know that."

"But you can't steal me," replied the mailman.

"No," Kent confessed. "You are your own. Still, you are wanted at the den, and you are loved by the one behind the mirror. He would not have sent me otherwise."

The mailman quivered.

"You should know something," added Kent. "It wasn't just you who drew me to the den. You played an important role, to be sure. Your clues definitely got my attention. But I've come to realize through all of this

235

that I haven't really been chasing you. I've been chasing the same one you have. And I've been chasing all my life."

Just then another figure turned the corner and entered the parking lot through the gate. He slipped right past Malcolm and Kent.

Something was not right. He was too familiar.

"It's about time you got here," the mailman snapped.

"Yeah, traffic, you know…"

Kent tilted his head in confusion.

The green eyes flashed.

Suddenly Kent felt an awful chill race through his body. He saw the blade, but it was too late.

Without saying another word, Jim grabbed the mailman and punched a knife between his ribs. The dull thump of the blow was accentuated by a grunting gasp, and the mailman's eyes went wide with pain and confusion.

"No!" Malcolm cried out, rushing forward to catch the mailman as he crumpled to the ground.

"Sorry old bud," Jim turned to Kent and winked, "can't have a menace like that out on the streets. There's too much at stake." He backed out of the parking lot with his palms up, then spun away and disappeared.

"Kent!" Malcolm shouted. The huge man was holding the mailman in his arms, watching him struggle for air.

Kent raced over and without hesitation grabbed the mailman by the throat. His fingers tightened around the darkness growing there and he tore the guard straight out. There was a great ripping sound, followed by a terrible screeching, and Malcolm retreated in horror at the sight of the same darkness that had ridden him so long. The guard thrashed wildly as it began to burn in the sunlight, but it could not escape Kent's grip.

The mailman gasped, fresh air pouring into his lungs for the first time in years.

Number Ten felt the sweet rush of victory as the mailman began to breathe, but it was a tempered joy. The guard had begun to burrow in through his skin. Ten smiled a sad and peaceful smile, weary courage lighting his face.

This was no normal guard. There was only one way to put it down.

"I'm going to need those wounds of yours," Kent whispered to the mailman.

The mailman squinted up at him. It was strange. He had toyed with the idea of destroying this man for so long... Now, as he watched the darkness digging into Kent and felt his own life draining out through his fingers, his demand for an answer from the den didn't seem all that important. It certainly wasn't worth the man's life.

"No," the mailman answered, gripping the gash in his side. "I'm afraid you can't have this one. This one would kill you."

"I know."

The voice was no longer Kent's.

"I'm here for your wounds," the Sweet Thief declared. "Hand them over."

The mailman clenched his teeth. He wasn't ready for this. Convinced that the den had betrayed him, he had been operating ever since on rage and indignation. Now suddenly that abscess was sliced open. He couldn't hate the den for not coming for him. They had come. It just wasn't on his terms.

The mailman groaned in agony. All the damage he had done, the pain he had dished out in retribution, it was... baseless. The den had not left him to die. They were here!

The mailman felt a searing pain in his chest, and once again he couldn't breathe. Eyes bulging, he looked up at the Sweet Thief, then groaned and lay back in Malcolm's arms.

"Oh no you don't!" The Sweet Thief grabbed the mailman's arm. "You aren't getting out that easy. You have work to do. Now give me your wounds before this darkness returns to you and takes you forever."

"I can't," the mailman thought, lacking the air to form the words.

"You can! Now stop fighting me. You've been carrying all this for far too long. It's time to surrender."

The light was dimming. Soon it would be dark and the guard would be free to move. Already the mailman could feel it staring at him from its burrow in the body of the Thief, just waiting to leap back across the gap and drag him off for good. He knew he could not fight it. There was only one way to get right; only one who could steal all of the pain that was crushing him.

"OK," he grunted as he looked up. "You win. Take it."

The guard cowered. Time bent. The scene rewound.

It all rolled back to the moment when Jim slipped in past the fence.

This time, however, Kent moved faster… He leapt between the mailman and the blade. He took the knife. He stole the wound.

The mailman stared in shock as Jim turned and fled. It all happened so fast, but the mailman knew what had happened. He'd seen the blade. He knew the wound was his. With tears rolling down his cheeks, he watched the thief gasp for air as the price was paid. There was no darkness in his throat. Number Ten had swiped it all.

A moment later Kent lay still.

"What in the world are we supposed to do now?" the mailman whispered. He and Malcolm were alone in the parking lot.

"I don't know," Malcolm murmured. "I never watched nobody die before."

The mailman hadn't either. "We can't leave him like this," he said.

"No," Malcolm agreed. "This don't feel right. People should have the chance to say goodbye. He has friends at the den."

"He's the Sweet Thief," the mailman observed, not wanting to go back and face that place. "He has friends everywhere."

"The Sweet Thief?" Malcolm looked up in surprise. "No, that ain't the Sweet Thief. That's Kent!"

The mailman looked down in alarm. Sure enough, the face was that of the young truck driver he had lured in to the den.

"No," the mailman murmured. "I saw him. He took my wounds."

"Yeah. He did."

"But it was the Sweet Thief," the mailman insisted.

Malcolm shrugged his shoulders. "That's Kent, man."

There was no time for the mailman to sit in his confusion. Someone could walk by at any moment and see the body on the ground. He reached down to pick Kent up, but he struggled to even move him. Thankfully, Malcolm was there. The big man stepped in and easily hoisted the body into the back of the mail truck.

35

Special Delivery

The mailman drove to the den in a fog, hearing no music at all. Static dominated the airwaves.

The desire for vengeance that served as his compass for years had been erased in an instant, leaving him with nothing to focus on but the blood on his hands. Had the knife been intended for Kent? No. But that didn't change the fact that thief's body was in the back of his mail truck, and that it was there because of him.

The mailman felt sick as he pulled up to the curb.

2212 Bismuth Vale.

He had sworn never to come back.

"I can't go in there," he said.

"Oh yes you will." Malcolm's words left no room for compromise. "You owe him that much."

The mailman began to object, but the big man cut him off. "I will not carry him in there without you." Malcolm crossed his huge arms and sat back in the seat, staring straight ahead.

"Fine." The mailman stepped out of the truck. He shuffled around to the back and found Malcolm already there, ready and waiting.

The truck door rolled up loudly, sounding harsh and final as the panels slid up the tracks and slammed into place. Then the mailman and Malcolm lifted Kent's body from the truck. Together they ascended the three short steps to the den, the mailman even more terrified than he was the first time he had climbed them. But there was no slowing down or turning around this time.

The door opened and they stepped inside.

They made it past the front door, but that was it. There was no room for them to take even one more step. The entrance hall was packed with thieves!

So much for hoping to sneak in and out unseen...

Someone had clearly tipped the den off about them coming, for not only had the thieves gathered, but the walls of the hallway had been pushed out dramatically to accommodate the crowd. Yet even with the extra space it was bursting at the seams.

The mailman looked around guiltily. He had brought a lot of pain to these people. But the glares he expected were not there. The eyes of the thieves, and those in the faces in the portraits on the walls, were all gazing at the one he and Malcolm were carrying. And they were beaming!

In the center of the hall there was a casket. Lined in silk and ringed in flowers, it waited to receive the body. Behind the casket stood the escort. She smiled and beckoned them forward. The crowd parted and the mailman staggered ahead numbly until he and Malcolm laid Kent's body down. Then the mailman stepped away and tried to melt into the crowd.

The funeral that followed was a joyous thing. Many who had known Kent stepped forward to share a word or two in celebration of his life.

"He fought off my attackers on his first day!" proclaimed an old woman.

"He showed me a different way to treat people," added Mrs. Sullivan.

"He gave me his muddy clothes," joked a man in a stunning suit. The den chuckled.

"He gave me hope that my friend would be OK," said Malcolm, his deep voice resonating throughout the hall. He looked at the mailman with a smile.

The barkeep stepped forward. He didn't say anything – just pointed at Malcolm, nodded in agreement, and patted Kent's head. Then he looked over at the mailman, smiled, and stuck two thumbs up in the air.

Next came a young woman, and the room went silent as Adelle put her hand on the casket. She didn't say anything out loud, but a tear or two got away and spattered the thickly lacquered wood.

Unlike almost everyone gathered in the hall, Adelle was not at peace with Kent's death. Her grief was raw, and it tore at the mailman's heart as he realized what he had done. To Kent. To Adelle. To all of them.

After Adelle, a few others came forward. There was no script, no order of service. They spoke until there was nothing more to say. Then each thief came forward and laid a hand on his, placing on Kent one last human touch before they sent him upstairs.

When the last thief had said farewell, the escort threw open the door that led into the den. That was when the celebration really started.

The room was alive!

The mailman had never heard such music and the banquet that had been set up had Malcolm grinning ear to ear.

It was as if they were all allowed, for a moment, to sample the sweet homecoming that Kent was experiencing now. The burden was shed. The heart was free. Kent was home! The thieves celebrated with him, looking forward to the bright reunion that waited up ahead.

The mailman was swept up in it, but his heart was not at peace. He still had to talk to Adelle. He had to tell her. She would hate him forever, but he had to tell her. She had to know the truth. The mailman searched throughout the den, finding her at last sitting beside a man with a scarred face. He began walking toward their table – then he stopped. What would he say? How could he tell her all that he had done? His heart burned with shame and he hadn't even begun.

"That will have to wait."

The mailman knew the voice at once, though he hadn't heard it in a long, long time. He turned to face the escort as only a returning prodigal can. "I don't deserve to be here."

"No," she said. "You don't." But before the mailman could sink any lower the escort added, "Point out one person here who does."

The mailman said nothing. He looked at all the other thieves and wondered how many of them knew what had happened to Kent.

"There is something you have to do," the escort informed him. "Follow me."

The mailman obeyed, but his heart began racing as he saw that the escort was marching straight toward the mirror. He was already drowning in what he had done to Kent without being shown what he had done to himself.

Thankfully the escort did not stop. Without so much as a pause, she passed by the mirror and continued out into the hall. The mailman breathed a sigh of relief and stayed right on her heels, careful not to glance over at the glass as they slipped by.

As the door swung closed behind them a powerful silence took hold of the hallway. There was no one around but the two of them. The thieves had all filed out. Even the casket was gone. But it was not quite empty.

A single portrait stood on an easel in the middle of the hall. The escort walked up to it and stopped, then turned toward the mailman and motioned him forward. The mailman knew at once whose face was painted there. He didn't need to look. But that was not an option. The escort commanded him to approach, and there he was confronted with everything that he had done to injure Kent.

The mailman watched the portrait being painted, every detail poured out on the canvas in vivid clarity. A few of those details were of himself, and the mailman saw himself plotting and scheming. He saw himself poring over letters on his desk, skillfully loading poisonous words into envelopes. The clues he sent to push Kent toward the den; the deals he made with Jim; it had all been planned out. None of it was an accident. He'd set up the ambush with Trina. Then he viciously attacked Kent when he fell. He even sent lies in Kent's name to the woman he actually cared for, destroying their relationship and smearing his reputation in the den.

The mailman watched it all again, as without provocation he had set himself against someone who might have been a powerful ally and a dear friend. Now that person was gone. The full scope of his wickedness met the mailman head on as he stood before the portrait of the one he had destroyed.

The escort reached out her hand. In her fingers was a pen.

"What is this?" the mailman asked.

"Your signature is required," she said matter-of-factly.

"For what?"

"To complete his assignment."

The mailman's hands began to shake.

"This thief voluntarily laid down his life for you – one who treated him like an enemy. As there is no greater act of love a person can offer, in that instant Kent was one with the Sweet Thief, for that is exactly what the Sweet Thief does. The guards have no answer for such love, and everything they have taken is stolen away. Your signature will testify that you saw Kent pay this price for you."

The mailman stared at the eyes in the portrait. He had always thought of Kent as a pawn, but this man had given his life to heal the very person that was attacking him! The mailman was in awe. He would sign whatever they asked.

The mailman took the pen and pressed it to the canvas. The ink ran rich and red, neatly clinging to the portrait and sealing what Kent had done. Then he handed the pen back to the escort.

Smiling with indescribable joy, the escort lifted the portrait and placed it with great care in its place on the wall, Kent's image now at home with all the others who had chased. Of course, it was just a symbol. She knew where he really was. Kent had been invited back into the green tiled corridor upstairs.

The cell and the tomb both broke open, and the cloudy green tiles shattered to reveal the great expanse. Kent was on the heights. Forever.

The mailman was thrilled for the thief, happy to see him where he belonged. But he was also immediately flooded with concern for those who were not yet there. Racing back into the den, the mailman made a beeline for the table where he had seen Adelle.

She was gone.

Only one man still sat at the table.

"I need to know where Adelle is," the mailman uttered breathlessly as he arrived at the table.

243

"I'm afraid not," Samuel answered darkly. "You've done quite enough already." He motioned angrily to the scars on his face.

The mailman looked down in silent confession, but then pressed on, "Does she know it wasn't Kent? Does she know that Kent didn't send those letters?"

"She's not sure. You messed her up pretty good. You messed us all up pretty good." Samuel wilted as he finished, "Adelle just got your latest message."

"What message?" Suddenly the mailman's eyes went wide. "Oh no."

He rushed through the room, looking for Malcolm. He found the huge man sitting with the barkeep, talking about sailboats. Both men lit up at his approach.

"Can't even tell you how g-g-good it is to see you again," the barkeep gushed.

"You too, Swabby," the mailman returned fondly. "We will have to catch up soon. Right now, though, I need to steal Malcolm away for a bit. Is that OK?"

"OK, you come back though."

"I will."

"Promise?"

"Promise."

The mailman pulled Malcolm aside and whispered frantically, "We've got to find Adelle! Jim is not who everyone thinks he is."

Malcolm's face was serious. "How do we find her?"

"I have all her information at my place, but it is going to be a nightmare going back there. I stacked the pain from floor to ceiling, and I invited in more guards than I can handle."

"Well, it looks like you are in the right place..." Malcolm indicated the den, and the mailman knew instantly what he had in mind.

The mailman shuddered as he surveyed the tables full of thieves. Then he leaned over and whispered apprehensively, "They hate me, Malcom. And they should."

"Only some of em hate you," Malcolm said. "Most of us love you. And many of em love Adelle, too."

"But this means..." The mailman's face was pale.

"You gotta to do it sooner or later," Malcolm said. "Might as well be sooner."

The mailman hung there, roasting on the spit. The right choice was clear, but it meant being completely vulnerable in front of those who had every reason to hate him. There would be no place to hide. Not there.

Clutching the backs of chairs to keep himself moving forward, the mailman began the daunting journey across the room. It was a voyage long in coming, and a hush fell over the den as one by one the thieves abandoned their conversations to watch the mailman haul himself along. Ten steps left, now five, now two...

The entire room was silent as the mailman stepped before the mirror.

"Welcome back," came a whisper. Tears were audible in the voice of the one behind the glass.

The mailman looked up in fear, terrified to find out what kind of monster would be staring back at him. But all he saw in the mirror was a small man in a postman's uniform; a sharp crease in his shirt and new shine on his shoes. A mailbag was slung over one shoulder, and on his hip swung a small bag filled with checkers.

Grateful tears blurred the mailman's vision. It was more merciful than he could have hoped for.

"Have you completed your assignment?"

"I have," he stammered, wiping his eyes until the green shone clear once more.

"Well done. You are now Number Seventy Five Thousand Four Hundred and Ninety-Two."

Awe swept over the den. No one blinked.

"Do you have anything to turn in?" inquired the voice.

"I do," the mailman answered. "But it is more than I can carry." There was a deep, important pause. "May I ask a question?"

"You may ask your question."

"I need help," the mailman trembled. "Can I ask for help?"

"Of course," the mirror whispered. "Would that you had asked earlier..."

The mailman turned toward the den. This was it. He did not need to ask for their attention. Even the flies on the wall were watching.

"I am a traitor," he began. "I betrayed this place, all of you, and the Sweet Thief himself. I despise myself for that. I hate what I've done."

The mailman felt a great and powerful rage roiling in the den, but he pressed on. "I am embarrassed to think of how shallow my motives have been. I regret every lying letter. There are no good reasons for the pain I've caused."

"No there aren't!" cried someone far back in the den.

"Cheap apologies don't fix a thing!" screamed someone else.

Malcolm stood up, his massive frame immediately drawing every eye. He looked to the ceiling and shouted, "Manuel!" Guards throughout the room were vaporized and those that remained fell back. When the room was silent again, Malcolm turned and pointed to the mailman.

"I do not deserve your forgiveness," the mailman began again, still standing before the mirror. "But I beg for it. Please forgive me. Forgive me for all the wicked things I've done."

The room was frozen, hearts leaning this way and that.

"I am also in desperate need of your help," added the mailman.

Hearts swayed further, all in different directions.

"Since the last time I stood before the mirror I have wandered in some very dark places. I invited an army of guards to live with me and even helped them build a fortress in my house. None of that is anyone's fault but my own. However, there is information inside that fortress about Adelle. Those of you who know her can testify that Adelle is a true thief. That's why I went after her in the first place. That's also why I intend to do whatever I can to disarm the weapon I designed. But I can't take down the fortress and retrieve my files alone. I need help. I have no right to even stand here and ask, but I'm begging you. Please help. Not for me, but to stop the havoc that I've unleashed on Adelle."

No one moved.

The mailman bowed his head. He didn't blame them. After all of his lies and scheming, why would anyone believe that this wasn't just another trap? That was the hard reality. He had done this. If it weren't for him none of this would even be happening. It was his mess, and he would have to deal with it himself.

The mailman turned again toward the mirror. "I request a new assignment."

"Your new assignment is Adelle," replied the mirror.

The mailman nodded. He had known it before he asked. He adjusted the strap of his mailbag, took a deep breath, and turned to leave.

Malcolm met him at the door and began to follow him out into the hallway, but the mailman stopped him. "This is not something we can do by ourselves, my friend." The look on the mailman's face was sad, but resolved. "I'm walking into a trap. It's one that I set myself. If we had the whole den we might have a chance, but two is not enough. You can't come with me."

Malcolm towered over the mailman. "Oh, I'm coming with you. That's my choice. Not yours."

The mailman looked up at Malcolm and shook his head. "No! I will not lead you back into the darkness. Getting you out is the one thing I've done right."

"And if you hadn't I would still be – " Malcolm shuddered at the thought. "I'm coming with you. That's that. Feeling not alone is all kinds of important when you're heading into the pit."

The mailman closed his eyes in relief. Then he smiled gratefully at Malcolm and the two of them turned toward the door.

"STOP!" cried the one behind the mirror. The walls shook and every heart quaked. "You have not been trained for nothing!" the voice boomed through the den.

The thieves looked around, wondering who the voice was talking to.

From the other end of the room the escort shouted, "Broken hearts are passed around and pain is handed down. That cycle must be broken. Who will go in and take the heartache on themselves? Who will bear the cost and bring new life? Who will endure chains willingly so that others may go free? Which of you will steal another's pain?"

It was the Thieves' Call, and it spread through the room like fire.

The barkeep was over the rail in an instant. Others rose more slowly. The old men in the room winced. The old women pursed their lips and wiped away silent tears, already counting the cost. Then, slowly, one by one, they stood. In the end, about half of the thieves were on their feet.

The mailman looked out over the den. Newly inspired by the escort's words, he strode back to face the room.

Those who saw him were surprised. They recognized him now. They had seen this thief before; a long, long time ago. Their eyes fell upon him with an odd mixture of pride and pity, hope and scorn.

What a beautiful, brave fool he was.

36

Assault on the Vault

An army of sweet thieves left the den with the setting sun, joyful songs from Kent's sending banquet still echoing in their ears. None of them had ever been part of something that felt so momentous. They moved like a tidal wave, their common strength swelling with each step.

"How will anything be able to resist such a force?" the first darts came raining down.

The mailman saw them coming and called out a warning. "Vanity!" he shouted. "Self-worship!"

The thieves responded immediately. Focusing in on where their strength truly came from, most watched the darts fall harmlessly to the ground. A few, however, were unable to get themselves out of the way and went rigid as they took the first hits.

"Why are you following this traitor?" Mortar shells came shrieking. "Division!" the mailman cried.

The thieves formed up and turned the blast aside, but with attacks showering them already, before they'd even reached the fortress, the coming battle seemed abysmally heavy. Several thieves turned and fled.

The remaining army turned the corner and the mailman's house came into view. Rising up like an ancient stronghold, it cast an oppressive shadow over the cul-de-sac at the end of the street, and it felt even more ominous than it looked.

"Remember who we fight for," the mailman cried as the thieves squared their shoulders and prepared to charge. "Remember those we free!"

"MANUEL!" the thieves roared, then took off toward the house. Their shout slammed into the fortress with such force that cracks spread instantly through the walls. Every exposed guard fell dead.

An eerie shriek rose from within the tower, and an instant later a horde of flying creatures poured into the sky. They dove over the wall and came screaming in fast and low, tearing with their talons. The mailman raced between them with fantastic speed, taking down as many as he could reach.

Some of the younger thieves, however, were not so fast. Sprawling on the ground, they clutched fresh wounds and cried for help.

"Medic!" screamed the mailman.

Two veteran thieves raced up to tend the injured. The rest charged on. They reached the outer wall and slipped between spotlight circles to begin testing the façade. The mailman looked on in admiration as one of the thieves clambered up the wall without a moment's hesitation. Was it recklessness or courage? It was always hard to tell from the outside. Only the thief really knew. Watching his example, a few more did the same. Others found a gap in the wall. Still others assaulted the gate itself.

The mailman moved in as well and immediately found himself staring face to face with a guard lurking just outside the wall.

"If even one of them falls it will be your doing," the guard raised its weapon. "You brought them all here." The guard paused thoughtfully, its mouth opening in a twisted smile. "Come to think of it, you brought us here as well. This entire war is your creation!" The darts were so close that the mailman felt the air tearing around him.

"That's true. And I can't change that." He dove to the ground, rolled sideways, and came up firing. "All I have is today, and today I fight for the Sweet Thief."

Its arms and legs deftly removed, the guard was left behind.

The mailman scaled the wall quickly, only to look over and discover a horde of guards assembling behind the gate, preparing to charge out and ambush the thieves. He had only an instant to decide: leap down behind the guards and take them by surprise, or let his comrades know what was coming. Gritting his teeth, he leapt down from the wall and sprinted toward the gate, whistling loudly and waving his hands above his head.

The thieves retreated, taking up a defensive position just in time to see the gate explode outward. A dozen guards came out furiously, expecting easy prey. What they found was a line of thieves staring at them through the sights of their weapons. The first volley ripped half of the guards off their feet. The rest were cut down as they tried to flee.

The thieves leapt up and charged the gate, breaching the wall in minutes. Guards shrieked and retreated from every corner into the inner courtyard of the fortress where they prepared to make their stand.

The mailman took on guard after guard as he faced the darkness of his past. A few went down easy. Others not so much. There was no way to avoid some of the hits. Halfway through the battle, the fight had taken its toll. Wounded and exhausted, the mailman found himself alone in the middle of the courtyard. Feeling exposed out in the open, he sprinted fast and low toward the nearest wall, intending to take cover in the shadows.

It was a costly mistake.

A guard was waiting in the alcove. Crouched among the shadows like a frog, it held the detonator that would spring the final trap.

"Kill the mailman!"

With those words the courtyard exploded. The earth came apart and rocks were sent spinning, trailing ribbons of smoke and fire. Clouds of dust filled the air and barking shouts rang out as guards charged in from all directions with riot shields and automatic weapons. A few of the guards looked somewhat human. Most did not.

The mailman met them head on, flowing through the storm of claws and bullets as if he knew each move ahead of time.

Fatigue, however, was one enemy he could not dodge.

The mailman could feel himself slowing. Soon he would miss a step and a strike would get through. That's all it would take. He had to get out soon. But how? The courtyard was packed.

He considered leaping to the wall, but as he glanced up he found that the sky was filled with the talons and beaks of all kinds of twisted creatures. On the ground the ring of guards had him surrounded, and in the midst of it all a greater darkness continued to stare out from the alcove.

"Kill the mailman!" it croaked again.

The den seemed a world away.

"This is real danger. Belief is worthless here!"

"Death will not stop to ask which side you are on!"

"There is no escape this time!"

The darts poured in, trying to weaken his resolve, but the mailman had done enough doubting. He danced through the shrapnel like liquid lightning. Each step flowed into the next. Each strike demanded another just after. There was no time to pause, and his attention was no longer open to the doubting voices. Everything he had was required for the moment at hand; his highest level of concentration only a sliver away from not being enough.

A slice burned through his arm. Then a shot ripped across his chest. He moved on, pushing the pain to the back of his mind, refocusing on the dodge - parry - strike that the coming second demanded. It felt as if his hand was hit by a blowtorch as a piece of a finger spun away. He did not have time to grieve the loss. Survival of the whole became paramount to all other concerns, eclipsing the loss of its parts. Teeth clamped down on an arm, which he freed an instant later by separating the attacker's mouth from the rest of its face. He was breathing heavy now, lungs hungrily sucking in air as he forced his body through, around, and over the mass of guards.

The walls of the courtyard became his allies. They covered his back. They welcomed his feet as he planted and pushed off. They penned in the enemy for him to slaughter.

The mailman slammed the nearest guard into the wall and watched its shark eyes shrink in terror. The terror was short lived. The guard quickly joined its lifeless cohorts on the floor of the yard. The mailman stepped over the body and moved on.

"Kill the mailman!" the dark frog bellowed, hopping up to the wall above the alcove.

Gunfire ripped through the courtyard as the guards made another push. The mailman was punched three times in the chest, thrown onto his back by the force of the impact.

Breath gone, blinded by pain, the mailman had nothing left. He lay back and surrendered to whatever end awaited him, looking forward to the chance to make amends with Kent face to face. The last thing he saw was the ring of the guards rushing over, crowding in, and finally blocking out the light. Then the world went dark.

The guards saw the mailman fall and raced to devour him, but their inattention to the thieves behind them proved fatal.

Shoulder to shoulder the thieves advanced. They cut through the distracted guards as if they were grass in a field, striking them all down in one pass. The guards tried to recover, but it was too late. The barkeep put his spear through the frog-like body of the dark commander, and moments later there was not a guard left alive.

37

Blackmail

Adelle raced home, determined to get there before the bomb went off. There was no telling how much time she had.

She pounded the steering wheel with the palm of her hand.

"Why Kent? Why?!"

She had no idea what had made Kent join the mailman. Perhaps they had been in league from the beginning. But why did they choose her? She hadn't done anything to either of them. And now they were going after her family! For what?

Her heart caught between pity and rage, it was hard for Adelle not to feel like Kent deserved exactly what he had gotten. Still, seeing him lying there in the casket... She fought the tears off. There was no time for that now. The accelerator was on the floor. If that letter arrived before she did it would destroy everything.

Adelle could smell trouble before she turned into the drive. Something was wrong. Slamming the car in park, she left the engine running and the door hanging open as she leapt out and raced across the lawn.

She never saw the tripwire.

Adelle crashed inside and found her family all seated together in the living room, an open letter in her sister's hand. There was a profound silence in the house, and her parents looked up at her with puffy red eyes.

They were not alone.

"Jim!" Adelle exclaimed, confused. "What are you doing here?"

"I came as soon as I heard. I'm so sorry."

Adelle blinked. "Yes," she nodded slowly, thinking he was talking about Kent. "It's terrible."

"Then it's true?" her mother asked, wringing her hands on her skirt.

"Well, yes," Adelle answered haltingly. "But how would you know about that?"

"This man just told us everything," her father said flatly. "Adelle, how could you?"

"Wait, what?"

Her mother fled from the room and the rest of the family stormed out after her. Adelle stood stunned.

"What did you tell them?" she asked hesitantly, her hands beginning to shake.

"Only the truth, Adelle. One wicked little truth." The green eyes flashed ruthlessly.

Adelle's legs were suddenly gone. She hit the floor and buried her face in her hands. "Why are you doing this? Why are you all doing this?" Her wailing was so full of hurt and confusion that she sounded manic.

"Oh, there there, Adelle. It's not so bad. At least Kent isn't around to see this. You see? There's always a bright side." Jim laughed as he stepped over her and followed her family from the room.

38

Postmaster General

The mailman lay in a corner of the courtyard, his wounds beyond repair. Malcolm cradled his friend's head in his lap, doing all he could to make his passing as easy as possible. Every breath the mailman took was weaker than the one before.

"You be easy now," Malcolm whispered. "The guards are gone. It's just us now."

The mailman shuddered softly as his body drew close to the end.

Just then one of the other thieves ran up to Malcolm, having come from inside the fortress.

"Did you find anything?" Malcolm asked.

"Did we ever!" the thief exclaimed, still amazed by what he had seen. "You're not going to believe this place. I've never seen anything like it. It's going to take us a month to haul it all back to the den."

"There's that much?" Malcolm asked.

"Sure is," said the thief, shaking his head at the fortune piled up inside. "I can't believe he survived so long carrying all that pain."

"I can," Malcolm whispered, hovering over the mailman protectively.

Another thief ran up to Malcolm, eyes scanning the horizon beyond the fence. "Not to be disrespectful, sir, but what's the next objective?"

Malcolm nodded. "We gotta get a crew and go after Adelle."

"Can we do that?" asked the thief, pointing at the mailman. "She's his assignment."

"I'm afraid he ain't gonna be able to do this one," Malcom murmured.

"Should we take him back to the den?" asked the first thief.

"I don't know…" Malcolm shook his head. "I ain't sure what to do."

"Are you willing to do what is required?" a different voice asked.

Malcolm looked up immediately. That voice was one he had heard before, and he found that the other two thieves had gone, leaving only one. Standing in the courtyard, a jet black tunic wrapped tight around his agile frame, was the thief Kent had described. The rest of the world seemed to fade away.

"It's you, ain't it?" Malcolm couldn't close his mouth.

The Sweet Thief smiled. "Malcolm, are you willing to take his place?"

The huge man looked down at his friend and saw the mailman's life slipping away.

"Yeah," Malcolm whispered without hesitating. "I'll do it. Will you tell my momma… tell my momma I love her?"

"She knows, Malcolm." The Sweet Thief couldn't hide the delighted chuckle in his voice. "She knows."

"Alright," Malcolm nodded, swallowing hard. "What do I do?"

"You're a sweet thief, right?" came the surprised response.

"Proud of it," Malcolm looked up, wearing determination like war paint.

"Then steal those wounds," the Thief said plainly.

"I never done that before…" Malcolm looked back down at his friend as if he was holding an unsolvable puzzle.

"I know," the Sweet Thief agreed. "But you are one of the very few people around who still can. Not everyone allows their heart to grow big enough to do it. But you have… I'm proud of you, Malcolm."

The big man looked up in surprise. Then he turned back to the mailman and put his huge hands on his friend's chest…

When the mailman woke up he felt much better than he expected. It was so strange – he clearly remembered being critically wounded, but now it felt like nothing was wrong. Baffled, he leapt up and examined his arms and legs. A host of new scars littered his skin, but that was it. There was no pain at all. He even had all of his fingers back.

Had he died? Was he just waking up on the other side? The mailman glanced around the empty courtyard trying to figure out what had happened, but there wasn't a soul to be found. Not a guard. Not a thief. No one.

Curious and slightly alarmed, the mailman sped into his house and bounded up the stairs. Enormous bags of loot still covered the floor in every room. Though tons of pain had already been hauled back to the den, the thieves were only just beginning to make a dent. The mailman skirted the mountains that remained and headed for his desk. Reaching out over the desk to the wall, he pulled down the bulletin board and started prying thumbtacks from the cork, filling his free hand with a stack of note cards. Then he spent a few moments loading folders from the filing cabinet near the door into his mailbag. When he could not fit one more sheet of paper in the bag, he threw the strap over his shoulder, grabbed two small sacks full of dark coins, and began the hike back to the den.

It wasn't far. Less than a half hour later he was standing out front, looking up at the door.

2212

The mailman climbed the steps and ducked inside, urgently racing down the hallway to the den. He wasted no time unloading his two bags of coins, watching in relief as they disappeared in the mirror. It had been a long time since he'd done that.

The mailman let out a deep sigh. There would be more to haul – a lot more – but he actually felt the burden beginning to lighten already.

Smiling gratefully at the one behind the mirror, he walked over to the long bar and sat down on a high round stool. Heaving his mailbag up on the bar, he began leafing briskly through the files inside. He found the card he was looking for and pulled out Adelle's address. Then he looked up to the barkeep, who was once more wiping down the rail.

"Hey Swabby, have you seen Malcolm?"

The barkeep's bloodhound eyes looked down. "Naw. Ain't seen no Malcolm."

"Did he come back here after the battle?"

"Aww, no." A sad look crossed the man's face and he began to fidget with his hands.

A feeling of dread clawed at the back of the mailman's neck. "Swabby. Look at me now. Where is Malcolm?"

"Don't know b-b-bout no Malcolm. He went way."

"Away where?"

"D-d-don't know. Just went."

The mailman lowered his mailbag behind the bar, slipped Adelle's card into his shirt pocket, and hopped to his feet.

He hurried from table to table, taking a quick survey of the thieves remaining in the den, but none of them had seen Malcolm either.

There was only one place left to go.

"I want to see the Thief," the mailman stammered as he stepped before the mirror.

"The whole world wants to see the Thief."

"But this is important," the mailman insisted.

"It's always important."

"But this isn't about me!" cried the mailman. "I'm not doing this for myself."

"No, you're not," the mirror agreed. "Your motives are flawless. However, just because you aren't doing this for yourself, that doesn't mean you aren't still trying to do it your own way."

"But someone's life is in danger!" the mailman argued.

"And you think you care about that more than I do…"

The mailman blinked and stopped talking. He even went silent in his mind. What could he say to that?

When the one behind the mirror finally spoke again, it was with a voice that was at once both unyielding and warm. "There are much greater things at stake than what you understand as being life. For that reason I must tell you no. This line, though you do not yet see it, is vastly more significant than a heartbeat. We do not make exceptions every time someone longs for the line to be moved. We don't redefine it every time someone wants it to look differently. And we certainly will not cheapen it just because we like you. That would be cheating you – all of you – in the worst way."

The mailman did not understand what the mirror was talking about, but he was now almost certain that something terrible had happened to Malcolm. "Please," he whispered. He could not handle the thought of having to say goodbye and send him off already. Even a thieves' funeral contained more grief than he could deal with right now. "Please!"

There was no wavering. The mirror stayed true. The line was held.

"Have you completed your assignment?" the mirror asked.

"No," the mailman replied in soft surrender. "May I ask a question?"

"You may ask your question."

"Do you know where Malcolm is?"

"Of course," said the mirror.

"Where is he?" the mailman gasped.

"He is with the Sweet Thief."

The mailman was instantly thrilled and emptied. His friend was home and his friend was gone. It was fantastic. And it was awful.

"Can I ask another question?" The mailman's voice quivered with trepidation, dreading the answer.

"You may ask another question."

"How did Malcolm die?" He had to know.

"That depends," the mirror replied cryptically.

"Depends?" the mailman repeated. "Depends on what?!"

"On what you mean when you say the word die."

Word games? Now?

More than a little irritated, the mailman tried again, "How did Malcolm cease to be alive?"

"Malcolm has not ceased to be alive. He is very much alive."

"But with the Sweet Thief?"

"Yes."

"And where is the Sweet Thief?"

The mailman squinted, as he could have sworn that he heard the mirror chuckle.

"He and Malcolm are out looking for Adelle."

39

Forwarding Address

"So I didn't really have to die?"

"Oh, you did," the Sweet Thief nodded in confirmation. "But life... Well, it's highly underestimated. Even those in the midst of it have a hard time grasping the fact that life really does win in the end."

Malcolm looked at him sideways.

"Invincible, Malcolm," the Sweet Thief explained. "That is what you are. You just don't realize it yet. But one day you are going to look back and realize that you were actually part of an army that overwhelmed the opposition, not by blowing their heads off, but by winning them over through sacrifice – an army that saved lives by giving up their own."

"I thought you said we was invincible."

"You are, Malcolm! While you spend your life stealing pain and freeing people, your enemies plot and scheme and work and fight against you until they finally kill you. You lose, right? But what if, after all that, your life is simply handed right back to you? What effect does killing have then? Where is the power of death if death is a temporary thing?"

"But death ain't temporary," Malcolm said, unable to make sense of it.

The Sweet Thief smiled and put his hand on the big man's shoulder. "You died today, Malcolm. I was standing right there when you did it. I watched you give up your life to save your friend." The Sweet Thief looked him in the eye. "So how do you feel?"

"Not very dead," Malcolm confessed.

"And there you go."

"But not everyone gets up," the big man protested. "Kent didn't get up."

"Not everyone gets up when you think they should. That's just a time issue. But make no mistake, every one of my thieves gets up and stays up. Every single one."

"So we are…"

"Invincible," smiled the Sweet Thief. "You cannot lose."

"Then why does it look like we lose?"

"So you can steal," the Sweet Thief shrugged. It was as plain and simple as that. "If you couldn't suffer, then you couldn't steal the pain of those who are suffering. You are allowed to join them in their suffering now so that they can join us in the end."

"But why?" Malcolm scowled, struggling to see the whole picture.

"Ah, that big question… Everyone always wants to know why." The Sweet Thief gave him a wink and a grin. "Don't worry, Malcolm. You'll find it. Just keep your eyes open."

"Keep my eyes open? What am I supposed to be looking for?"

"Right now you should be looking for Adelle. The mailman will need your help."

"Where do I find her? And him? And when I find them, what do I do?"

The Sweet Thief laughed fondly and laid his hands on top of the big man's head. "Easy, Malcolm. One thing at a time. Don't freak yourself out."

"But what do I tell the mailman?" Malcolm cried.

The Sweet Thief smiled. "Tell him I said hi…"

Then, just like that, he was gone.

"Malcolm!" a voice rang out, electric with relief.

Malcolm spun around just in time to see a boxy little mail truck come skidding to a stop in the street beside him.

"Am I ever glad to see you!" The mailman leapt out and ran to meet his friend, giving Malcolm as much of a hug as his little arms would allow. "I had a terrible feeling you were dead."

"Dead?" Malcolm looked down at the mailman like he was crazy. "Please… I'm a sweet thief, son." Malcolm's attempted wink looked ridiculous, but it didn't matter. The mailman apparently didn't get what he meant anyway.

"I can't tell you how good it is to see you!" the mailman gushed.

"You too," grinned Malcolm.

The mailman stepped back and straightened his hat. "Alright, now maybe you can answer a question for me."

Malcolm held up his hands. "You can go ahead and stop right there. I don't get it. All I can tell you is the Sweet Thief says hi."

The mailman stood dumbfounded.

"Now, we got work to do." Malcom stopped smiling and grew serious. "Did you figure out where we can find Adelle?"

That snapped everything back to the moment.

"Oh Yeah! I've got that right here!" The mailman reached into his shirt pocket and pulled out the card with Adelle's address.

They both hurried back to the truck and the mailman showed Malcolm where the place was on a folded paper map.

"You ain't got GPS?" Malcolm asked.

"Come on, Malcolm. I'm old school."

"You're old school all right," Malcolm shook his head. "Too old to be saying things like old school."

"You got that right," muttered the mailman. He buckled his seat belt and checked his mirrors. Then he turned the key and punched the pedal to the floor. It was the first time the mailman's truck ever left rubber on the road.

Forty-five minutes later the little white truck – complete with red and blue stripes and a blue eagle head – pulled up to Adelle's house. A man stepped out onto the curb. His uniform was well pressed and sharply creased, and his mailbag hung easily from his shoulder. He whistled as he walked; his song keeping perfect time with the cracks in the sidewalk.

The mailman stepped onto the front porch.

"He's here," the guards reported.

"He's here," the warning was relayed further in.

The doorbell rang out.

"This is no time for company!" the guards screamed at the hostages cowering within the house. "Don't you have enough to deal with right now? Whoever it is has no right to be here. Just ignore it until they go away."

The hostages withered at the guards' orders and they stayed where they were. Adelle's mother sat despondent on the bed in her room. Her father was there as well, anxiously staring at his wife. A brother was stewing, hearing more and more of what the guards were saying about vengeance. A sister was tired of it all and was packing a suitcase.

Jim glanced coldly toward the door. He certainly was not going to answer it. He was still fuming over the fact that the mailman was alive. Kent had made things much more complicated than they needed to be!

Out on the porch, the mailman knocked again.

Guards opened fire from their posts behind the windows.

"You aren't wanted here."

"It's ridiculous to keep on knocking. No one is coming."

"They will hate you if you don't leave."

"You've already been standing here too long."

The mailman saw the darts in flight, but this time he did not dodge. Instead he simply allowed them to bite in.

"Your attacks are accepted," said the mailman. "Do what you will. I will not withdraw."

The guards in the windows looked at each other in alarm. They had nothing else to throw at him. Out of ammo, they tried to reload and fire the same rounds, but the shells were spent. The darts would no longer fly, and they fluttered to the ground like maple seeds.

The mailman knocked again. And again. He would not leave. The guards at the windows retreated, going inside to secure the hostages.

"Go away!" an angry voice finally yelled from inside.

The mailman knocked again.

"Are you deaf?! I said go away!"

The mailman could hear the pain and anger in the brother's voice. The guards were working him over.

That changed the game. The mailman was content to take hits himself, but he was not here to add to the pain of his targets, and forcing the issue right now would only help the guards erect their towers inside.

The mailman stepped off of the porch.

From behind the door, Jim paused. That was it? That was the attack of the great mailman? Surely that couldn't be all there was. The darts that had repelled him were nothing.

Jim frowned. He had been deeply disturbed to see the infamous thief walking toward the house, especially after he had been unable to take the disgraced letter carrier out himself. But now it seemed that all the hype was just that. For all the things that people said about him, the mailman was surprisingly unimpressive. Unless... Jim moved to the window and pulled back the curtain just enough to allow him to peek out, convinced that he would see the mailman trying a different approach. But all he saw was the mail truck pulling away. The thief had gone soft.

Adelle was still crumpled on the floor. Dark bars were welded in place around her, encircling her in a cage far stronger than steel. Past failings that she thought were long buried had been exhumed and packaged for all to see, as shrapnel from the mail bomb tore through those she loved most. The secrets she had tried to keep from their eyes, secrets she had paid for a thousand times over, exploded fresh from their hiding places, and she hated herself for having betrayed them. The load was crushing.

"Manuel. Manuel." Adelle whispered the name over and over as she rocked herself on the floor, her arms wrapped around her knees, her face buried in her arms. If only he would show up. Just this once. They all said he would; that when there was too much pain to carry he would be there to take it. But he wasn't. Her heart cracked and bled. It had all turned on her, and she was left hanging like a criminal – the criminal she was...

"You are the worst," the guards whispered.

Jim walked back into the room and joined them. "Look at you," he taunted. "You wasted all your strength for nothing!"

Adelle sobbed. She had given all she had as a thief. But now, when she needed someone to steal her pain, there was no one to be found. She had trusted Kent and had been betrayed. She'd trusted Jim and had been set up. The mailman had singled her out for no reason at all, and Samuel, the

265

one she looked to so often for answers, had refused to leave the den. All alone, with her family shattered by her own hand, Adelle was broken.

Jim turned away. His work here was done. There were still other thieves to take out, but this one was finished. She would never crawl out of this pit, and her family would fall in right behind her. It was amazing what a few well-placed words could do.

Leaving behind a large number of troops to keep the hostages in line, Jim walked to the front door. He was hungry to go finish off the mailman while he was still weak, and Adelle's destruction would only make that easier.

Yanking the door open, Jim stepped onto the front porch, only to find an envelope hanging from a string. Dangling at eye level, it twirled slowly right in front of his face.

Jim scanned the front yard from one side to the other, looking for the mailman. But he saw no one. There was only this envelope.

"Funny," he thought toward the mailman. "This is the best you've got?"

There was no need to play the mailman's games. Jim had already won. All he had to do was walk past it. That would be checkmate. Unless, of course, the envelope was not for him. If the mailman was indeed trying to steal from Adelle and her family, then whatever was in the envelope could be intended for them. There's no telling what the mailman might have put inside. He could have supplies and weapons in there that would help Adelle file through the bars of her cage and begin to take out the guards. He couldn't leave her here alone with that envelope!

Maybe that was what the mailman was up to... Maybe he was trying to trap him here at the house, forcing him to guard the place himself to prevent his hostages from escaping. Why? What was the mailman doing that he would want him to stay here? No, Jim shook his head. That was too complicated. The mailman wasn't that smart. This wasn't about keeping him here. It was something else. But who was the letter for? Was it for Adelle or was it for him? Did the mailman even know he was here?

"Some mailman," Jim smirked. "...didn't even put a name on it." Then he went quiet. For while there was no name or address on the envelope, there was a stamp.

"What are you playing at?" Jim whispered out loud. He snatched the letter down and gave it a shake. There was definitely something inside, but when he held the envelope up to the light he couldn't make out a thing.

Suddenly he realized what he was doing.

He was playing the mailman's game.

"Oh, good!" Jim cried out. "Very good. But I'm not biting!" He threw the envelope to the ground, but then he immediately picked it back up. He couldn't leave the envelope at the house; not if it was for Adelle. But he couldn't open it either, in case it was one of the mailman's traps. That left one simple option: he would destroy it.

Burn it. Tear it up. Take it out of circulation.

Jim paused. If he was going to destroy it anyway, he might as well know what was in it. Knowledge is power, after all. If it was for Adelle, it could tell him the mailman's next move. If it was for him, well that could also help him to know what was coming next. He doubted the mailman could say anything that would hurt him.

He looked again at the envelope. It was just paper. What was there to worry about? One little strip of glue. That's all that held it closed. The questions could all be laid to rest. All he had to do was break the seal. He didn't even have to read the whole thing. He could just read the first line. If it was for him, he could destroy it without reading another word and dodge any trap the mailman had hidden within. If it was for Adelle, then he could see whether there was any information that he could use to his advantage.

But no! The mailman had left the envelope hanging. He wanted Jim to find it. It was a trap! Wait! No, there was no way the mailman could have known he would be there. It was for Adelle! And whatever was inside was important and urgent enough that he wanted to make sure she found it now. Otherwise he could have just slipped it in the mailbox. It was important and urgent. But who was it for?

Burn it and be done with it! He was winning. Why change things? But if he was just going to burn it there was no point in not looking! Unless he thought the mailman could get in his head. Then he should certainly not read it. But the mailman would not get in his head. He was too smart for that. Besides, he could always stop reading. There were a hundred ways to do this safely. If it was a bomb it could be defused. If it was intelligence for Adelle it could be used. Either way, what could it hurt? He was not afraid of the mailman.

The strip of glue was so thin. It was almost nothing at all.

Dear Adelle,

I did all of this and I am sorry. I've made a huge disaster out of everything. I was trying to dig out the truth about the den, and I was angry and desperate enough to hurt whoever I needed to in order to get to the bottom of things. I used Kent to get to the Sweet Thief, and I used you to help me trap Kent. I wish I could undo it all. I was wrong about everything. You should know that Kent had nothing to do with any of this. It was all me. I'm also sorry that I dug up what I did about you, and I wish I could rebury it. Hopefully no one else sees it. I'll destroy what I have, so you don't have to worry about that. But beware of Jim. He is not who you think he is. I have some dirt on him too, and am about to make it public. Soon he won't be able to hurt anyone anymore, once everyone knows who he is. I know I can't undo the damage I have done, but I want you to know that I won't do you any more harm. Your forgiveness? I don't expect that. I don't even have the right to ask for it. But hopefully this will give you a little peace. I am not after you. My only focus now is to put a stack of letters in the mail. The world will know who Jim is.

-The Mailman

P.S. Dear Jim, Catch me if you can.

40

The Heist

Jim dropped the note, wishing he had burned it.

Two minutes later a motorcycle shot out from behind Adelle's house, the engine shredding the stillness in the air. Jim kept the throttle open all the way into town.

Back at the house, Adelle's sister dragged a rolling suitcase out onto the porch. She pulled the door shut behind her, turned around, and almost jumped out of her skin. A giant of a man was looking up at her from the front steps. Even sitting down he was massive.

"Please, miss," Malcolm said softly, "I need to speak with Adelle. It's an emergency."

"Yeah, I bet it is…" the woman murmured. She sounded both irate and terrified. "You go on, get out of here, or I'm calling the police."

"But Adelle's got my medicine," the man said weakly. He man did not say another word, but grabbed his chest with his hands and collapsed face down in the yard.

An army of guards surrounded the woman. They were arranged in rows that ran four and five deep, armed to the teeth and ready to repel any attempt to get through. They were ready to turn Malcolm in. They were ready to lash out and strike. What they were not ready for was for him to be helpless. The surprise attack was perfect, and the guards were routed by the woman's own troops.

Rushing forward to the man on the ground, the nurse's instincts went into overdrive. She quickly checked for breathing and a pulse, the guards of fear and anger pinned down by the suppressive fire of her concern for the man possibly having a heart attack right in front of her.

With the guards momentarily out of commission, Adelle's sister was free to act. "Adelle!" she yelled over her shoulder.

The unmistakable sound of alarm in her sister's voice sent a rocket screaming into the house. It slammed into the living room wall and the shockwave from the blast loosened the hinges of the cage around Adelle. Half of the bars fell outward. Her sister called again, panic rising, and Adelle was up on her knees. She was moving by habit now, leaning heavily on the experience of her battle hardened militia. She may be critically wounded, but her troops still knew what to do. Compassion drove her out of the cage and she stumbled to the front door, still half blind with tears.

"What is it?" Adelle whimpered. "Are you OK?"

Her sister turned halfway around as she continued to work on Malcolm. "This man said something about you having his medicine and then collapsed in the yard. I need you to tell me what medicine he is taking and go call 911."

Confused, Adelle wiped her eyes. The immense form lying beside her sister was unmistakable. "Malcolm!" She raced down the steps and knelt beside the enormous thief, frantic to find out what was wrong.

"Adelle!" her sister cried. "Call 911! We need…"

Macolm gently grabbed her arm.

Still reeling from the morning's attack on her family and now stunned and confused by the presence of Malcolm at her house, Adelle sat staring.

"Adelle, we got to get you loose," the deep voice said.

"What are you doing here?" It was as if Adelle hadn't even heard him.

"Adelle," he repeated, sitting up. "We're all here."

It was true. She saw them now. The house was crawling with sweet thieves. They looked like commandos, and the guards inside had no clue they were coming.

Adelle shook her head and looked down. "You don't understand. I'm not who you think."

"Yeah, I know. The mailman told me everything."

She looked at him in horror, shame's dark bars erupting up from the ground around her. Malcolm stomped them back down beneath a huge boot.

"I don't care about none of that," Malcolm said. "That's not who you are now. Besides, every one of us has some of those stories. You just ease up now. You ain't the bad guy, and we're all here."

The words sounded true. They felt true.

"There's more," Malcolm said, recapturing her attention. "The mailman told us everything he did, too. Kent didn't know. He didn't know about none of this. And he never knew about the things in that letter. That was all the mailman."

Adelle's face was still smeared with hurt and confusion.

"He did it to trap Kent. It was the mailman's letters that brought Kent to the den. He was using Kent like a hostage, to make the Sweet Thief show himself. He wanted to see. He wanted answers for his wounds. Like you do now."

Adelle swallowed hard.

"Look, we know there's gonna be damage from all this. There's gonna be wounds. But it's out in the open now and we're all still here. We ain't goin away." He wrapped a huge arm protectively around her shoulders.

Adelle wished his arms were even bigger. She leaned against him and allowed him to take an immense pile of coins.

Her sister watched the whole thing, softening as she saw Adelle so completely broken. What Adelle had done was unspeakable, but she was still her sister.

μ̄ μ̄

41

Caught Red-Handed

Dozens of thieves sped from Adelle's parent's house to the post office downtown, but by the time they pulled into the parking lot the battle was already raging. Jim's forces were deployed all across the asphalt and the mailman's soldiers had taken up defensive positions among the mail trucks.

Hatred shot back and forth like the non-stop clapping of gunfire. It rose and fell in intensity, vacillating between tiny bursts and full on storms of wrath. Accusations flew like blistering missiles, and barricades of excuses sprang up to meet them. Both combatants were done listening, all lines of communication cut. Chunks of asphalt and pillars of dirt flew up from the ground as heavy artillery sent raging shells in both directions. Neither side would yield. Neither was able to gain the upper hand. It was a stalemate of mutual destruction.

Ignoring the warnings of the friends around her, Adelle walked into the thick of the battle and took her stand in the center of the parking lot. The angry fire whipped past, but she was immune to it now. They had both already spent their worst ammunition. Nothing they had left in their arsenal could touch her.

As she continued to stand between them, her mere presence proving their impotence, the battlefield slowly went quiet. Adelle raised her hands, determined to be heard. In the presence of everyone involved, there would be some accountability today. Almost effortlessly, she tore the coverings off of the fortifications and filled in the trenches and foxholes, forcing both Jim and the mailman to the surface. They had no choice but to hear her as she spoke. Their earlier attacks bound them to her now.

"I don't understand..." Adelle looked at Jim. Was this really the same person who had spent so many sweet moments with them in the den, who appeared to be such a part of what was going on? He seemed a million miles away now. Still, she asked the question she knew he wouldn't answer. "Why?"

"Everyone always wants to know why," he fired back flippantly. No charm remained in the green eyes. The only true answers to her question were shallow and wicked, and he would not say them out loud.

She pressed her advantage with confident grace, wielding truth like a hammer. "What did I ever do to you? Tell everyone here what I did to make you hurt me like you have."

Jim's grin was ruthless. Adelle had stepped on a hidden mine, one she should have known was there, and the click beneath her feet echoed through the parking lot. Jim leveled his rifle at his target, knowing that she was now anchored to the spot. Slowly, he pulled the trigger. "What you did to me has nothing to do with it. What you did to others... now that's a different story. I just picked up the ammunition you left behind and used it. You can accuse me all you want. You did this to yourself. You built the bomb that blew your family apart."

Desperately she tried to dodge the familiar bullet, but she dared not move her feet. "You didn't answer the question," she fired back instead. "What did I do to YOU?"

It was pathetic how helpless she was. Jim was almost bored. How many times would he have to destroy this thief before she got tired of being humiliated? "To me? Nothing. Nothing at all."

"Then why did you have to hurt me?"

"It was never about you," Jim shrugged coldly. "That's the most tragic part about you even being here. You're just collateral damage. In fact, you would have never been involved, but when I saw the effect you had on Kent, well, I couldn't help myself."

"But we were friends!" Adelle cried, outraged at his treachery.

"We were?" Jim looked at her with mock surprise.

"You were with us," Adelle wailed. "We trusted you."

"Yeah, you did."

"Wasn't that enough for you?"

"No."

Adelle was frozen, disarmed on the battlefield. She was out of ammunition. Her target could not be killed because her target had no heart. Jim took careful aim, training in his sights for the kill shot, deciding just how to phrase the question... Accusing him of betrayal after what she'd done to her family? The question wrote itself. She could say all she wanted about him being a traitor, but at least he was only guilty of betraying strangers. She had betrayed her blood. The sights aligned, his finger went tight.

Then it all went red.

Heat seared his hands as a bullet ricocheted off his rifle and lodged in his shoulder.

"How could he be friends with you?" the mailman broke in, looking past the smoking barrel of his weapon. "He never stole a thing in his life. He has no idea what it is to be a thief because he's never actually been one. I put him in the den. I taught him what to say. I taught him how to dress the part and got him in the door. But he never did a job. He never had a target of his own. He never once stood before the mirror. He was only playing a role, and he hated the den from the beginning."

Adelle spun on the mailman, but she never got her question out.

"Because I told him to," the mailman confessed.

Jim turned toward the gathered thieves and sent a spray of darts into the crowd. "Don't look so shocked. You all made me. Every one of you brought me in! You want to do great things, but you're too afraid of the cost. So you do things that only look great, protecting yourselves the whole time. Don't you recognize me?"

The thieves shuddered as they finally saw it... Jim was a little piece of all of them. He was their demand for answers. He was their love of their own portrait in the hall. He was their longing for an important place in the den and the feeling they got when they kept a few dark coins off to the side as a memento – a trophy to show the price they'd paid and to celebrate how good they were.

Jim was their catch phrases that had become hollow with empty repetition. He was their rituals that had stepped in front of and replaced the truths behind them. He was the safe distance they kept from the hurting and the dirty and the wicked. He was their failure to steal, and in order to comfort themselves... they ate with him. There was a Jim at every table in the den.

Jim's darts were reckless but true, and thieves throughout the crowd went down until he ran out of bullets. His empty rifle clattered on the asphalt as he cast it aside. Then he drew his knife and raced across the parking lot. He moved nearly as fast as the Sweet Thief himself as he began slicing through the crowd, attacking thieves individually. He struck the places where each thief was weakest; those places he had seen at the tables. Each failure, each instance where the higher calling had been abandoned for easier or more profitable ones... Jim knew them all and he called them all out.

The thieves fell like leaves. Even their greatest thefts were shown to be tainted with selfishness; the stolen treasure all for them. In the long run they had done nothing. All of their strivings were pointless.

Suddenly the lies went silent as Jim was yanked to the ground from behind, a garrotte of truth going tight around his throat. In his vicious charge against the thieves, he had forgotten one small thing.

The mailman had written it all down. All of it. He captured every thought and word, laying it out clearly in a letter to the world.

Jim would no longer be able to hide among them. Thieves everywhere would know him. He would no longer be able to slip in beside them at the table. The mailman poured it all out on paper – his great confession – and then signed his name at the bottom. It was the same name as the one on his postman's uniform. Three little letters. J-I-M.

"Excuse me," he whispered. "I need to go drop something in the mail." The battle was intimate now.

"I can't let you do that," Jim growled, twisting and trying to get loose.

"Can and will," the mailman returned, gritting his teeth.

"What makes you think I'm going to be OK with that?" Jim grunted, trying to wedge his fingers between his throat and the strangling letter.

"Because you are tired of being trapped," replied the mailman, pulling back hard. "We both know that you've never actually seen your guards; that everything you understand about them is what I've told you… but I can see them. I see the strings they pull. I see the chains and prods. I know you live every day as a hostage, doing nothing but putting on a show. And even though you don't like me right now, I know you want to be free of all that."

"We're all putting on a show…" Jim strained.

The mailman crossed his arms behind Jim's head, locking the hold in tight. "Let me fight this one. I've done it before. I've seen a lot of people go free. Let's finally do it for you. Let's get it all out in the open. Let me mail this letter. Let me take down your guards."

"There's only one problem with that," Jim thrashed. His face was bright purple. "My guards are your guards. Yeah, you can see them. But they've got chains on you just like they've got chains on me."

"That's true," the mailman allowed. "But I know someone…"

"Oh, so you believe that now? I thought you weren't sure. I thought you wanted to see him."

"I have."

"Only because you wanted to."

"No. I see him now. Look around. He's here."

"Where?"

"In them," the mailman looked toward the wounded thieves.

"That's your evidence? These thieves I just cut down?"

"Yeah," whispered the mailman. "These sweet thieves. They will admit that they are nothing without him. But with him…"

"No! They are just blindly hoping the same way you are! It's ludicrous; you are all just looking around at each other, each one convinced because the other one believes. But underneath it all there is nothing really there!"

"What if there is?" the mailman loosened his grip.

"That would be just lovely," Jim taunted. "Wouldn't it?" Without warning he swung his knife backward.

The mailman smiled sadly, accepting the blade as it plunged into his heart. He would not hate Jim. He would not strike back in revenge. He would do what the Sweet Thief had taught him to do. He would steal pain and hand it over. Never again would he stockpile it or try to carry it himself. He knew at last that he wasn't built for that. He released Jim at last and took hold of the knife in his chest.

The blade came out slowly, but it did come out, and the mailman handed it to the one standing beside him.

The gathered thieves gasped in relief and recognition. He was there. He was actually there!

Adelle stood trembling, overwhelmed with relief.

Malcolm was beaming, his smile almost too big for his face.

Swabby and Samuel and the crowd of other thieves... for a moment it was clear, as they realized he had been there the whole time.

As for Jim, he was gone. No one looked for him, though from time to time someone would check with the mailman just to make sure.

"I hear from him once in a while," was the mailman's answer. "His voice is quiet now, though. He knows I'm onto him. Still, he tries to sneak back in occasionally – usually when things are going really well or when I'm tired. But now that the den knows his face, he shows up less and less."

$\overline{\mu}$ $\overline{\mu}$

Epilogue

The Sorting Room

The mailman sat at his old desk, though it was no longer in the fortress. The thieves had hauled it back to the den with the rest of the loot. Upon the desk was a stack of blank stationery, a mailbag stuffed with files, and the mailman's ancient typewriter.

He had a lot of damage to undo and he was eager to get started.

> *Dear Francis,*
> *There is someplace you just have to see...*

The keystrokes hammered down the rhythm of a brand new song. The mailman whistled along as he typed. There were no cracks in this music.

> *Dear Trina,*
> *You have beauty that the world knows nothing about.*
> *But there is someone who does...*

The words felt good. With every letter the mailman's bag grew lighter.

> *Dear Kent,*
> *"A few will spend their days etching eternity.*
> *The rest are merely scribbling on the wind."*
> *Thank you for etching. It mattered.*
> *-The Mailman*

$\overline{\mu}$ $\overline{\mu}$

μ   μ

About the Author

Brian Wallace spent most of his childhood in southern Maryland, where he grew up chasing turtles, blue crabs, and footballs.

After earning a biology degree from Roanoke College in Virginia, he set out with a team on a two year music ministry adventure that took him all around the United States, India, and Nepal. A love for the road was born that continues to this day. *Psalm 84:5*

Brian has since been a science teacher, a volleyball coach, a cancer survivor, an occasional bass player, a speaker at youth events, and an author. Sweet Thieves is his fourth novel.

*"Many thanks to family and friends for lending support
in all of its various forms throughout the years!
Your heartprints are in here..."*

www.brianwallacebooks.com

281

59348194R00157

Made in the USA
Lexington, KY
05 January 2017